THE BAYING OF WOLVES WAS ALL AROUND THEM—

"The cliff, it's our only chance!"

Plunging forward, Crystal and Raulin almost crashed into Jago who had stopped and stood staring at their intended refuge. "I think not," he said quietly. Raulin and Crystal rocked to a halt beside him.

The black wolf stood on the cliff top. Its teeth gleamed white even in the dusk and its open mouth made it look almost as if it laughed. Then it leaped.

Raulin raised the crossbow and pulled the trigger.

The wolf's scream, when the quarrel drove into its haunch, sounded like nothing out of an animal's throat and when the body hit the ground almost at Raulin's feet, a young man snarled up at them.

"Wer," Crystal said. "They're wer." And she remembered what she had been told of the wer: *The wer hate the wizards with an intensity hard to imagine. The names of the wizards are curses to them.*

And then, as if in confirmation, a voice said, "We don't like wizards on our land."

Turning, they saw four wolves, two mountain cats, and a man standing between them and their abandoned sleigh. The man carried a rod of amethyst and bronze which he pointed at Crystal. And suddenly her thoughts ran out like water, her vision fogged, and she felt herself slide to the ground. . . .

THE
LAST WIZARD

TANYA HUFF

DAW BOOKS, INC.
DONALD A. WOLLHEIM, PUBLISHER

375 Hudson Street, New York, NY 10014

First Printing, March 1989

3   4   5   6   7   8   9

Printed in the U.S.A.

For Fe, who freed the emotions and refuses to let me lock them away again.

ACKNOWLEDGMENTS:

I'd like to take this opportunity to thank Doris Bercarich for technical assistance above and beyond the call of friendship. *I* wouldn't have lent me a disk drive.

Progenitor

Seven were the goddesses remaining when the gods were destroyed. Seven they were and these were their degrees:

Nashawryn was the eldest; ebony haired and silver eyed, ruler of night and darkness, concealment and safety held in one cupped hand, a dagger of fear clenched tight in the other fist.

Zarsheiy, who closely followed night in age, ruled fire, and, claimed her dark sister, was ruled by it. Flame her hair and flame her eyes and flame, they said, her heart. Passionate and unpredictable, one moment giving, the next destroying, Zarsheiy's temper was legend amongst both Mortals and the deities they had created.

Most loved of all the seven was Geta, Freedom, who watched her twin brother Getan, god of Justice, destroyed by his Wizard son and so hid her grieving face from Mortals all the long years the Wizards ruled.

Gentle Sholah held hearth and harvest in the bowl of her two hands. Her dance turned the seasons, and she was the first who dared deny Nashawryn and have Zarsheiy heed her call.

Tayja was Sholah's daughter, carved for her of mahogany from the heart of a single tree by

Pejore, the god of art. It was Tayja who dared go into Chaos and bring out the skill to harness Zarsheiy and she who fought always to strike the dagger from Nashawryn's hand. Craft and learning were her dominion and although she demanded much of those who worshiped her, of all the goddesses, save perhaps Geta, she gave the most in return.

Youngest of the seven was Eegri, and on her realm of chance even Tayja's reason blunted. She went where she would; into night; into flame; now revering freedom, now denying it; tripping through field and forge with equal abandon. She had no temples and no priesthood, but her symbol was etched over every door and among Mortalkind there were many who lived by her favor.

The last of the seven claimed to have been present when the Mother-creator lay with Chaos and bore him Lord Death, her one true son. She claimed to be more passionate than fire, to be more necessary than freedom, to be the moving force of hearth and harvest, to be more a fickle power than even chance herself. Of craft and learning she claimed to be the strength, lending to poor Mortals the incentive to succeed. Her name was Avreen, and she wore both the face of love and of her darker aspect, lust.

As the dark age of Wizards ended, these seven were all of the pantheon that survived; no longer worshiped, seldom remembered. But a goddess once created does not disappear merely because her creator has moved beyond and closer to the truth. As they watched the Wizards rule, so they watched the Wizards die. And they saw that one did not. The most powerful of the Wizards, his father the most powerful of the gods long destroyed, still lived. Throughout the many thousand years during which he hid, the seven watched. When he emerged to rule the earth again, they were ready.

The gods had stood alone, each against his child; and lost. They would stand together.

The Mother-creator's eldest child, immortal first created, died for love of a mortal man. The seven used that love—for was not Love one of them—and formed a vessel into which they poured all that they were. They caused that vessel to present their essence back to the Mother's youngest, to a mortal woman, to the only aspect of all the Mother's creation that was in turn able to create, and she formed that essence into a child.

And the child, unique in creation, won whcre the gods had failed.

One

"You waitin' for someone?"

"No."

"Mind if I set?"

"Yes."

The beefy faced man opened and closed his mouth a few times and a wave of red washed out the freckles sprinkled liberally across his nose and cheeks. "Think you're too good ta set with me?" His hard miner's hands clenched the edge of the small table.

"No." But the tone said yes.

It said other things as well, spoke a coldness that caused the miner's balls to draw up, even under his thick sheepskin trousers.

She lifted her head just a little and let a ray of lantern light fall within the confines of her hood.

The man's eyes widened. For a moment his jaw went slack, and then his sandy brows drew down in a puzzled frown. He knew something was happening; he didn't know what. An instant later, he lost even that and turned away, knowing only that his advances had been rejected.

She lowered her head and her face was once again masked by darkness.

"Not very polite," said her companion as the miner returned to his own table amidst the jeers and catcalls of his friends. "I never thought to see you use your power on such a trivial thing."

Crystal shrugged but kept her voice low as she answered. Although she had no objection to being thought overly proud or even peculiar, it wouldn't do

12

to have the whole tavern think her insane; sitting and talking to a companion only she could see. She said as much to Lord Death, adding: "I wish to be left alone. That is not, to my mind, a trivial thing."

Lord Death drew his finger through a puddle of spilled ale, making no mark. "And your wish is to be that poor mortal's command?" His hair flickered to a bright red-gold, and for a heartbeat his eyes glowed a brilliant sapphire blue.

The hiss of breath through Crystal's teeth caused several patrons to turn and peer toward the dim corner. She quickly dropped her gaze to her mug of ale until, curiosity unsatisfied, they returned to their own concerns.

"You dare?" she growled when the attention had shifted away. "You dare show that face to me? To criticize *my* actions with it? To dare suggest I walk his road? Kraydak's road?" Kraydak of the red-gold hair and sapphire eyes and silken voice and blood-red hands. Kraydak, the most powerful of the ancient wizards, dead now these dozen years. Her hand had set his death in motion, but his arrogance had killed him in the end. His arrogance. His concern had been solely for himself, all others existing only to serve.

Lord Death sat quietly, chin on hands, watching the last of the wizards work her way through his accusation to the truth. In spite of a parentage that tied together all the threads of the Mother's creation, and more power than had ever been contained in a mortal shell, she was as capable of lying to herself as any other. But she seldom did and he doubted she would now. He'd spent a lot of time with her over the last few years, drawn by something he was not yet willing to name, and he'd come to respect her ability to see things as they were, not as she wanted them to be.

"I'm sorry." The whisper from the depths of the hood was truly contrite and both slender hands tightened about her mug. The pewter began to bend and she hurriedly stroked it straight. Forgetting how it must appear to anyone watching—and there had been inquisitive eyes on her since she entered the inn—she turned to face Lord Death. The shadows of the hood could not hide the brimming tears from one who walked in shadow. "I . . . I seem to be losing control of things lately."

The one true son of the Mother reached out to brush a tear away, but the drop of water slid through his finger and spun down to the scarred tabletop. He sighed and his mouth twisted as he withdrew his hand. "May I give you some advice?" he asked as they both stared down at the fallen tear.

She sniffed and managed a smile. "I don't guarantee I'll take it."

He smiled back but kept his voice carefully neutral, not letting the worry show. "Find something to do. Kraydak committed his worst excesses because he was bored." He waved his hand. "Go back to the Empire, there's enough to fix there to keep any number of wizards busy."

Crystal shook her head and pushed a spill of silver hair back beneath her hood. "I can't. The people of the Empire are too aware of the evil a wizard can do and I am too obviously—" she sighed, "—too obviously what I am. When they see me, they see Kraydak."

"You destroyed him. They'll come to see you in time."

"If you expect one act of good to wipe out ten centuries of evil, you expect too much of your people, milord. Even if I tried to make amends for every horror he ever committed—and I did try, in the beginning—they would still see only that I was a wizard, like him."

"Not like him," Lord Death reminded her.

"No," she agreed. "But in his Empire, wizard means terror and they see me as potential threat not savior." Her voice trailed off as she remembered how her help had been received; how she'd come to use her powers in secret if at all, hiding who and what she was rather than trying to fight the inheritance of fear

Kraydak had left her, afraid herself that she would one day lash back and so become what they accused her of being.

Even here in Halda, even though King Jeffrey was a cousin of sorts, she kept her identity hidden. Kraydak's legions had cut through the valley country and a wizard would not be looked on kindly. Amid the small crowd of men and women who'd braved the weather for companionship's sake, she could see a hook where a hand should be, a patch covering an empty socket—the eye seared out by fire if the puckered ridges surrounding it were any sign—and scars beyond counting. High in the northern mountains, this mining village had been hit less hard than others she'd seen, but once having felt a wizard's power they would not likely welcome it again. Fortunately, the bitter cold—noticeable in the tavern even though fires roared at both ends of the long room—wrapped everyone in the anonymity of heavy clothing and she was not the only one huddled deep within a hood.

A problem to involve her mind and her power would go a long way toward settling the turmoil she'd lived in lately; thoughts and feelings boiling beneath the surface, occasionally bubbling up as they had with that poor miner. It seemed, sometimes, as if each individual facet of her personality fought for a life of its own, only rarely coming together to work as one harmonious whole. There were days when she dreaded opening her mouth for fear of what would come out.

"Perhaps," Lord Death broke into her thoughts, "you should go home."

She briefly considered it. Her twelve-year-old brother and the seven-year-old twins were enough to keep an army of wizards busy. "No," she said aloud, "it's too soon. Mother would be sure something was wrong and she'd fuss."

"Maybe she could help."

"Help with what? There's nothing wrong." Crystal wondered if he could see the heat rising in her cheeks. He sat silently, smiling slightly. *He knows me too well,* she thought, but for some strange reason that pleased her. "There's nothing wrong my mother can help with," she amended and was rewarded by a fuller smile. "And besides, the adulation of the Ardhan people is as hard to take in its own way as fear and suspicion."

Fear and suspicion.

Which brought it full circle back to the Empire. Without her help, it would be many, many years before the effects of Kraydak's tyranny were erased from the land and the people—but she suspected that this slow healing was for the best. Only time would convince those who'd survived the crushing weight of Kraydak's yoke that they were their own masters again.

"The trouble is," she said at last, "no one needs me."

Lord Death had no response to that so he merely sat and watched the last of the wizards drink her ale. He enjoyed watching her, not only because she was stunningly beautiful and inhumanly graceful, not only because she was intelligent, witty, and powerful, but because . . . He broke off the thought, as he always did at that point, and glanced around the room. An ancient man, sitting as close to the fire as he could without igniting his old bones, lifting his mug in salute. Lord Death smiled and returned the salutation. He appreciated a graceful exit. A number of the relic's friends peered about, wondering whom he greeted. By the coarse jokes and ribald poking at the old man's supposed gallantry, it was obvious they saw only Crystal. After living their lives in a land where winters were often eight months long, they were well practiced at judging a person's gender despite the heavy clothing.

If Crystal noticed any of this, she chose to ignore it as she ignored the other noises of the crowd, letting sounds wash over her in an undifferentiated rumble. Her table, back in a corner and away from the fires, was isolated, cold, and a little dark. Save for the one miner who'd approached at the drunken urging of his friends, she'd been left alone from the moment she'd slipped quietly back there and sat down. Even the young man who served her ale came back as seldom as he thought he could and shivered the entire time he was forced to linger so far from the fires. He'd asked her once if she wouldn't like to move closer, more for his sake, she suspected, than hers. She'd told him no, and he hadn't brought it up again. If she thought about the cold at all, she welcomed the drafts that skirted her ankles and tugged at the edges of her cloak; they kept the odors of humanity, steaming woolens, and stale beer down to a bearable level. An enhanced sense of smell, part of her heritage from the Mother's Eldest, could be a distinct disadvantage at times.

She wasn't sure why she'd even entered the inn. She had no need of food or warmth; she had no wish for companionship; but when the last light from the setting sun had picked out the gilding on the tavern's hanging sign and it had flared like a beacon in the fog she'd taken it as an omen.

What kind of omen an inn called The Wrong Nugget would be, Crystal had no idea.

She sighed and let her gaze drift over to the stairs that led to the second floor. Each step dipped from the wearing of countless footsteps and the wood was polished almost white. Any place that kept the stairs so clean, she decided, could be trusted to keep the bugs in the beds to a minimum. Perhaps she would stay the night.

But tomorrow?

Maybe she could return to the centaurs. It had been seven years since they'd taught her the delicate manipulations of the dreamworld. Perhaps enough time had passed that she could handle their pompous and pedantic utterances again. She thought of C'Tal. *"Are you entirely certain that your spiritual growth has proceeded sufficiently for you to be instructed in . . ."* No, seven years wasn't long enough. There had to be something else.

She sighed.

"No one needs me," she said again, and finished her ale.

"Self-pity makes me sick!" The voice blazed between her ears, disgust and anger about equally mixed.

Crystal flicked a glance behind her. Only her shadow grayed the rough log wall. Only Lord Death was close enough to have made the remark.

"I beg your pardon?"

Lord Death looked startled at the frosty tone. "I didn't say anything," he protested.

"You didn't?"

"No."

She had to believe him. He had never, to her knowledge, lied. She wasn't sure he could. "Then who . . ." She rubbed her forehead with a pale hand. Wonderful, now she was hearing things. Just what the world needed: a useless, *crazy* wizard.

With a scream of frozen hinges and a roar of winter wind, the outer door burst open and slammed back against the wall. After an instant of stunned silence, the sudden blast of freezing air brought a number of the patrons to their feet and a bellow of: "Close the Chaos damned door!" ripped out of a dozen throats.

The man who staggered into the light wore furs so rimed with ice it was only common sense that said he wore furs at all. He half dragged, half carried a man-sized bundle, equally white. Just over the threshold, he stopped and swayed and stared, eddies of snow swirling about his feet through the open door.

The men and women in the tavern stared back, caught by his desperation but not knowing how to respond, as the room grew colder and the lamps guttered. Finally, the young server pushed through the crowd and wrestled shut the door, alternately kicking and cursing at the lumps of ice that had followed the stranger inside. When warmth no longer leeched out of the tavern, he placed a tentative hand on the stranger's arm. The man didn't appear to notice. Even blurred by layers of clothing, every line of his body screamed exhaustion. His sway grew more pronounced and he toppled to the floor, curled protectively around his burden.

"Get the poor bugger a brandy," someone suggested, breaking the silence.

"If yer buyin', I could use one meself."

"Brandy'll kill'im. Have Inga here give'im a kiss."

"That'll kill'im fer sure."

Amid appreciative laughter at this string of wit, the server knelt down beside the body, advice and drunken speculation continuing until one voice above the babble, sharp and clear:

"What is going on out here?"

The tavern fell as close to silent as taverns ever fall, and every head still capable of the motion turned to the kitchen door. Physically, the woman who waited there for an answer was not the type to inspire such quiet. She was short, thin, with close cropped red curls, and a wide mouth—currently pressed into a disapproving line. The apron she wore over winter woolens was stained, for, proprietor or not, she did much of the cooking herself. A smudge of ash marked her nose. "Who," she demanded, dusting flour off her hands, "left the damned door open? We can feel the cold all the way into the kitchen. I've told you lot before that I've no intention of heating all of Halda."

"It's a stranger, Dorses," the barman called out and the rest of the explanation was lost as everyone tried to shout out their version of events.

She sighed, signaled the barman to stay put—his skill with beer or brandy was undeniable, but the man was useless in an emergency—and made her way across to the door. Experience told her it would be faster to see for herself than to try and sort out over twenty voices. When she reached the stranger, she touched his shoulder with the toe of her shoe.

"Is he dead, Ivan?" she asked the server.

"No." Pale brows drew down toward a snub nose. "But he's not good."

Dorses shook her head and turned a withering gaze on her clientele. "And I suppose it occurred to none of you to get him over by the fire and out of those wet furs?''

As several of the more sober blushed and muttered excuses, she looked back to her server. ''What are you trying to do?'' she demanded as Ivan continued to tug on the stranger's arms.

''I can't get him to let go of his bundle,'' he grunted, lower lip caught up between his teeth.

''Then let him be.'' She scanned the faces present. ''Nad?''

''He's in the pot.''

''Nay, I'm back.''

The man who pushed his way forward was of average height and anything but average width. His shoulders were so broad he seemed a foot or so shorter than he actually stood. Pleasant features were arranged about a mashed caricature of a nose in an expression of eager curiosity.

Dorses twitched Ivan out of Nad's way and said: ''See what you can do.''

Nad flexed his massive shoulders, bent over the stranger, and taking each fur covered arm in a callused hand, lifted. A foot, then two, the stranger rose and although he maintained his grip the bundle's own weight pulled it free. Nad grunted in satisfaction, moved a bit to the left, and gently lowered the man back to the floor.

''Chaos,'' breathed Ivan, his eyes widening. ''That's a brindle pelt he was carryin'. Looks fresh killed, too.''

The stranger lay forgotten in a puddle of melting snow while they all examined what he'd been clutching so tightly. Dorses bent and stroked the long, brown and black fur.

''It's brindle all right,'' she said, lifting a corner and looking beneath. Her tone remained unchanged as she added, 'It's also a body.'' After eight years of running this tavern, she'd pretty much lost her ability to be surprised by anything.

''My brother,'' the stranger's voice was a reedy gasp.

He rose shakily to one elbow and removed the half-frozen wool scarf from in front of his mouth. "Wounded in the mountains." Beneath a drooping mustache his lips were pinched and white. "Needs . . ." Then he collapsed back to the floor.

"Help," Dorses finished, her hand slipping beneath the fur and resting on the throat of the wounded man. His pulse barely shivered against her fingers. "Ivan, take care of . . ." Without a name, she waved a hand in the general direction of the stranger. "I want his brother here up on that table. Don't unwrap him, Nad!" she snapped as huge hands reached down and started to roll the brindle free. "Lift him as he is."

"But Dorses!" Nad protested, scarred fingers sinking into the plush fur. "Just think on it! A week at my forge wouldn't bring in what this pelt will. You don't use brindle as a stretcher! You can't!" His tone was horrified.

"Why not? It's almost a shroud. Now move!"

With a miner on each side of the torso and another lifting the legs, the body and the pelt were hoisted onto a hastily cleared table. Nad bit back a cry as the preferred fur of kings settled gently on top of biscuit crumbs and spilled beer. At a curt nod from Dorses, he almost reverently folded back the outer edge, and then the inner, pulling slowly but steadily for the pelt was frozen stiff and stuck to something beneath.

"Mother who made us all," he breathed, and his hands dropped to his sides.

Even Dorses paled.

The stranger's brother looked about thirty and was a slightly built man, thin but muscular. A week's beard glinted gold in the lamplight, some shades darker than the wire-bound braids. His skin was pale and he had a delicate beauty seldom achieved by men; just barely saved from being effeminate by the stern line of his mouth, uncompromising even so close to death. Above the waist, his clothes bore russet brown stains. Below, they were shredded and the flesh beneath was no better. Not even the stiff and reddened strips of hide that bound them could disguise the extent of the injuries. Only by courtesy could these hunks of meat still be called legs.

The tavern fell silent. One of the men, up on a neighboring table for a better view, scrambled down off his perch and vomited into a bucket. Everyone ignored him, their eyes on the dead man. Oh, he still clung to life, although the Mother only knew how, but there wasn't a person watching who would grant him a place amongst the living.

"Jago?" Pulling free of Ivan's help and leaving the young man holding his sodden furs, the stranger fell onto the bench by the table and took his brother's face in cracked and bleeding hands. His hair was nearer brown than blond and pulled back into a greasy tail. Although pain and exhaustion made it difficult to tell for certain, he appeared five to seven years older than the wounded man. "Jago?"

"Give me your knife," Dorses said quietly to Nad. "Those bindings have to come off."

"Those bindin's are all that's holdin' the flesh on his bones," observed a woman in the crowd.

"Aye," Nad agreed from his vantage point. "You'll have a right mess if you cut him free. And the whole lot's froze so you'll have ta pry the bindings up and likely take a bit of leg with it. Would't be surprised if what's left is frostbit too." He handed Dorses his knife and added, " 'Course, far as he's concerned it won't make much difference either way."

"While he lives, we do what we can." And her tone left no room for argument.

The knife was sharp but the bindings were tight, wet, and becoming slimy as they thawed. Only the shallow and infrequent rise and fall of his chest said Jago still breathed. Although her eyes never left the delicate maneuvering of the blade, Dorses checked between each repositioning of the point; just in case. She'd fight to save the living, but she'd not waste her time on one already gone to Lord Death.

"Are you a healer?" The stranger looked up from

his brother's face, his eyes and the circles beneath them nearly the same shade of purplish gray. His accent gave the words an almost musical inflection but did nothing to hide the desperation.

"No." Dorses' mouth pressed into a thin white line and the tendons of her neck bulged as she forced the knife through the hide.

"We've no healer here," Nad explained, putting one foot up on the bench and leaning a forearm on his thigh. "And few anywhere in Halda. When the Wizard's Horde went through twelve year ago, they were all killed, from apprentice ta master. When the wizard fell, and the horde with him, there was no one left ta teach the youngsters until Ardhan sent aid. E'en then there was so much healin' needed doin' they'd no time ta teach at first. Dorses was joined ta a healer though and he . . ."

"He couldn't have done anything here." As the flesh beneath the bindings began to warm, her nose told her what she'd find. She had hoped it was the untanned brindle hide she smelled, and in part it was, but with even a small fraction of leg exposed the putrid stench rising from the black bits of flesh could only mean gangrene. The one question remaining was how the man still lived with legs clawed to shreds and rotting off his body.

"Have you a name?" She asked the stranger.

The stranger nodded. "Raulin. This," he added, "is my brother Jago. We were traveling north across the mountains when we were attacked by the brindle. Jago screamed and screamed, but I got my dagger in its eye . . ."

"In its eye?" More than one eye in the tavern measured the length of the pelt. A full grown brindle stood more than seven feet high at the shoulder and its eyes were two feet higher than that. Of course, if it was feeding . . .

"I climbed on its back," Raulin continued, as jaws dropped throughout his audience, "and put my dagger into its eye. It's a long dagger. It died. Jago stopped screaming." Tears dripped from his face onto his brother's. "Five days ago. Maybe four. He hasn't screamed since. I did what I could. I promised to get him to a healer." He began to struggle to his feet. "You said no healers. We have to go on."

Dorses' hand on his shoulder pushed him back down and a steady pressure kept him there. She was stronger than she looked.

"You're in no condition to go anywhere," she said, her voice as gentle as anyone had ever heard it. "And your brother is well on his way to Lord Death."

In the quiet corner, as far removed from the drama near the door as was possible while still remaining in the room, Crystal raised her head and met Lord Death's eyes. He nodded.

"He's mine, or yours," he said.

She peered through the nearly solid wall of wool and leather covered backs and then at the Mother's one true son. Already his hair was beginning to lighten and a faint line of beard coarsened his jaw as the features of the young man on the table moved onto Death. She couldn't save every handsome young man destined to die. But she could save this one.

She made up her mind.

"He's mine."

The scrape of her chair, moving away from the table as she stood, sounded unnaturally loud. A miner turned, nudged his neighbor, and in seconds the crowd had spun on its collective heel to look at Crystal.

There was no longer any point in avoiding attention.

She threw back her hood and let the cloak slip from her shoulders. Hair, the silver-white of moonlight, flowed almost to her waist and danced languidly about in the still air as though glad to be free. She stood taller than the tallest man in the room. As she stepped forward, her eyes began to glow; green as strong summer sunlight through leaves. There could be no mistaking who she was.

The ancient wizards had been bred of gods and mortal women and they'd ruled the earth for millennia until their arrogance destroyed them. All but one. All but Kraydak. And in less than a thousand years on his own, Kraydak had engendered as much carnage as all of the others had accomplished together over five times as long.

But from Ardhan came a prophecy, that from Ardhan would come Kraydak's doom.

Crystal. A weapon forged by the goddesses in a mortal womb, shaped by the strength of the Eldest.

Crystal. The last wizard. Only seventeen when she'd faced Kraydak and defeated him. Only seventeen when she'd saved the world. Twelve years later, she looked barely older.

The crowd parted, moved by surprise and other emotions, less well defined, with a guttural, multitoned murmur. Her gaze shifting neither left nor right—the tavern might have been empty from the way she moved—she approached the table, a song of power building in the back of her throat. It wasn't a sound yet, but the hair on every neck in the room stood up. She looked down at the wounded man and then at his brother.

For the first time in five days, Raulin's eyes held hope.

"Save him," he said.

She nodded, laid long pale fingers on the torn and rotting legs, and sang.

Two

The soft crackle and hiss of flame, the pervasive scent of smoke mixed with wool and wood, the warm weight of blankets shielding her body against the chill that touched her uncovered face, the musty taste of time's passage in her mouth . . . Crystal opened her eyes.

Above her, parallel lines of logs, bark still clinging, slanted down to the right. She turned her head and followed their length until they ended in a wall, also of rough log, and liberally chinked with mud and moss. Barely below the eaves, two small windows made of glass so thick it appeared green let in weak and watery winter sunlight. She shifted and heard the rustle of straw as the mattress moved below her.

Inside. And in bed. What else?

Rolling her head back to the left, she saw another wall, with a door, and close beside the bed a small table that held a half burned candle, a heavy ceramic pitcher and a matching mug. Her nose wrinkled. There was water in the pitcher.

Moving carefully, for muscles shrieked protest at the gentlest activity, Crystal managed to free an arm from the constricting bedclothes. She reached out, a long pale finger touched the edge of the jug, and she paused.

As much as she needed to drink—and her mouth felt as though a family of mice had moved in for the winter—she knew the water, or more specifically the swallowing and the weight in her stomach, would only intensify the craving for food she could feel beginning. Until she could satisfy *that* she'd best not make it any worse. Whoever put her here—in this bed, in this room—would soon return, for the fire sounded as if it had almost burned down.

She let her hand fall and concentrated instead on remembering what had happened. There'd been a man. No, two men. And a healing. Frowning in disgust over her lack of recall, she grabbed at the memory and yanked it forward. Jago. She'd healed Jago's legs. Or more accurately, rebuilt them, and then rebuilt Jago. She remembered his life-force fluttering beneath her power like a wounded bird trying to beat its way free. But she'd held and healed it, pouring her own life-force into it until it could manage alone. The last thing she remembered was hitting the floor, the fall closely followed by a confused babble of voices. She grimaced. No, two confused babbles of voices; one of them reverberating inside her head.

"So. You're awake." Dorses said, and paused in the room's doorway to study the wizard.

Long silver hair spilled across the pillow, not moving now but not exactly lifeless either. Green eyes were partially hooded by pale lids, and the one hand that lay outside the covers seemed almost translucent. It was easy to believe that this ethereal beauty was a child of the Mother's Eldest, less easy to believe that she held the power of life and death in those ivory hands.

"Please . . ." Crystal's voice had an unused rasp. "Please, I need food."

Dorses watched for an instant longer, keeping her expression carefully neutral. Did feeding this wizard indicate approval beyond what she had already? And if it did, did it matter? No, she realized, it did not. A moral judgment had been made when she'd had the helpless woman carried upstairs. That would have been the time to deny her, not now. She twisted her head and called over her shoulder, "Ivan, fill a tray and bring it up."

The half-lidded eyes opened a bit wider and a definite twinkle sparkled in the emerald depths. ''Rather a lot of food.''

''Ivan!'' The yell was a practiced, long-distance command. ''Fill the large tray.''

Crystal's lips flickered into a smile, but the expression took too much effort to maintain. She sighed and tried to move the taste of mold out of her mouth.

''Can you use a drink?'' Dorses assumed nothing, but the wizard certainly looked like she *needed* a drink. Hardly surprising, all things considered.

''Will Ivan be long?''

''No.''

''Then I would love a drink.''

The intense longing in Crystal's voice made Dorses thirsty as well. She moved to the bed licking her lips, filled the mug, and held it to the wizard's mouth.

The water had sat in the pitcher for some hours and was beginning to go stale and flat, but it couldn't have tasted better to Crystal had it just been drawn fresh from a mountain spring. She drained the mug and with the strength it gave her pulled herself shakily up to recline against the headboard of the bed. The fire, she could now see, burned in a small black stove, squatting against the opposite wall.

''If I may . . .'' Dorses offered. Slipping an arm between back and headboard—and the wizard was not as light as she looked—she rearranged both wizard and pillows in a more comfortable position.

''Thank you.''

''More water?''

''Please.''

Using both hands, Crystal managed to hold the mug and drink. She tried to ignore the spasms of hunger, concentrating instead on the very real pleasure in her mouth and throat. When the cup was empty again, she carefully put it on the table, and turned to the innkeeper.

''How long?'' she asked.

As she'd already asked about the food, Dorses assumed the wizard wanted to know how long since the healing. "Two and a half days." She moved to tend the fire, going over all she wanted to know, ordering the questions, wondering how best to begin. When a wizard, the last of all the wizards, collapses in your common room, a number of questions need answering. She opened the stove's door and began to rebuild the fire. Two and a half days ago she'd seen a dead man come back to life, blackened and rotting legs made whole and pink, but the why of *that* was wizard's work and no business of hers. "Why," she finally asked without turning, "did you fall?"

For the shelter and the food, Crystal felt the innkeeper was entitled to an answer. Her fists clenched against the hunger, she tried to explain. "He was too close to Death. Healing the legs wasn't enough. I had to give some of my life to keep him alive." She forced the fingers of her right hand to relax so she could indicate the room with a wave. "Why did you . . ." Why did you have me carried upstairs? Why did you see that I was comfortable and protected? Why did you shield me from those who would take advantage of my helplessness? And there would be those, there always were. All that conveyed in only three words.

Closing the stove door, wiping the wood dust from her hands, Dorses considered the question. This was not the first time she'd been asked it in the last two and a half days. Perhaps it was time she found an answer. After a moment, she stood and met the wizard's eyes. The motion of her hand was a reflection of Crystal's. "You gave some of your life to keep him alive," she said.

There were more questions in the silence but Ivan, arriving with the laden tray, pushed them into another time.

"I brought some of everything that was ready," he panted, maneuvering his bulky load through the door with the ease of long practice, " 'cause you never said what you wanted on . . ." He stopped as he felt Crystal's eyes on him and all the color drained from his face. *It's one thing to know you serve a wizard; it's another thing entirely when that wizard sits up in bed and stares at you.* He took a step backward and his mouth worked soundlessly.

"Put it by the bed," Dorses ordered sharply, afraid he was going to turn and run.

Ivan's gaze snapped to Dorses, and finding nothing there, at least, he didn't understand, he moved tentatively forward and eased the tray down on the small table.

No longer able to control herself, Crystal grabbed for the steaming bowl of soup.

Moving backward much faster than he'd advanced, Ivan retreated out of arm's reach, then paused to watch. His pale face grew paler as the hot soup disappeared, but he stood his ground, fascinated.

"Ivan!"

He jumped. He'd forgotten that Dorses still stood by the stove. "Yes, Dorses?"

"Haven't you anything to do?"

"Uh, aye."

She waited, arms folded across her chest.

"Uh . . . right. I'll get ta it now." After a last astounded look at Crystal, who had finished the soup and was reaching for the tray, he ran from the room.

"Your apprentice?" Crystal asked as she broke open a fresh biscuit and spread it thickly with butter.

"Aye." Dorses hooked the room's one chair out of the corner with a toe and sat. "He's a good worker when he remembers there's work to be done." A nod at the tray. "Enough?"

Besides the soup and biscuits, the tray held a meat pie, a bowl of rabbit stew thick with potatoes and carrots, a small baked squash, and two apple tarts.

"It should be, thank you."

Dorses peered a little nearsightedly at the woman on the bed. "I'm curious; did you know this would happen? The collapse? The hunger?"

"The hunger, yes. The energy I use has to be replaced." Crystal flushed. "But the other, I'd forgotten. It's been a long time since I've healed someone so close to Death. I forgot what it would cost to bring him back." She paused and licked a bit of gravy from her lip. Suddenly it occurred to her that Lord Death had suggested the healing. Somehow, she doubted he'd forgotten and she wondered why he'd put her in such a position. "By the time I remembered," she continued, resolving to question the Mother's son when next he appeared, "it was too late to stop."

"Could you?"

"Have stopped? Yes."

"Why didn't you when you realized that this," Dorses waved a hand at the bed, "would come of it?"

Finished with the stew, Crystal started on the meat pie while she searched for a way to make her position clear. "Once I'd started, it wouldn't have been right to stop. I'd made him my responsibility by beginning and I couldn't just let him die. Giving him the life-force he needed, even knowing it would leave me helpless while it kept him alive, seemed the lesser of two evils." She sighed, blowing pastry crumbs over the bed. "Although I'd have rather not had to do it."

"Ah." Dorses thought about that for a moment. This was the first wizard she'd ever heard of who considered the *lesser* of two evils. For that matter, she could think of very few people who would save a stranger at their own expense. "And what would you have done," she asked at last, "had you just been hungry?"

The wizard grinned. "I'd have staggered outside to the nearest grove and become a tree until spring when the body of the Mother would feed me."

"If you weren't chopped up for firewood," Dorses reminded her dryly. "Winters are long here."

Crystal acknowledged the truth of that with a smile. What a way for a wizard to die. She licked bits of squash from her fingers. "When I fell, what happened?"

Dorses shrugged thin shoulders. "Nothing much. No one wanted to touch you, which wasn't surprising considering who and what you are. So, after we got our other invalids up into bedrooms, I had Nad carry you up here before liquor overcame common sense.''

''Nad wasn't afraid to touch me.''

''Nad does what I ask.''

Crystal had a pretty good idea that most of the village did what this strong-minded woman asked. ''Thank you.''

''You're welcome.'' She spread her hands. ''Now what?''

Crystal flushed again and put down the second tart. ''I can pay you for all of this.''

Dorses cut at the air with a dismissive gesture. ''It isn't a problem. There could be blizzards every night and the place'd still be packed. You're good for business. You could eat that way for another five or six days and still not eat up all the profits you've made me in the last two nights. What I meant was, now you're here, do you plan to stay?''

Crystal thought about the aimless wandering she'd been doing lately, about the fear that greeted her wherever she went save home and the mindless adoration that greeted her there. So far, there'd been none of that here. She had spoken more to Dorses than she had to anyone outside her immediate family in years. Except, of course, Lord Death. It felt good.

''If you don't mind,'' she decided suddenly, ''I'd like to stay for a bit.''

''Mind? Weren't you listening? You're good for business.'' The innkeeper rose, glad to have it settled, and pleased the wizard was staying; not solely for the increase in custom. ''Ivan!'' she called down the stairs. ''Come up for the tray.''

He must've been waiting at the bottom of the stairs for the summons, he reached the room so quickly.

''Chaos,'' he breathed, spotting the empty dishes. He lifted the tray gingerly, it had been used by a wizard, after all. ''I only ever saw Nad eat that much before.'' It was this, not the miraculous healing, that marked her as truly powerful in his mind. Food, he understood. He tried a tentative smile. To his shock and joy it was returned.

"Thank you, Ivan." Her voice was a summer breeze.

"You're welcome, L–Lady," Ivan stammered and floated from the room, so totally oblivious to his surroundings Dorses had to move out of his way.

Puzzled by the young man's behavior, Dorses glanced questioningly toward the woman on the bed and suddenly saw what Ivan had; a soft, exotic beauty with a hint of need and a promise of passion. A beauty more a matter of expression than eyes or lips or cheek. She pursed her own lips in admiration; this was a power *she* understood.

"At least he no longer fears me," Crystal explained softly, letting the expression fall, becoming no less beautiful but certainly less accessible.

"If you think Ivan in love will be easier to manage," the other woman said dryly, "I wish you joy of him. Do you thus lay the fear in all men?"

"No." Her laugh was a little embarrassed. "Two years older or two years younger and that wouldn't have worked." She remembered other men who'd howled curses at her, or pleas, or just howled. Ivan's uncomplicated sweetness was like a balm across the memories.

"Well, if you're well enough," Dorses spoke over her thought, "there's one man I wish you'd see. That Raulin's been driving me crazy trying to get into your room."

"Raulin? The brother?" She wondered what he wanted. Over the last twelve years she'd learned they always wanted something. "I guess I'd better see him."

"Good, I'll tell him . . ." Dorses paused in the doorway, nodded once, and added, ". . . Crystal." Then she was gone.

A long time, the wizard thought sadly, *since someone said my name in friendship. Except,* she added upon reflection, *for Lord Death.*

It was too soon for the food to do any good, even in a wizard's system, but Crystal imagined that she could feel her power grow. It frightened her being helpless; there were too many who would love to make wizard pay for a wizard's crimes. She studied the ceiling and reached out just a little.

The logs were pine. The branch now growing into the room at her urging, fully needled, and tipped with a pair of pinecones, proved it.

"More power back than I thought," Crystal muttered. She'd only intended a light touch. "This could be embarrassing to explain."

Out in the hall she heard Dorses trying to make an impression on someone who didn't appear to be listening.

". . . and you will not stay long. She'll be here for a few days, you'll likely see her again before you leave."

"I only want to thank her. That's all."

Crystal wasn't sure, but she thought she recognized the voice, although when she'd heard it last, it had quavered with pain and exhaustion. Raulin. He spoke in a kind of lazy drawl she found pleasing. The voice of a man who smiles a lot she decided; smiles and means every one.

"Lady?"

Rested and fed, Raulin was much more attractive than he'd been that night in the tavern. It wasn't so much the features—the nose a bit large, the gray eyes a bit deep, the brows a bit too definite, the mustache more than a bit . . . Crystal paused, uncertain of how to describe the mustache but it was more than a bit, that was for sure—but rather how he wore them: with laugh lines, and a twinkle, and a willingness to be delighted by life.

"Lady?" he repeated and stepped into the room. "Mind if I come in?"

"You're in," she pointed out.

He smiled. "And you don't seem to mind."

No, she didn't. She returned the smile and said, "You wanted to see me?"

"I've been trying for the last two days," he admitted. "In fact," his smile grew broader, "Dorses would say I've been very trying."

Crystal gave a gurgle of laughter, the sort of uncomplicated response she thought only her younger brother could evoke. "I really doubt Dorses would," she told him.

"Maybe not." He reached the edge of the bed and dropped to his knees. His face grew serious and his eyes stared fearlessly into hers. "You saved my brother's life," he said. "I can never thank you for that, there aren't the words, but I wish you could know how I feel."

Maybe later she would warn him about the dangers of looking into a wizard's eyes.

An emerald spark appeared and Crystal took the gift Raulin so innocently offered, moving across their gaze into his heart. It held little darkness, she found, and much light. At the center of the light was Jago. The younger brother, much loved and protected. The companion, the right arm, the other half. A man to guard his back, a friend to guard his dreams. Could he lose this much of his life and still have a life remaining?

Crystal didn't know she was crying until a gentle finger wiped away a tear.

"Lady?"

She caught his reaching hand and held it for a moment. "I do know how you feel," she said, so softly he had to lean forward to catch the words. "And I am well thanked for your brother's life."

To her astonishment, he brought the hand that held his to his lips and kissed its back, his mustache drawing fine lines of sensation across the skin.

"Lady," he told her, allowing her to reclaim her arm, "I will continue thanking you all the days I live." His smile returned. "And never has gratitude been expressed so willingly."

Was he flirting with her? Crystal tilted her head and gazed at the man in puzzlement.

"And if my thanks could be expressed in some more tangible way . . ."

She recognized that tone. He *was* flirting with her.

"You have only to command me, Lady. I long to fulfill your every wish." The florid words were accompanied by a mighty flourish of an imaginary hat.

"Uh, no wishes at the moment."

"Well, then . . ." He stood and dusted off his knees. "I'd best get back to Jago." The smile became a grin. "He's not as pretty, but I don't want him to spill soup in the bed. We can't afford a second one." He bowed, winked—she was quite sure he winked—and left.

Crystal shook her head. What an unusual man. His gratitude seemed truly to come with no strings. And Dorses appeared to want her around only because, for some unsaid reason, she liked her. Did everyone she'd met today play a very deep game or were they actually aware of her as a separate being, not necessarily evil because she was a wizard and not some thing to take advantage of because she had power? Had she stumbled on a small pocket of crazy people? Or perhaps, her expression grew slightly wistful, had she found the last of the sane?

Lord Death stood in a corner of the room and watched Crystal's face, wishing he could read her mind to see what prompted such a soft and dreamy look. She wasn't aware he could be with her unseen and he had no intention of telling her. If there were dead or dying present, she always saw him, but at other times he often chose to just spend time invisibly watching.

He was pleased to see he'd been right about Dorses. This woman could accept what Crystal was. He'd thought as much when he'd urged Crystal to heal that young man, knowing what it would take out of her, knowing it would throw her on the mercy of the innkeeper. The wizard needed to spend more time with people and less time brooding about her future. Brooding would lead her nowhere good.

He wished she'd confide in him about what had been bothering her lately. He wanted to help but didn't know how. Perhaps she'd say something to mortal ears. Once it was in the open he'd be able to do something.

The pleasure faded as he considered Raulin. It was so easy to forget Crystal had a mortal heritage as well and he greatly feared she now found herself in the company of one who would appeal to that side.

He didn't want to understand the pain he'd felt when the mortal touched her.

He was Lord Death and pain was not a part of that.

He looked up and the pine branch died.

The next morning, Crystal left her room, wandered down to the kitchens, and astounded the innkeeper by not only suggesting a new way of doing turnips, a staple in the local diet, but by then preparing the dish herself.

Dorses, knowing Crystal's background as both Princess and Wizard, for who in that part of the world did not, assumed it was something she'd learned in the dozen years since the defeat of Kraydak, made a note of the recipe, and asked no questions.

Crystal, thanking the vegetarian centaurs for teaching her at least one skill that served some purpose in the mortal world, offered no explanations. She had no wish to underline differences, not when she felt so content.

While they worked, the two women talked, and firmed their tentative feelings of friendship.

When Ivan came in from morning chores, he brought a dried and delicate wild rose, found perfectly preserved, mixed in with the summer's hay. Wordlessly he presented it to Crystal, accepted her thanks with glowing eyes—few wizards' had ever been so bright— and pink with pleasure, watched her wind it in her hair where it slowly softened and lived again.

The afternoon, Crystal spent with Raulin. He made

her laugh with his wild flattery, and she felt herself beginning to respond to his obvious interest. In his own way he was as single-minded as those who saw only the wizard, but it was a single-mindedness she couldn't help but appreciate. It was a nice change.

Although he never mentioned it, his accent told her he came from the Empire. She wondered how he'd managed to survive the long years of Kraydak's rule with his good nature intact.

That evening, she lay on her bed, listening to the sounds rising up from the common room, one hand gently stroking the velvet petals of Ivan's rose. Dorses had asked her to come down, but she hadn't the courage to face the locals and risk their almost certain fear and rejection.

"There," Nad sat back on his heels and beamed down at his handiwork. He'd just set new andirons into one of the common room's giant hearths and he was pleased with the way the design looked. "You see," he said, "they've got ta be large enough ta carry the load but not so large young Ivan here can't move them out ta clean the ashes like. And as this is a public place," he looked up at his audience and smiled, "then best make 'em easy on the eyes."

Crystal grinned back and tucked one foot up under her on the bench. With both hearths unlit, the room was far from warm. "They're certainly very pretty," she agreed. "I've never seen irons shaped like stag horns before."

"Stag horns!" Dorses snorted from behind the bar where she was counting stock. "All I asked was that they be thick enough not to melt out of shape and he brings me stag horns!"

"Actually, they don't look very thick," Crystal said softly to Nad, not wanting to get him in trouble with the innkeeper and her quest for durability. "Are they likely to melt?"

"Nay." The blacksmith's brow puckered and he scratched at the bald patch on top of his head. "But they may sag a tad the next time we have a cold snap and some stonehead overloads the fire.''

"That would be a definite shame." She slid off the bench and onto her knees beside him. "May I?"

"Be my guest." Nad waved a hand, puzzled but gracious.

Crystal leaned forward and lightly touched both antlers. The iron flared a sudden brilliant green. "No fire built in this hearth can affect them now," she explained as the glow faded. "They'll always be as lovely as they are today."

"Well, I'm much obliged," Nad's broad features were rosy. Praise always made him blush, for he could see the flaws he'd left even if no one else could, and this was high praise indeed. "That's a right handy trick." He gave her a sly grin. "Can you straighten nails?"

She laughed and held out her hand.

The nail Nad dropped on her palm had certainly seen better days. It was bent not once but twice, and touched with rust as well.

She held it gently by the head and stroked the index finger of her other hand down its length. No green glow answered. The nail turned cherry red and melted into slag.

"Good thing we were on the hearth," Nad observed philosophically.

Crystal stared down at the tiny puddle of molten metal. She didn't understand; the power had begun to answer, then it had twisted off as if responding to another call. She wiped suddenly sweaty hands on her thighs. "That's . . . that's never happened before."

"*Idiot,*" sneered a voice in her head.

"You shouldn't get upset about it." Nad grasped her shoulder lightly with a warm and comforting hand, misinterpreting Crystal's bleak expression. He liked the girl. Let others argue the mortality of wizards—and they had been for the three days this one had been at the Nugget—she was kind and she was beautiful and that was enough for him. He loved beauty and tried to put a little into everything he made; from pickaxes, to plows, to andirons. "I couldn't have used that nail agin anyway, not bent as it was," he continued, smiling sympathetically. "I guess you were still fired up." His blunt chin pointed at the stag horns. "From doin' t'other."

"I guess." She managed a small smile in return because the blacksmith looked so upset at her distress. She wanted to accept his explanation. She hadn't been paying much attention to the nail, it was such a small thing, and she could easily believe she'd used too much power. Foolish, for attention should be paid to the smallest of power uses, but not frightening. Except for the voice.

"Well now, look who's comin' down ta join us," Nad got to his feet and extended a massive hand to Crystal.

She took it and stood, fortunately enough taller so that Nad's huge shoulders weren't blocking her view.

Slowly descending the stairs, placing each foot firmly but with care, was Jago. He'd been shaved, his hair washed and rebraided, and no trace of his injuries was apparent, but knuckles showed white in the hand that gripped the banister and his gaze never rose from his path. Raulin followed closely behind, his expression as proud as if he'd taught Jago to walk.

"Well, you certainly look a sight better than you did," Nad boomed, striding forward to meet the brothers at the foot of the stairs. "Just tryin' out the new pins are you?"

"Yes," Jago said shortly. He was out of banister and it was a good five feet to the nearest bench.

Nad looked at Jago, looked at the open space he must cross, and understood the hesitation. "You've nothin' ta worry about, them legs of yours are as good as new."

"I know that," Jago's tone was polite, but only just barely.

"I've been telling him the same thing," Raulin put in. "Not that they ever were much . . ."

"Raulin . . ."

"And it'd not be polite to let the lady wizard think you didn't trust her healin'," Nad added.

Jago's lips narrowed. "It's not that, I . . ." He trailed off, unsure how to explain.

"It's just you saw your legs," Crystal said gently, stepping into his line of sight. "Before you lost consciousness you saw and you knew what you had to look forward to if you woke. And no healing can erase a memory like that, not if the Mother-creator Herself had been the healer. You know your legs are whole, but you can't believe; not quite, not yet."

"Yes." He nodded, both with respect and relief that someone understood. "That's it exactly." He took a deep breath, avoided Raulin's reaching hand, and walked to the bench. Then he sat, visibly unclenched his jaw, and smiled up at his brother. "What do you mean they never were much?" he demanded.

Below his mustache, Raulin's smile was identical. It was the one feature they held in common. "I meant in comparison, of course."

"I think," Nad turned a beaming face on Dorses, who watched from behind the bar, "this calls for a drink."

"Not surprising," the innkeeper said dryly, "you think everything calls for a drink." But she filled five tankards with ale and joined the others at a table.

Crystal studied Jago's face while he drank, and when he lowered his tankard he caught her at it. He met her eyes as forthrightly as his brother had, his own holding neither fear nor suspicion, only a cautious reserve. Raulin had laid himself open for her taking; Jago only acknowledged that she could. His eyes were a very dark violet and he was among the handsomest men Crystal had ever met. She looked away first, found Raulin studying her, flushed, and ended up staring into her ale. This showed all the signs of becoming very complicated.

". . . certainly the most excitin' night we've ever had at the Nugget," Nad was saying. "As if you three weren't enough, we found at closin' time old Timon had already left with Lord Death.''

"What?"

"Oh, nothing ta worry about," the blacksmith hastened to explain, "he had ta be ninety if he was a day. Just his time." He took another drink of his ale. "Still, the Nugget's not likely to see another night like that in a hurry."

"Nor want to," Dorses said emphatically.

"Now I don't know about that," Raulin drawled, winking in Crystal's direction. "Everything turned out for the best."

Jago raised his tankard to his brother. "Next time *you* distract the brindle."

"Brindle tried to eat me, I'd choke him."

"You've always been hard to swallow." Jago's tone was light, but his face had tensed. It didn't take a wizard to see memories crowding up against the banter.

"Dorses?" Ivan stuck his head in from the kitchen. "It's near sunset and the biscuits aren't . . ."

"Near sunset? As late as that?" Dorses leaped to her feet and scooped the tankards from the table. "Put the dry ingredients together, I'll be there in a minute."

Ivan's head disappeared.

"You lot can stay or go as you please," Dorses told them, dumping the tankards behind the bar and heading for the kitchen. "But sunset's when I unbolt the doors. Crystal, if you don't mind, the fires, we've not much time . . ." And she was gone.

Crystal, if you don't mind, the fires . . . She turned the words over in her mind, oblivious to the others in the room. *Crystal, if you don't mind, the fires* . . . Of all her many acquaintances, over all the years, only the old Duke of Belkar had treated her power as though it was a useful tool.

"Lady?" Jago's worried voice brought her back to the Nugget's common room. "Are you all right?"

"Yes," she turned the brilliance of her joy on him.

"I've seldom been better." *Crystal, if you don't mind, the fires* . . .

She waved a hand at the new andirons and they disappeared beneath a load of wood. She turned to the other hearth, found the wood already laid, pointed a finger at each and said, "Burn."

A flare of green and both hearths filled with flame.

"She's good with fires," Nad confided to the brothers as the room began to warm.

"Ah," sighed the voice in her head.

It sounded pleased, but Crystal was too pleased herself to notice.

"Will you stay a while and enjoy the fruits of your labors?" Raulin asked, more than one invitation apparent in his voice. "Seems like a pity to waste such heat."

Pleasure faded and Crystal headed for the stairs. "No," she said without turning, "I can't."

"Crystal . . ."

A murmur from Jago cut off Raulin's next words, and she escaped to her room.

"I have had it with this!"

Crystal glanced up from the potato she was dicing. "Had it with what?" she asked.

"This!" Dorses glared at the disassembled pieces of the water pump. "Nothing but trouble and Nad's off at the mine today." She rubbed at her forehead, leaving a smudge of rust behind. "I don't suppose you could fix it."

"Sorry." Crystal shrugged. "But pump repairs were never something they taught me."

Dorses sighed. "I didn't think so."

After the incident with the nail, the strange and sudden twist, Crystal was hesitant to use her power on the pump, but neither did she want to let Dorses down. "Perhaps I could look at it anyway."

"Couldn't hurt," the innkeeper admitted standing aside. "I'm out of ideas."

With her index finger, Crystal pushed a metal ring

along the counter. It clinked against a stubby cylinder. The wizard took a deep breath. There had to be almost twenty bits and pieces of metal spread out in front of her and she had no idea of what to do with any of them. She wanted desperately to repay some small part of Dorses' kindness.

Her left hand lifted a tiny bolt and fitted it into the plate in her right hand. Crystal bit back a scream. Her hand had moved; she hadn't moved it.

"Crystal? Are you all right?"

"Fine," she managed, watching her fingers screw two totally incomprehensible things together. Dorses must not find out what was happening. Her right hand attached something to the pipe at the top of the pump. She couldn't bear it if this pushed Dorses away, as it must. Her left hand placed a second piece on the first. Her mind still seemed her own, but her hands moved at another's command. Strangest of all, behind her surface terror stood a wall of competence and calm.

"Relax," suggested a voice.

"React," sneered another.

The first voice was new, but the second she'd heard before.

With a sharp snick of metal against metal, her hands fixed the rebuilt cap onto the pump, tightened the collar, then fell limply to her sides. For a very long moment, they burned and itched with the not exactly unpleasant sensation of returning blood, then that faded and they were hers again. She raised them to her face, studied the palms, turned them over and studied the backs. Fortunately, the feeling of calm remained, distancing her still from what had just happened.

"You didn't cut yourself?" Dorses was a little worried; Crystal stood there so quietly, staring at her hands.

"Uh . . . no."

"Lets see what . . ." The innkeeper moved around the wizard's motionless body. "Mother-creator, you've rebuilt it!" She grabbed the handle and began to pump vigorously. "Let's hope it wasn't in pieces long enough for the pipes to freeze."

"Do they?" Crystal asked, only because she felt she must say something.

"Chaos, yes. Once the cold weather sets in, Ivan's up every couple hours in the night keeping the water moving." A cough and a sputter and a splash of cold liquid shot out the mouth of the pump. Dorses smiled in satisfaction. "I hate having to melt snow," she confided to Crystal. "I thank you from the bottom of my heart."

Crystal opened her mouth, unsure of what she was going to say but uneasy over taking credit for something she hadn't done. To her horror, words spilled out without her willing them. "Consider it a gift from the goddess." And the calm disappeared.

"Think highly of yourself, don't you," Dorses laughed, still facing the pump, not seeing the fear that robbed all power from the wizard's features. "I've a barrel of beer that could use a blessing then; it's going skunky."

"Maybe later . . ." Crystal choked out, and fled. For one of the few times in her life, she thanked the centaurs for their insistence on emotional control—although for them control meant denial—drummed over and over into the child she had been until it became almost second nature to hide what she felt. Those lessons served her now, keeping all the terrified bits of her together and moving.

"Crystal?" Dorses turned, but the kitchen was empty. She wondered if she should follow. Had she said something wrong? But the soup boiled over on the stove, and once that was taken care of the pies needed finishing, and the moment for following passed.

Up in her room, Crystal lay in the center of the bed, knees drawn up to her chest, eyes squeezed shut, arms wrapped tightly around her head, and her hair a silver veil over all. Only her lips moved. Over and over they formed a denial, of the voices that whispered and roared and of the knowledge of what those voices meant. "No, no, no, no. . . ."

Unseen beside her, Lord Death reached out a hand. It hovered a moment close above a shoulder he couldn't touch and when he withdrew it, the fingers closed to form a fist. *The comfort of Death,* he thought, *is a cruel joke.*

"Crystal?"

The banging on her door was persistent and loud.

"Crystal, open the door!"

Slowly she unfolded and still more slowly stood. She waved a hand and the door swung open.

Raulin, his hand raised to bang again, took a quick step into the room. "Are you all right?" he demanded anxiously. "Dorses says you've been up here since morning. She figured if you could keep the door closed you must be fine, but me, I wanted proof." He moved forward and brushed her hair back off her face, leaving his hand resting gently against her cheek. He had to tilt his head slightly to meet her eyes. "What's wrong?"

Crystal wet her lips. She'd fought all day, banishing the voices, building and reinforcing shields in her mind. Her nerves hung balanced on the dagger's edge and she could not allow herself the luxury of hysterics, not inside, not where others could be hurt. "I think," she said softly, "I don't want to be alone." Then, as Raulin continued to meet her eyes, she blushed deeply.

His answering smile banished much of the day's terror.

"No," she corrected hurriedly, "not that." She moved her face against the warmth of his hand. "Not yet."

"Then come down to the common room," he suggested, marveling at the satin feel of her skin, daring to trace one finger down the curve of her throat. Not yet meant later. He could wait. "Jago's down there now; he's enough of a wonder to hold them. They won't even notice you."

She cocked her head to listen and noticed for the first time the noise sifting through the floor. "Is it as late as that . . ."

As she obviously didn't require an answer, Raulin concentrated instead on coaxing her to the door. When she balked on the threshold, he slipped an arm around her waist. "You did say you didn't want to be alone," he reminded her. He withdrew his arm as an emerald glow reminded him who he held. Cautioned but undaunted, he tucked her arm in his and, when that provoked no objection, kept her moving toward the stairs.

The common room was packed and, as Raulin had said, Jago stood in the center of an admiring court, the more vocal of whom were trying to get him out of his pants.

"Come on, laddie," called an old woman with a voice like crushed stone, "let's see them legs!"

"Let's have some skin," cried out a much younger one.

Most of the crowd had obviously been drinking heavily. Jago did not appear to be having a particularly good time.

"He hates being the center of attention," Raulin confided to Crystal as he steered her to a table in the back, the same table she'd sat at the night it all began.

"And you'd have your pants off?"

"In a minute." He grinned. "There's little I hate more than false modesty."

Over the multitude of heads, Jago—boosted up on a table by Nad, partially to give everyone a good view, partially to keep him safe—met Crystal's eyes. She knew he saw her, it wasn't a mistake she could make, but in no way did he acknowledge her presence. It showed a sensitivity to her feelings she hadn't expected and she found herself warming to the younger man. With nothing to draw their attention, the crowd indeed didn't notice her and she sat unseen until Nad innocently gave it away, only wanting Crystal to share in the glory. "And there's the Lady," he called, with a happy smile and a pointing finger. ''The one who did the healin'.''

The crowd fell silent as they turned and the weight of their gaze pushed Crystal to her feet. She felt her power build in answer to theirs. A crowd could become a mob very quickly, she knew, and quicker still when drink had blurred the boundaries.

''Wizard?''

The sound rose in a questioning wave and could still break either way when a man with an eye patched pushed to the front of the pack and said, ''Where's my son, wizard. Where's my boy?''

Crystal kept silent. No answer she could give would satisfy. It never had before. She felt the familiar tightness in her stomach.

A woman, with a steel hook where her right hand should be, stepped forward to stand by the one-eyed man and the mob took them as their center and formed about them. Some murmured names. Others rubbed scars. They all remembered the day, twelve years before, when the Wizard's Horde had come.

''Wizard.''

A growl now, an unpleasant rumble.

The funny thing was, if she actually was what they accused her of, they wouldn't dare accuse.

She saw Jago tense, his place on the table giving him an advantage in the fight that was sure to begin. Nad, his honest face puzzled, looked from one friend to another, unsure of what was happening. Beside her, she heard Raulin stand, and felt him ready for battle. She was very glad Ivan stayed safely in the kitchen.

''Wizard!''

Their common voice rising to a howl the crowd surged forward, arms reaching to clutch, but they slammed against a barrier and continued to slam against it as the wizard walked through them and up the stairs.

In the upper hall she paused. The crowd had not yet turned its attention on those who'd stood beside her. Before it could she reached out, wrapped Raulin and

Jago in her power, and twitched them to safety; one heartbeat there, the next gone. Even if Raulin hadn't enough sense to stay in their room, Jago, she strongly suspected, would keep him locked inside. She heard Dorses' voice, falling like cold water on the din, slapping down and relocking the passion.

Not until she reached the safety of her own room did she allow the barrier to fall. They were all the same, the ones who hated, they never realized they couldn't hurt her.

Physically.

The voices kept her company all through the long night that followed. Not until morning did she regain enough power to push them back in their place.

Three

"Chaos, Jago, you owe her! The least we can do is tell her and let her choose." Raulin stuffed a heavy wool shirt into his pack, and reached for a pair of thick gray socks. His brother's hand clamped down just above his wrist.

"Those," Jago pointed out, grabbing the socks and tossing them in his own pack, "are mine." He released Raulin's arm and returned to methodically folding his own spare clothes and neatly placing them inside the oilcloth bag.

"I don't believe you, that you'd begrudge your own brother a pair of socks," Raulin muttered. "Your own brother . . ."

"*I* remember what old Dector told us; up in the mountains a pair of warm, dry socks could save your life."

Raulin released his pack and threw both arms up into the air. "Which is exactly the point I'm trying to make. Do you *want* to depend on a pair of socks? She's a wizard, Jago! For the Mother's sake, think of what that means!"

"I have thought of it, which is obviously more than you've done."

"Look," Raulin managed to keep his voice reasonable as he began ticking points off on his fingers, "she saved your life. If that sort of thing happens again wouldn't you want to have her around?"

Jago's lips tightened. "Yes," he admitted.

"And then last night, you know as well as I do that she pulled our asses out of the fire with that trick. We'd have been sleeping with Lord Death if she'd left us there.''

''That's *not* what you said last night.''

When the brothers had found themselves suddenly up in their room instead of in the middle of a howling crowd, Raulin had been furious. First, at the crowd for daring to raise a hand against the woman who'd cured his brother. Second, at Crystal for removing him before he could lift his hands in return. Had Jago not kicked his feet out from under him and then sat on him until he settled down, Raulin would've stormed back down the stairs and thrown himself into the fray.

Causing exactly the sort of riot Jago suspected Crystal was trying to prevent.

Raulin, once calmed and convinced Crystal would not want to see him, went to bed and fell quickly asleep. Knowing *why,* he didn't care *how* she'd gotten them out of the tavern and into their room, nor did he worry about the implications of the act.

Jago, however, lay for hours, staring at the ceiling, his thoughts tumbling to the cadence of his brother's snoring. Such power expended on their behalf made him nervous. One hand dropped to rest on his thigh. They already owed this wizard more than they could repay and now the debt had grown. With Raulin so ready to take up arms in her defense, he'd have no choice but to stand by the wizard's side. Although, he was forced to admit, he'd have stood there for the debt's sake as well. And for hers . . .

For two and a half days he'd carried a piece of her life and that tied them in ways he had no wish to be tied. Not to a wizard. Not even this one, beautiful and desirable as she undeniably was.

Their city had been conquered by Kraydak's Horde in their great-grandfather's time—although Kraydak was not known as a wizard then—and by the time of Jago's birth the excesses of the conqueror were an accepted part of existence. People lived their lives and did what they could to avoid coming to his attention. During the Great War, when Kraydak had stood revealed as what he was, nothing had changed. People tried harder not to be noticed and prayed to whatever they still believed in that they wouldn't be called upon to serve.

"And now," Jago had muttered to himself, "twelve years after surviving *that* we're not only noticed but serving." He'd sighed, elbowed Raulin to stop the snoring, and finally fallen asleep.

"I said, last night was different!"

Jago started, snapped out of his reverie by Raulin's voice. "Sorry. I was thinking."

Raulin tied down the last thong on his pack. "You think too much."

"Yeah? Well, I'm thinking for two."

"And," Raulin continued, ignoring the dig, "you never listen."

"I never . . ." Jago yanked at the cord around his neck and pulled a small leather pouch up from under his shirt. "Well, all right then." He whipped it over his head and threw it across the room. The pouch smacked in the center of Raulin's chest. "Go ahead. Give it to her. But don't be surprised if she thanks you very kindly, tells us we've no business meddling, and pops off with it. Remember your own words; she's a wizard."

"And so, in spite of everything she's done for us, we're not to trust her?"

"I didn't say that!"

"You think she'll betray us?"

"I didn't say that either."

"Then what are you saying?"

Jago opened his mouth to remind his brother of the creed they'd lived their lives by and then closed it again. They'd been noticed; there was no retreating from that. And he did trust her; he couldn't not. But still, she was a wizard and accepting her did not deny that wizards had always, without exception, made their own rules. "I don't know," he said finally.

Raulin reached out and gave one of Jago's braids an affectionate tug. "Don't worry, little brother. We'll just ask her, she'll say yes or no, and that'll be the end of it.'' He slipped the cord over his own head but left the pouch hanging loose. ''We'll pack the sled later.'' He headed out the door. ''Come on.''

''Who never listens?'' Jago sighed, grabbed up his vest, and followed.

''So you're really goin' then?''

Crystal nodded, gray circles beneath her eyes mute testimony to a sleepless night.

''I wish you wouldn't,'' Nad muttered, staring down into the deep mahogany of his morning tea. ''I'm sure they'd come ta like you in time.'' Then his lips twisted and he shook his head. ''Nay, they wouldn't either.'' He looked up and sighed. ''It's too bad there's nothin' great for you ta do, like a shaft collapsin' or the plague or somethin' that'd bring them ta need you.''

''You're not suggesting she collapse a shaft, are you?'' Dorses asked, wrapping Crystal's nearly unresponsive fingers about a mug of steaming tea. She kept her tone light, hoping to lift the pall of gloom that hung about the woman. A half smile rewarded the attempt while Nad sputtered and tried to explain.

''I understand,'' Crystal said finally as Nad's sentences became more and more confused, ''but it doesn't matter, not really. If a shaft collapsed while I was here, no matter how many lives I saved the fault would end up mine. And any plague I cured I would also be accused of causing.''

Nad's eyes glistened. ''You can't win.'' He blinked back tears and cleared his throat. ''You just can't win.''

Crystal felt his own eyes fill and bit her lip to keep the tears from spilling. Nothing undid her control faster than sympathy and understanding. She took a hurried gulp of tea, scalding her mouth but glad of an action to hide behind.

''Yo, Crystal!'' Raulin peered in from the empty common room. ''Can we talk to you a moment?'' His brows waggled and beneath his mustache was an enthusiastic grin.

The Nugget's kitchen was warm and safe and with the prospect of leaving the inn before her, Crystal wanted to stay both warm and safe for as long as she could. But Raulin had stood beside her and Jago had shared her life so she set down her mug and got slowly to her feet.

As she brushed by Raulin—he remained in the doorway holding open the door, leaving very little room for her—she wished for an instant he'd come to her last night and she could have lost the pain in his arms. Except she wouldn't have, and she knew it. Too late now . . .

"We . . ." He pushed the door shut and stepped away from it into the common room. "Jago and I have a proposition for you."

Crystal looked from one to the other; from Raulin's enthusiasm to Jago's wary stare. "What?" she asked finally.

"We have a map that will lead us to one of the ancient wizards' old towers." Raulin patted the pouch hanging on his chest. "We want you to go with us."

Emerald eyes blinked twice and Crystal shook her head. "What?" she repeated but with an entirely different emphasis.

Raulin put a foot up on a bench and propped his elbow on his thigh. "Look, I know it's hard to believe, but it's true. After you defeated Kraydak, things went a little crazy in the Empire, every two copper power mogul trying to gain control. While things were, well, stirred up, we found this map."

"We stole it from the office of Kraydak's city governor."

"Jago!"

"If you're telling her at all, tell her the truth."

"He was dead. He didn't need it."

"Wait." Crystal held up her hand, cutting the incipient argument short. "Did you kill him?"

Jago showed teeth in an unpleasant smile. "Not exactly."

"While I warned His Excellency that a lynch mob waited out front," Raulin explained in a flat voice, "Jago led them to the rear exit."

"And when he tried to slip out the back they ripped him to shreds?" Crystal asked, although she didn't really need to.

Once again Raulin's smile matched his brother's. "Eventually."

The city governor had been Kraydak's hand, a hand holding Kraydak's whip; Crystal spared him little sympathy. After twelve years of being the only wizard in a mortal world, Crystal had come to feel there was almost an excuse for what Kraydak had become; there wasn't so much as a rationalization for the mortals who had turned on their own kind. What the brothers had done had been as necessary as stepping on a roach.

"You *found* a map?" she prodded.

"Oh, yeah." Raulin pulled himself free of memories. "I only noticed it because the Right Honorable Scumsucker dropped it scurrying out the door. I grabbed it . . ." He paused, decided the rest of what he'd stripped from the room had no real relevance to the tale, and continued. "Mother wanted to be a Scholar, couldn't of course, it was an outlawed discipline, but she read constantly and even managed to get her hands on a number of the forbidden texts. She recognized the sigil on the map."

"A bleeding hand," Jago interjected, "on a circle of black. Aryalan. One of the ancient wizards." His tone, unlike Raulin's, held no enthusiasm, no excitement. Raulin told a story. He reported facts.

Crystal felt Jago's disapproval, it surrounded him like a fog, but she was uncertain whether he disapproved of the weight of history that accompanied the wizard's name, the situation he and his brother now found themselves in, or her hearing of it.

"How can you be sure," she asked, "that the map leads to her tower."

"We can't," Raulin admitted cheerfully. "No one can read the script. What's more, it must have been recopied so many times over the centuries it's got a virgin's chance in Chaos of retaining any of the original wording. But it does lead to something of the wizard's, something important and big. That much we're sure of. Think of it, Crystal," he leaned forward and his hands clutched at dreams, "a treasure house of the ancients, lost since the Age of Wizards ended. Ours for the taking. Yours too if you'll come. Chaos knows, your talents could come in handy." Then his voice softened. "And we'd like your company."

For an instant Crystal thought, *So, he would find use for me after all*, then realized she did Raulin a disservice. It took no wizard to see that he wanted her more than he wanted her power. The power was only a useful addition. She glanced at Jago and he answered her silent question with a terse nod; more conscious of the wizard than his brother and therefore more wary of the woman.

This was what she'd been looking for, a new venture to involve her power now that the purpose she'd been created for was done. Something to give her life direction; for she had no doubt that although this pair of mortals might be able to breach the wizard's tower, there'd be power within it only she could handle. If she went with them, she'd be necessary again.

And more than that.

Companionship on the trail, laughter to chase away the loneliness, warm arms instead of cold power wrapped around her at night.

Raulin's gaze was a caress and, behind the caution in Jago's eyes, warmth lurked.

She felt herself respond, an answering heat rising. To her horror, she felt something rise with it, stirring behind the heavy shields that blocked the voices, felt it through the barriers, its strength bringing all the other bits and pieces with it and threatening to fling them free.

Crystal clutched at her concept of self. "I can't,"

she gasped, turning and fleeing. Halfway up the stairs she paused and let go enough to face them again, saying softly, "Be careful."

Raulin only stared, but Jago answered in tones matching hers, "You also."

And then she was gone.

"Well," Raulin said after standing a moment in stunned silence, "you were a lot of help."

"Huh?"

"I'm not surprised she ran, with you glowering at her like that."

"I wasn't glowering."

"You certainly weren't being too encouraging."

"Yeah? At least I wasn't leering."

"And I was?"

"When aren't you? Every woman we meet, it's the same story."

"I don't leer."

They started up the stairs, both very aware of having given Crystal enough time to reach the safety of her room, both well aware that bickering covered concern there seemed to be no way to express. They'd seen fear enough to know it, even on a wizard's face.

"Lady?" Ivan slid out from behind the tree and moved tentatively forward. "I, I just wanted ta say good-bye."

From somewhere, Crystal found a smile for him. She'd slipped through the village unnoticed—those not at the mines were blind behind the heavy felt pads that covered the windows, blocking the winter drafts—and wondered how he knew she'd take this path. Known in advance, she realized. He'd been waiting for her to arrive.

" 'Twas easy," he told her when she asked. "You wouldn't want ta pass the mines, not after . . ." He colored and continued, leaving the sentence hanging. "And I heard you tell Nad that you were headin' north when you stopped. If you were still goin' north, well," he shrugged, the motion almost buried under his heavy furs, "unless you changed ta a bird, this is the way you had ta come."

They both turned and looked down the only negotiable way up the cliffs that shielded the village from the furies of the north wind.

"And if I had turned to a bird?"

Ivan smiled. "Then I'd seen that," he said simply, "and have waved." His eyes dropped to snowy boot toes. "But I'm glad you didn't," he added.

"I am too," Crystal told him, and meant it. In the small pouch that held the few things she treasured—a birch leaf, withered and brown, a strand of her mother's hair, a smooth gray stone from Riven Pass—was Ivan's wild rose still, and always, blooming. She suddenly wanted to give him something that would mean as much to him, regardless of what the power use might open within her.

The heavy clothes she wore were more for comformity than necessity and although every breath hung in a frosty cloud and the sky had the brittle clarity that only comes with bitter cold, her hands and head were bare. She pulled free two long, silver hairs and, brows drawn down in concentration, braided them into a ring.

"Give me your hand."

Ivan obediently removed his mitten and extended his arm.

Crystal slipped the ring on his smallest finger. It fit perfectly.

Speechless, Ivan stared at his hand like he'd never seen it before. Then he gasped as he took a closer look at the ring. From an arm's length, it appeared no more than a thin silver band such as anyone might wear, but up close the solid metal became again the intricate weaving of two of the wizard's long silver hairs.

"I, I don't know what ta say," he managed at last.

"Well," Crystal gently slipped the mitt back on his hand as he seemed incapable of doing it himself, "you came to say good-bye."

The youth nodded and bit his lip. "Good-bye, Lady." He took courage from the warm feel of the ring about his finger and met her eyes. "I hope you find what you're lookin' for."

When he came up out of the emerald glow that had enveloped him, he was alone on the cliff top and his were the only tracks that marked the snow. He slid his thumb inside the larger part of his mitten and touched the ring. It was a beautiful gift but not the greatest the wizard had given him, for before he'd lost himself in her power he'd seen tears glisten in her eyes and he still felt the soft pressure of her silent good-bye.

Suddenly, he grinned and threw himself down the steep trail back to the village, bounding and leaping like a crazed mountain goat, his whoops echoing back from the cliff face and filling the valley with sound.

The last piece of equipment lashed tight to the sled, Raulin straightened and stared to the north. They'd follow the path young Ivan said she'd taken only to the top of the cliff and then swing west. He sighed and his breath laid a patina of frost on his mustache.

Jago stepped out of the Nugget, pulling on his mittens, and followed the direction of his brother's gaze. He couldn't help but be glad they were going on alone. Breaching a wizard's tower with another wizard in tow struck him as one wizard too many. Probably *two* too many, but he hadn't been able to convince Raulin of that and going along had seemed the answer. Besides, if they did win through . . .

"Jago?"

"What?" He slapped his pockets until he found his snow goggles and slipped them on.

"I wasn't leering, was I?"

"Afraid you scared her away?"

Raulin turned to face the younger man, his expression hard to read. "Yes," he said simply.

Jago shook his head. "No," he put as much conviction in his voice as he could, "you weren't leering. You didn't scare her away." He shrugged. "If one of us scared her, it was me. She knew, in spite of everything, that I didn't completely trust her. But I think she had her own reasons for running.''

''Yeah. Me too. Did you pay the innkeeper?''

''Of course.'' Jago went to his place behind the sled and got a firm grip on the pushing bar while Raulin slipped the leather traces over his shoulders. ''I gave her the brindle pelt.''

''You what?'' Forgetting he was now held to the sled, Raulin turned so quickly he almost threw himself to the ground.

''Why waste our coin?'' Jago asked practically. ''We had no time to have it tanned and it was beginning to go gamy.''

''If I'd known you were going to throw that much payment at her,'' Raulin growled straightening himself out, ''I'd have asked for another bed.''

''I don't know what you're complaining about,'' Jago muttered, rocking the sled from side to side to break the runners free. ''You're the one who snores.''

''I don't snore!'' Raulin threw his weight against the harness and the sled jerked forward, cutting the start of the path shown on the ancient map in the snow.

The great white owl drifted silently on a breeze, the tip of each wing barely sculling to keep it aloft. Its shadow kept pace, a sharp edged silhouette running along the moon silvered snow. Suddenly, with powerful beats of huge wings, it dove for the ground, talons extended.

Had the hare frozen it might have lived, for owls hunt by sound more than sight, but it panicked and fled, kicking up a plume of snow that clearly marked its position. The shadow reached it first. Frantically, it twisted and spun and died as the talons closed and the weight of the owl drove it into the ground and snapped its back with a single clear crack.

The owl shook itself free of snow and bent its head to feed.

Perhaps the bird's bad eyesight explained why it continued to eat, apparently unaware of the man who stood less than a wingspan away, observing it with distaste. Perhaps.

"How," Lord Death asked with a shudder. "can you eat raw rabbit in the middle of the night?"

The owl clicked its beak in Lord Death's direction but made no other answer, save to eat a bit more raw rabbit. Not until its meal had been reduced to a patch of blood on the snow did it turn, blink great green eyes, and change.

"It could be worse," Crystal told him, spinning herself new clothes made of snow and moonlight—the cloak she clasped round her shoulders was red. "Compared to some, owls have fairly civilized eating habits."

"You realize that with no time to digest you have a stomach full of . . ."

"I realize."

"And?"

"I try not to think about it." She smiled. "I'm glad to see you."

Lord Death smiled back; he couldn't help it. He hoped she never discovered how much a slave to her smile he was. Except for the times he hoped she would discover it, and therefore smile more often.

Occasionally—this moment—Crystal wished she could trust the expressions on Lord Death's face. Did it mean anything when he smiled at her in that way, his eyes soft and questioning? Or did it merely mean that one of mortalkind had died wearing that expression?

They walked in silence for a time and then both began to speak at once.

Crystal laughed and waved a regal hand. "You first, milord."

"I merely wondered why you continue to travel alone." He'd put some effort into choosing the phrasing and it had, he thought, just the right touch of curiosity mixed with polite interest. Enough to get an answer but not to give away how much the answer meant. He wished he knew why the answer meant so much.

"There was . . . I mean, I . . ." She sputtered into silence and came to a halt.

Momentum moved Lord Death a farther pace or two, then he stopped, turned, and studied the wizard's face. "What are you afraid of," he asked, recognizing her expression. His voice grew cold. "What did he do to you?"

Puzzlement replaced fear for an instant then realization replaced that. "He didn't do anything." Crystal wondered what Lord Death had thought to turn his cheeks so red.

"Then what?"

Should she tell him what she suspected was happening? That the threads of power that made her what she was were one by one coming untied. He couldn't help. But then no one could and didn't friends tell each other what troubled them? Still, they weren't the usual friends, not the last surviving wizard and the Mother's one true son. Or should she just make something up to satisfy him?

"I can't tell you," she said at last, gifting him at least with no lie.

His voice deepened to a growl. "Why not?"

Helplessly she spread her hands. Why didn't she want Lord Death to know she was, perhaps literally, going to pieces? Why did it matter so much that she not shatter the image she knew he held of the perfect Crystal?

"Could you tell him?"

"Him? Raulin?" Strange question. She considered it. She hadn't told him, but could she? Raulin held no image of her the news could break and their friendship hadn't had the chance to develop to where what he thought of her mattered. "Yes," she said thoughtfully, "I could tell Raulin . . ."

Lord Death's face flickered through several expressions and ended up wearing none at all. "Oh," he said. And vanished.

Crystal stared at the place Lord Death had stood, her hand half raised to pull him back. "He wanted me involved in mortal lives again," she told the wind. "How could I betray him when I answered the question he asked?" she demanded of the shadows. "I never knew he carried mortal feelings," she confessed to the moonlight and opened her mind to call him back.

Across the meadow a tree burst into flame as the presences in her mind surged out of the place where the shields had penned them and grabbed for her power. Crystal screamed and dropped to her knees as burning hands beat at the inside of her skull. Below her, the snow hissed and melted. Voices howled and voices shrieked and voices screamed at other voices, but outside Crystal's head the night continued quiet and serene save for the one tree consumed in a tower of orange and gold.

Crystal felt her body rise, the movements small and sharp, directed by an unskilled puppeteer, or by one whose efforts were hindered by another fouling the strings. She staggered, almost fell and felt her feet jerked back beneath her. One voice, its cadences the hiss and crackle of the dying tree, shouted defiance.

"I will have her!"

"No," purred another equally heated but infinitely more controlled. *"Mine, for I was the key."*

Arms flailing, Crystal lurched first one way then the other, every two or three steps leaving a steaming hole in the snow. Her clothes, power created, dissolved, leaving her wearing only the pouch of memories on a leather belt around her waist and a blue-green opal, hanging from a silver chain about her neck. She felt the cold and then she didn't and then the pain was too intense for her to tell.

Then a third voice moved from the tumult to the forefront of her mind and the burning within became almost bearable. Her legs steadied and lengthened into a runner's stride.

With her fists clenched so tightly the nails cut half

moons into her palms, Crystal clutched at the shards of her power and tried to force her shields back into place. Nothing remained to force; the shields had been obliterated and the voices fought over the ruins. When she tried instead to regain control of her body, something slammed her against a tree with enough violence to have her cry out in purely physical pain. Muscles and joints protested as the voices battled among themselves, twisting her from side to side. When the running began again, she let it.

Through the forest, across a small meadow, up a rocky cliff face and down an impossible trail, all done at close to full speed, the third voice fighting off the others while directing Crystal's feet. In shattered bits and pieces, Crystal felt the calm that had cushioned her while her hands repaired the Nugget's kitchen pump.

A small building appeared at the edge of her vision, her body changed direction slightly and ran toward it.

"No!" howled a voice.

The leg just lifted off the ground spasmed and when it came forward again, refused to bear her weight. Crystal pitched forward, rolling at the last second to avoid slamming her face into a granite outcropping. Her body wracked with convulsions, she fed what little power she held to the third voice. She had to get to that building—she didn't know why, but its call nearly drowned out the chaos—and the third voice seemed also to be trying to get her there.

The convulsions eased and the puppeteer pulled her to her knees, then her feet, then she was running again. The second time she fell, she tasted blood as her teeth went through her tongue.

The building stood barely two body lengths away, maybe less.

The convulsions returned and locked her muscles. She couldn't rise, not even to her knees, so she rolled through snow and rock and blood and vomit, rolled to the threshold and slammed up against the door. With the last of her strength, with the third voice falling before the other two, she lifted her arm and fumbled at the latch.

Her fingers refused to obey so she slapped at the piece of metal, drove her hand up against it, used the pain as a focus to keep control of her arm.

The door swung open and she flopped inside. . . .

Silence.

No sound save the soft murmur of the wind in the trees and the beating of Crystal's own heart.

She dragged herself forward, and with a swollen and bleeding foot pushed closed the door.

The wood beneath her cheek was cedar and from the spicy smell masking the stink that she knew had entered with her, the rest of the building was as well. A silver square of moonlight marked the floor a handspan from her nose. She lay quietly, gathering together her splintered power, motionless until she held enough to feel whole again, then slowly, very slowly she pulled her legs beneath her and pushed herself up until she sat.

The building was small and square, a door in one wall, small windows in two others flanked by cupboards filled with the supplies a traveler might need. Opposite the door was a fireplace, and wood stacked floor to ceiling. At a comfortable distance from the hearth, sat the cabin's only piece of furniture: a chair, arms and back intricately carved with leaves and vines, the whole thing lovingly polished to a satin finish.

The Mother's chair.

The Mother's house.

Small cabins maintained by those who lived in the Mother's service. Blessed with the Mother's presence. A place of peace, not only for the mind and spirit but for the body as well for no weapon could pass the door and no hand could be lifted in anger within the walls.

Crystal had had no idea such a sanctuary existed here on Halda's frozen border.

Carefully, she reached within. The bedlam had been calmed by the Mother's presence although the pieces that had created it still remained apart. She searched among them gently until she touched the presence that spoke with the third voice. ''Thank you,'' she said to it.

''You're welcome, child,'' replied the voice. *''They called me Tayja when I had a life of my own. Know me as your friend.''* And then the presence withdrew, leaving Crystal to herself, but the calm that came with it lingered.

Moving gingerly, for she hadn't the power to repair the damage done, Crystal crawled toward the chair, wincing as a torn bit of flesh caught on a rough piece of flooring. She knew she needed to eat and sleep, but she needed to think even more. When she reached the chair she sighed, and rested her head where the Mother's lap would be.

Tayja. Goddess of craft and learning.

It was just as she feared.

When the Age of Wizards ended, there were few powers left in the world. Out of all the pantheon that mortals had created to help them understand the Mother's creation and their place within it, only the seven goddesses remained. In time they caused one last wizard to be formed, a power to fight an ancient evil, and into that vessel they poured all that they were.

''And now that the evil is defeated,'' Crystal realized, her aching head pillowed an abraded arms, ''some at least have no further use for the vessel.''

Fire. Zarsheiy. Now she could name the hissing and howling voice, the first she'd heard, the part of her that fought the hardest to be free.

''And *that* is the problem . . .'' Her eyes began to close and she sighed again. ''They are a part of me and without them I am not. I wish,'' she murmured sleepily, ''that just once there'd be an easy answer.''

As she drifted to sleep, still leaning against the Mother's chair, she thought she felt the soft touch of a sympathetic hand against her cheek.

Four

For two days Crystal did little but eat and sleep, slowly healing her damaged body as her returning power enabled her to do so. On the third day, she allowed the fire to die down to embers and, sitting with her back to the Mother's chair, slipped into trance and then deep within her own mind.

Green, a deep rich summer shade lightening to springtime as she went deeper still. A tendril of thought rose up to meet her and she paused, knowing that in the Mother's house only benevolent forces could stir.

"Why have you come?" Tayja asked, her tone sharp though not unkind.

"We need to talk." The wizard concentrated and the green light fractured into a forest grove, the two women standing within a circle of silver birch.

The goddess smiled, the white of her teeth startlingly bright against the darkness of her skin. "Ah . . ." She sank to the velvet grass and stroked a hand along the blades. "So long . . ." Then her face grew serious and when she looked up at Crystal it bore the stamp of the mahogany of which she had been made. "You are safe enough with me, but do not attempt this with the others. It will only intensify their struggle to be separate once again."

Crystal nodded and sat, folding her legs beneath her. The Grove was an image so much a part of her that it took little power to maintain. "What is happening to me?" she asked.

"I thought you had discovered it."

"Well, yes, but . . ."

"But you wish me to clarify? Very well." Tayja sat straighter and cupped her hands before her. "Consider yourself to be the crystal you are named." As she spoke a crystal appeared on her palms, rough cut, multifaceted, and a little smaller than a clenched fist. "You should be neither surprised nor fearful," she chided, for the living Crystal had stiffened at the other's manipulation of her mind. "I am, after all, a part of you." A green light shone through the stone. "As you can see, the joinings between the many facets are obvious and this one more so than the others." She traced a finger down the line and the portion of the crystal it delineated began to glow red.

"Zarsheiy?" Crystal guessed.

"Yes. A necessary but unenthusiastic part of your creation. She has always been unstable and had all our power not been necessary . . ." The goddess shrugged, a most ungoddesslike gesture, and continued. "While you were focused there was no problem." The crystal flared; green light submerging the red section back into the whole. "But as you lost purpose . . ." The green faded and the red glowed strongly once again. "Zarsheiy began to make her presence felt until . . ." A sharp crack and the red fragment of crystal broke free. "This weakened the structure and gave Avreen, who was always closest to Zarsheiy, ideas of her own." Tayja looked suddenly amused. "Actually, child, you gave her some ideas yourself."

Crystal felt her cheeks grow warm as she considered the aspects Avreen wore. "Raulin?" she asked.

"Raulin," Tayja agreed. "Not in itself a bad thing, but it strengthened Avreen and when next you used your power she twisted it, hoping to break free." Another facet flared along the edge of the larger stone, this one a deep flesh pink. "She didn't quite manage it, but her attempt and Zarsheiy's continuing fight to wrest control made the matrix increasingly unstable." The definition of the remaining contact lines intensified and each facet began to take on a color of its own, making the original crystal seem more a puzzle than a single piece. One, a deep brown, well marbled with green, became for a moment the dominant color.

Crystal touched the brown portion gently. "You?"

"Me," Tayja confirmed, her expression twisting slightly in embarrassment. "I found I could work on my own, and you wanted so badly to fix the pump. I am sorry though, I had no right." She sighed and shook her head. "Three nights ago, however, it became fortunate that I had strengthened my will or, if you wish, the part of your will which is mine.

"When you opened yourself to call Lord Death, you lowered all barriers and both Zarsheiy and Avreen took advantage of the opportunity." The red fragment grew suddenly radiant, the crystal writhed in Tayja's hands, and the pink fragment lay free as well. "They began to fight for control of your power. Because I have always been integrated more fully into your personality, I can call to my use a greater part of your power than either of them but in order to do it, I had to take their path."

Crystal noticed that even when the brown broke free of the larger mass, much of it remained green.

"With your help, I brought you to this house, where both of my ambitious sisters lie dormant and no others can break free to challenge you. Use this quiet time to rebuild your shields so that when you leave, as you must, they will be contained."

Crystal stared into the goddess' hands. The red and the pink had become colorless. The brown remained unchanged. Deep within the multihued stone—for four goddesses had not yet taken up their aspects—she saw a core of green. She realized that little bit of green would be all that remained if all the goddesses broke free and Crystal knew it wasn't enough to sustain a life.

"What must I do?" she asked, searching Tayja's face for the answer. "How do I become whole again?"

Tayja spread her hands, the stones vanished, and she

shook her head. "I do not know, child," she admitted, "but two things I can give you. First, as much as we seem separate we are all a part of you. We gave up our lives at your creation and now have none of our own. Second, the whole is always greater than the sum of its parts." She frowned. "Not a great deal of help, is it?" The goddess clasped Crystal's hands for a moment. "Now you know me, you better know one part of you and there is always strength in that."

The Mother's house was cold when Crystal returned to it, the embers she had left, mostly ash. Carefully, she rebuilt the fire using only mortal skills. Not until it roared red and gold, and heat began to rise again, did she consider her meeting with the goddess.

"I suppose," she said to the Mother's chair, thoughtfully nibbling on a handful of raisins, "that if Tayja truly is a part of me and *I* don't know what to do then *she* can't. I do know I can't go on like this." Not only for her own sake but for the sake of the world as well. The ancient wizards had refused to control their appetites; her lack was less a matter of choice, but the results were likely to be the same if any one of the goddesses gained control—death and destruction. She twisted a strand of hair about her fingers and frowned. As much as she disliked the idea, the centaurs seemed to be the only solution. Maybe they knew something that could help.

Our knowledge, C'Tal had often said, *begins with the Mother's creation of this world and we have constantly added to it ever since. This aside, we do, however, prefer you to work out your difficulties yourself. That is why we taught you to think.*

Crystal sighed. 'Oh, be quiet," she murmured at the memory and it obediently stilled.

She spent the rest of the day tidying the small cabin and restocking the woodpile. The night she spent in meditation, rebuilding her shields around the goddesses, using the knowledge Tayja had given her to anchor them securely. In the morning, in clothing made of cedar and woodsmoke, she closed the door of the Mother's house firmly behind her and headed west.

As she walked, her power-shod feet barely dimpling the snow, her thoughts turned back past her recent breakdown to Lord Death and his sudden departure. Going over their conversation once again, she was forced to conclude his actions most closely resembled those of a jealous man.

"Which," she pointed out to a curious chickadee watching from a juniper bush, "is ridiculous. Lord Death is . . . well, Lord Death." He *isn't* a man."

As she continued walking, she didn't see the small bird's panicked flight nor the evergreen wither and die.

Crystal had not been celibate in the twelve years since she'd defeated Kraydak, but men who could deal with all she was were few and far between. She remembered Raulin's solution and smiled; in his desire to deal with the woman he merely acknowledged the wizard and for him that was enough. She suspected Jago would not have settled for anything so simple.

Deep below the shields, Avreen stirred.

Startled, Crystal shifted her thoughts away from the brothers, a little embarrassed they affected her so strongly that even such gentle memories could cause the goddess of lust to rise. She almost conceded that, if Lord Death was indeed capable of jealousy, perhaps he had cause. She shied away from the thought for that would mean he had reason and somehow that frightened her more than all seven goddesses.

Puzzling over her reaction to the Mother's son—and his to her and hers to that—Crystal walked around a granite outcropping and nearly died. A high-pitched and undulating howl echoed off the mountains and shattered the silence into a thousand sharp edged pieces. Blind panic threw her back as a massive brown and black body slammed through the space where she had been. Her heart in her throat, she rolled and looked up, dashing the snow from her face.

Brindle. A young male, barely five feet high at the

shoulder. Small black eyes, well shaded beneath their protruding brow-ridge, glared down at her. His angry snorts made great gouts of steam in the frigid air. Muscles tensed and, silently this time, he charged.

Crystal just barely managed to avoid the strike. The soft whisper of fur against her cheek as she twisted to safety gave her an indication of the animal's speed. Had he been older and more practiced at judging distance, even the agility that came of Crystal's mythic heritage might not have been enough.

As his prey disappeared again, the brindle checked his lunge almost in midair, flipped his heavy body about with a fluid grace, and, growling in irritation, attacked once more.

Crystal caught hold of her power and slapped a portion at the brindle's nose.

He stopped dead, his eyes narrowed, and his upper lip drew back to show a mouth full of needle sharp teeth.

Trying to calm her breathing, Crystal began to back cautiously away. The brindle snarled a warning and she decided it was safest to stay right where she was. Slowly, so as not to provoke a response from the watching animal, she sat on a bit of windswept rock and wondered what to do.

She remembered hearing that brindles never abandoned their chosen prey; tracking it for days across hundreds of miles, worrying at its heels, waiting until a chance presented itself and then moving in for the kill.

Had it been night she could've turned into the owl and flown—not even brindles could track a trail through the air—but she daren't risk the bird's sensitive eyes to the glare of winter sunlight.

Raulin had killed the brindle that attacked Jago with only a dagger. Crystal studied this brindle, much as it studied her, made note of the claws, each a dagger's length and cruelly curved, and realized just what that meant. She measured its bulk against her memory of Raulin. This brindle could make four or five of the man and the beast that had attacked the brothers had been larger still. In her mind's eye she saw him, clinging to the thick fur at the animal's throat, driving the dagger into the eye again and again, desperation lending strength to the blows until finally one pierced the brain. She shuddered.

She couldn't use enough power to flip the brindle away, as she had Raulin and Jago at the inn, for that would weaken her shields and leave her helpless against Zarsheiy and Avreen. She doubted she could count on Tayja saving her again. If she had a choice, she preferred to face the brindle.

They were said to be intelligent, cunning, and ferocious; vulnerable only when feeding, for their gluttony made them careless. They did not peacefully coexist with any other living creatures and barely tolerated each other. Up to a dozen might live scattered throughout a clan range which was ruled absolutely by the oldest female, and if male brindles were thought to be bad tempered . . .

Crystal smiled.

The brindle howled at this display of fangs, puny through they were, then jerked what was to be his killing charge to a stop before it actually got moving. Where heartbeats before his prey had waited, an old scarred female, survivor of many matings, now reared and raked the sky with her claws.

Crystal opened her brindle mouth and roared.

The young male spared an instant to wonder what had gone wrong, then instinct took over and he ran.

The female brindle dwindled back to human form and the wizard grinned. A half grown male simply did not argue with a matriarch, no matter how unexpectedly she appeared. He would not stop running until he was miles away. From deep within, she felt the touch of seven smiles as the goddesses approved, for once in complete agreement, and just for an instant she knew how it would feel when she was whole once more.

?

Crystal's head snapped up and to the northwest. The touch came again.

?

Her power pulsed in response. The touch changed. Called.

!

Almost involuntarily, she stepped toward it. Something in the mountains, something with power, needed her help. She crossed the snow marked by the brindle's prints and walked into the fresh white beyond before she dug in her heels and asked the obvious question.

What called? Or who?

She knew the touch of all the Mother's Eldest, and this was none of them. She knew the sacred places where the Mother's power resided most strongly, and none were in these mountains. It had the feel of wizardy. But the ancient ones were long dead and even Kraydak, the one survivor from that earlier age, had joined them a dozen years ago.

!

Could she have triggered the relic Jago and Raulin searched for? She wished she'd asked for a look at their map.

!!

"All right." She picked up the thread of the call. "You needn't shout."

She checked her shields. They remained strong, for the illusion had taken little power. The centaurs would always be available for questioning, but this summons could end as abruptly as it began and Crystal *needed* to know where it came from. The goddesses would have to wait. She only hoped they would.

Throughout the day, as the mountain terrain grew bleaker, the call grew stronger. At sunset, she walked between towering peaks at the edge of the tree line. With moonrise, she flowed into her owl form and took to the air. It made no difference to the call, it stretched before her, a pathway of power, easy to follow.

Too easy? she wondered and took a moment to consider the idea that she might be moving into a trap. If the call did come from an ancient relic, this was a very real possibility. The wizards of old had thought as little of each other as they did of the world at large.

But if the call came from something else, if there was a power out there that could speak to hers, surely that was worth the risk? Not the promise perhaps, but the suggestion of companionship and perhaps help.

Yes, she decided, it was.

When her wings began to tire, she found shelter of a sort between two boulders, and, taking back her woman shape, wrapped herself in power and slept for the remainder of the night.

In the morning, with her stomach making imperious demands, Crystal glared around at the rock and snow and cursed herself for not having taken the time to hunt the night before.

She could safely feed off her power for a little time; the peak was no more than half a day away, if she reached it and the call came from farther on she would go back and hunt before continuing.

At midmorning she found a cave. The call came from within.

Long and narrow and twice the height of the wizard who stood just inside its mouth, the cave sloped downward into the mountain. It seemed a natural fissure, rough walled and rubble strewn, but when Crystal laid long fingers against the wall, the power that had formed it in the distant past still echoed faintly in the stone. So the call came from the ancient ones after all. For a long moment she stayed half in, half out of the cave, disappointment warring with curiosity. Then she sighed and stepped forward as curiosity won.

When a sharply angled turn cut off the light spilling in through the cave mouth, patches of lichen dappling the rock began to faintly glow silver-gray, keeping the path from total darkness.

Suddenly, the cave narrowed to a vertical slash leading into the mountain's heart. To follow the call, Crystal would have to slide sideways, her movements confined on either side by the mountain itself. If there was a trap this would be the place to set it. She paused and pushed her hair away from her face. Was curiosity reason enough to attempt such a passage? The call continued to tug at her power and, moistening dry lips, she pushed into the crack.

"As long as I've come this far . . ."

The weight of the mountain flattened her voice, making it small and toneless.

Forty sidling footsteps later, she realized the lichen patches no longer provided the only light. A few steps farther and it had lightened quite definitely to gray. Another step, a struggle around a corner that seemed to clutch at her chest and hips, and the end of the passage was in sight; a pinkish-gray ribbon of light. Heartened, she moved as quickly as she could toward it.

Five steps away, four, and a body blocked her view of the cavern beyond. Lord Death stood where the passage widened, his hands outstretched toward her, his features flickering through a multitude of faces each wearing an identical expression of horror.

Was this a warning, Crystal wondered, biting back a startled shriek. Why did Lord Death block her path and why didn't he speak?

And then he did.

"Free my people," he pleaded and vanished from her way.

As puzzled by his cryptic utterance as by his appearance, Crystal hesitantly advanced.

The cavern felt enormous after the confinement of the passage, but the opposite wall was actually no more than fifteen feet away. Before she could scan the rest of area, her attention was snagged by the pattern in the stone of the far wall. Set into it were hundreds, maybe thousands, of bones.

"I see," piped up a shrill voice, "that you admire my map."

Crouched in the corner where the wall of bones touched one of mere rock, was a twisted and misshapen parody of a man. Its back was humped so high its head appeared to come from the middle of its chest, its arms were too long, its legs too short, and mottled gray skin fell about it in wrinkled folds. Its eyes were black from lid to lid, two vertical slashes served it for a nose, and the mouth that split its face from ear to ear was as empty of teeth as a frog's.

Crystal felt her jaw drop as once again the power that had led her here touched her own. There could be no mistaking the source, not so close. This was what had called her. She stumbled back a step.

"Who?" she managed. "What?"

"It is called a demon," said Lord Death, now standing at her side, lives still playing across his face, "and it is quite mad."

"I am sane enough when I choose," the demon protested, clambering to its feet. "Madness is my escape."

"You're trapped here?" Crystal asked, trying to make some sense of what was going on.

The demon threw wide its arms. "I am imprisoned here!" it shrieked. It flung itself forward to land on its knees at Crystal's feet. "I beg of you, free me."

It smelled of cinnamon, sharp but not unpleasant.

"You have the power. You answered my call. Now you have seen me in my misery. You cannot leave me here."

Crystal glanced behind her. The narrow entrance to the tunnel was unbarred. She reached out with power. Red and black bands wrapped around and through the stone cocooning the cavern even to the small spring in one corner. Identical bands but black and red cocooned the demon. It was the oldest power she had ever felt.

"How long have you been here?"

"Eternity," sniffed the demon.

"Six thousand years," said Lord Death softly. "The wizard Aryalan bound it just to prove she could. Then she left it here."

"Left me," agreed the demon. "Bound me and forgot me." It turned from Crystal, crawled to the wall of bone, and began rubbing up against it.

The bones were not six thousand years old. Although many were yellowish gray with age, many more were still ivory.

The demon chuckled at Crystal's expression. "You like my map?" it asked. "He would not free me when I called to him, but he sent me things to do."

"Who did?"

"The sunny gold one. With eyes like bits of sky."

"Kraydak?"

Gray shoulders shrugged. "He never said his name. When there were two powers in the world he was one. Now there is only you." Its eyes narrowed. "And I do not want more man-things sent. I have finished my map."

It could have only been Kraydak, Crystal realized, called as she had been. He had refused to free the demon and later amused himself by sending mortals to it and to their deaths.

Raulin and Jago had gotten their map from Kraydak's city governor.

Desperately, Crystal searched the demon's prison for signs of a fresh kill. Even considering the three days she'd spent in the Mother's house, they could not have been that far ahead of her.

There were no bones except those in the wall. No blood, wet or dry. No bits of . . .

She jumped as the demon took her hand and pulled her forward. Its grasp was cool and dry.

"The bargain," it whispered to her, "was with the other. But if you free me, you may have the map instead."

"He said he would free you if you made him the map?"

"Yes, yes, he did."

"He lied." No guess but a surety. Kraydak always lied when he could.

The demon began to cry. "I know. Everyone lies to me. But it was all I had to offer him."

"What does the map show?"

"The way to her hole." It polished a bit of bone with a flap of skin. "To the Binding One's hidden place."

The way to Aryalan's tower. Kraydak had offered the demon freedom in exchange for the way to Aryalan's tower. He must have hoped to plunder it but had died before he got the chance.

Crystal reached out and lightly touched the wall.

DEATH!

She jerked her hand away and slowly turned to face the one the voices summoned.

"That which binds the demon in," Lord Death explained, "binds these mortal lives as well. I cannot take my children home. Free him, Crystal, and free them also."

She moved carefully away from the wall and looked down at the demon as sternly as she was able. "If I free you, what will you do?"

"Do?" Its mouth worked for a moment but no sound came out. "Do?" it repeated at last. "I shall go home. Go home. HOME!" The last word rose to a howl, a scream of anguish that ran up and down Crystal's spine with razor edges. The sound filled the cavern, thrummed within the rock, and was joined by the cries of the multitude in the wall.

The demon and those trapped with it shrieked out the agony of their long imprisonment.

Deep within Crystal's mind, darkness stirred and wakened. It surged outward, a roaring tide that slammed through shields and over defenses. Nashawryn answered the demon's call. Crystal added her scream to the others as the eldest goddess broke free within her.

Five

Blackness.

Screaming terror.

Fire in the darkness that gave no light.

A hundred knives that cut and twisted.

A thousand years of pain.

Driven deep within her own mind by the darkness and the fear, Crystal searched desperately for the core of self that Tayja had shown her. If it still existed, it lay beyond her reach. Nashawryn held sway over all.

Here, the nightmares that had dimmed her childhood.

There, the paralyzing dread of the young adult.

All about her the horror of the woman; madness, the shattering of her soul into a myriad of pieces that could never be joined again, each brittle shard dying cut off from the others.

A hundred voices wept and hers was more than one of them.

The noise pushed her this way and that, adding bits of her to the cacophony every time she tried to resist, moving her closer and closer to the precipice where fear and reality became one and Nashawryn would be all that remained.

And then . . . and then she cried alone.

The blackness trembled.

Crystal forced herself to be still.

Beyond the curtain, something called.

Her nose twitched as she smelled the soft leather of her father's jerkin. Her fingers curved as they held the silken masses of her mother's hair. She rested for a moment in the memory of their arms.

Then she stepped forward.

The blackness tore.

She gathered close the piece of self she had almost forgotten and opened her eyes.

Raulin was just forcing himself around a tight corner in the passage when the howling began. The sound echoed alarmingly within the corridor of rock. He winced, instinctively jerked his head away, and swore as the back of his skull slammed against the rough stone. He felt Jago's hand close on his shoulder, but any words were lost as a woman's screams began to weave a high-pitched descant of terror throughout the continuing howl.

Raulin ripped free of the mountain's grasp, leaving cloth and bits of skin behind, and flung himself down the last few feet of passage and into the cavern.

Crystal. He'd known it from the moment the screams began, though he didn't know how. Her head was thrown back, the lovely white column of her throat was ridged with strain, her eyes were clenched shut, her hands were fists that beat the air, and her mouth stretched wide to let the sound escape.

He wasn't quite in time to catch her when she crumpled to the ground but reached her side a second later, lifting her thrashing head and shoulders up off the rock and onto his lap. With one arm cradled protectively around her, for her constant movement threatened to throw her free, he reached up with the other and fumbled with the fastenings on his jacket. Her clothing had disappeared when she fell and she needed protection from more than just the winter air. Abrasions, slowly oozing red, already marked the satin skin. He wished he still wore his huge fur overcoat—removed before attempting the narrow passage—for that was more the kind of protection she needed.

The jacket was tight and hard to manage one-handed, harder yet when arms were full of a beautiful, naked woman who would not hold still, but Raulin managed to drag himself out of it and get the heavy fabric wrapped at least partially around Crystal's body.

On some level, his mind reacted to her desirability. He was only mortal man, after all. But those feelings were deeply buried and he held her as he would have held Jago in the same circumstances.

Her screams had died to whimpers. A trickle of blood, where teeth had scored her lip, trailed across her cheek. The jacket held her arms confined, for which Raulin gave thanks as his ears still rang from the force of one random blow. She kept trying to draw her knees up, to curl into a ball, to hide from whatever had done this.

Every time her knees came up, Raulin pushed them back. She was the stronger, he the more determined, finding what he needed to stop her in the memory of his father who had one day given up, curled into a ball, and while his wife and young sons watched, had died. He murmured soothing things to her, nonsense, bits of lullabies, anything to quiet her, to reach her.

And the howling that had started it all, went on and on.

He turned his head, saw the source, without really registering what he saw, and snapped "Shut up!" at the misshapen thing.

It did.

Now the only screams were Crystal's.

"Crystal?" He caught a flailing hand that had fought out of the jacket to freedom. "Crystal, it's Raulin. I have you. You're safe."

Suddenly she stilled; her breathing hoarse and labored, her body trembling with tension.

"That's it," he whispered and stroked her forehead with his cheek for both his hands were full. "Now come back. Come back, Crystal, I have you."

Her nose wrinkled and the tension went out of the free hand as the fingers curved around something he couldn't see.

"Crystal?"

She sighed, the warm weight of her settled onto his lap, and she opened her eyes.

The howl of loneliness hit Jago like a solid blow. He staggered and would have fallen had the mountain not held him so securely. He clutched at his brother's shoulder, seeking reassurance in that touch, reassurance that the emotions ripping through his head weren't his. When the thousand voices added their pain and the howl became a choir, his hands went to his ears. He saw Raulin throw himself forward and disappear out of the passage. The sound held him pinned and he could not follow. He was left alone with the lament.

Alone.

An eternity alone.

He ground his palms against his head. It made little difference.

Free us. Free us. Free us.

Fear.

The last was a single call, a silver thread running through the tumult. Jago inched himself forward. It was not the best of guides, but it was all he had to follow.

He squeezed around the tight corner, repeating over and over, "I will get to Raulin," using his brother's name as a talisman against the loneliness. And the fear.

When the passage widened and the mountain no longer supported him, he took only a single step before the howling beat him to his knees.

It went on and on and on and Jago felt an answering scream rising up within him to join it.

Then, just as suddenly as it began, it stopped, and only the silver thread of fear remained.

Crystal. He'd carried a bit of her life and could not mistake it.

He stood, and with one hand against the rock for support—his body still trembled in reaction—he made his way out of the passage and into the cavern.

Raulin knelt in the middle of the floor, his jacket off

and wrapped about the wizard who twisted in his grasp. A vaguely man-shaped thing crouched at the junction of two walls, one the bare bones of the mountain the other inlaid with a fantastic pattern of . . . of bone.

"Crystal?"

The screams had died to whimpers and he could hear his brother clearly.

"Crystal, it's Raulin. I have you. You're safe."

And behind him Jago heard a moan; a soft sound, pain filled.

Slowly, he turned.

An auburn haired man stood staring down at Raulin and Crystal, shoulders slumped in despair. Feeling Jago's gaze, he lifted his head. Surprise replaced the pain in the amber eyes so quickly Jago could not be sure he'd even seen it. Then the despair was gone as well and the new stance denied that it had ever existed. The man smiled slightly.

"Do you not know me, Jago?" he asked. "We were very close once."

Jago felt his mouth move. It took him a few seconds to manage an audible sound and even then the roar of blood in his ears threatened to drown it out. "Lord Death."

Lord Death inclined his head. "Our previous encounter seems to have given you something few mortals enjoy, the pleasure of my company."

There was nothing Jago could reply, so he inclined his head in turn.

Lord Death waved an aristocratic hand toward the center of the cavern. "Your brother is very clever," he said and to Jago's ears the words came out with an edge. "He appeals to her humanity. Gives her something with which to fight the fear." The Mother's son grimaced and Jago shuddered, the expression was such a strange mix of sorrow and anger. "It is lucky you arrived when you did."

Lucky. Jago heard the contradiction between the voice and the words. If Raulin, however he did it, pulled Crystal up out of the fear, then it *was* lucky they'd arrived at the cavern when they did. Lord Death had admitted as much but not with pleasure. No, not with pleasure.

"Crystal?"

Raulin's voice had softened, the tone so different, that both Jago and Lord Death turned.

Lord Death stepped forward, then jerked himself back.

Crystal sighed and opened her eyes.

Why did father grow that ridiculous mustache? Crystal wondered as focus returned. Then the face behind the mustache came out of shadow and she smiled and said weakly, "Raulin."

He returned the smile and stroked damp hair back from her face. "Welcome back."

"Jago?"

"Uh . . ." Raulin suddenly realized he had no idea if Jago had followed him, remained in the passage, or . . . He began to twist but stopped at the familiar feel of his brother at his back.

"I'm here." Jago kept his voice low, pitched to reassure, glancing back over his shoulder as he spoke. The features of the dead moved across Lord Death's face and he could get no idea of how the Mother's son felt. *Tread carefully, my brother,* he thought as Raulin shifted Crystal into a more comfortable position on his lap, *there is more here than even you will be able to deal with.*

"Are you better now?"

Crystal squeaked as Raulin's grip abruptly tightened. The concerned features of the demon poked into her line of sight.

"You were making a lot of noise," it accused. "Shrieking. Wailing."

"What in Chaos' balls is that?" Raulin demanded, trying to shield her body with his own.

"It's a demon." Crystal pushed against his arms

until they relaxed enough to let her breathe. "It's trapped here."

"Is it dangerous?"

"Maybe," the demon said cheerfully.

"Jago!"

Jago, his dagger in his hand, took a step toward the demon, putting the point of his knife between it and the two on the floor. "Go on," he commanded, "get back."

The demon opened wide its lipless mouth and closed it on the metal.

Startled, Jago snatched the dagger back and stood staring down at the hilt. A thin wisp of smoke was all that remained of the blade.

"Cheap," muttered the demon and retreated to the corner to sulk.

The brothers exchanged incredulous glances, then looked in unison down at Crystal who had begun to giggle softly.

"I'm sorry," she sputtered, "only the look on your faces . . ."

The laughter built until her body shook with it and the sound began to take on a hysterical edge.

"Crystal?" Raulin shook her gently, but she continued to laugh although tears ran from her eyes and she trembled uncontrollably. "Crystal!"

Jago dropped to one knee beside them. "Hold her," he said.

"I *am* holding her." He fell silent as Jago took the wizard's jaw in one hand, turned her head to face him, and slapped her, hard. Then again.

With a shuddering sob, Crystal buried her face against Raulin's chest, and clung. "I'm sorry," she said again, her voice even weaker than it had been, but calm. "I don't . . ."

"Shh." He stroked her back, murmuring the words into her hair. "It's all right. Do you want to get up?"

She shook her head and clung tighter.

Raulin met his brother's eyes.

"Perhaps you'd better go get the packs," he said softly.

Jago's eyebrows went up.

Raulin glared. "Don't be stupid," he snarled, his hands continuing to soothe the woman in his arms.

Jago flushed, touched his brother's shoulder in a wordless apology, rose, and slipped silently from the cavern.

They'd left the packs back where the passage had narrowed so suddenly. Their sled, with the bulk of their gear and supplies, they'd had to leave a short distance down the mountain when the way became more rock than snow and the trail too steep to wrestle it farther.

Jago studied what had to be moved; the two packs and both massive fur overcoats plus a pile of assorted hats, scarves, and mittens. The packs would have to be moved one at a time, and perhaps emptied to get them around that tight bit. He rubbed his chin, absently scratching at the golden stubble, and decided that since the packs contained no clothes it might be best if he got the coats through first. He remembered how little Raulin's jacket covered, added how quickly comfort could warm, and recalled the expression on Lord Death's face. Not the despair, the anger that had followed.

"Definitely the coats." He heaved them up into his arms and turned to face the narrow passage with gritted teeth. At least he had something to take his mind off the fear that being underground always evoked.

Dragging some forty pounds of uncooperative fur through the mountain's heart was among the less enjoyable things he'd done lately, but when Jago reached the cavern and saw the way in which the positions of Raulin and Crystal had subtly shifted while he was gone, he knew he'd made the right decision. Although Raulin would not take advantage—he'd deserved Raulin's anger for implying he would—Jago didn't doubt his brother would be willing to cooperate and this was neither the time nor place.

"Here." The fur flopped like a live thing to the ground, one arm draping over Crystal's legs. "This'll do you a lot more good than that little jacket."

"She doesn't get cold," Lord Death pointed out from his place by the passage.

"Perhaps not," Jago replied without thinking, "but Raulin does, and he needs his jacket."

Crystal's head snapped up and she stared from Jago to Lord Death.

Raulin merely stared at his brother. The demon crouched out of Jago's line of sight and as far as Raulin was concerned that left Jago talking to empty air. "What are you babbling about?"

"You can hear him?" Crystal asked, her arms sliding down from around Raulin's neck.

"Hear who?" Raulin wanted to know.

"And see him?"

"See who?"

The wizard's silver brows dove into a deep vee. "I've never heard of a mortal being able . . ."

"Able to what?"

Jago sighed. "Why don't you tell him while you dress," he suggested to Crystal, nudging the fur with a booted foot. "I'll go get the rest of the gear."

The packs, as he suspected, had to be unpacked, for neither force nor ingenuity could get them around that last tight corner before the cavern. Rather than reload everything, and then unload it again six meters away in order to use it, Jago carried the bits and pieces into the cavern in armloads. The tableau remained unchanging from trip to trip.

Crystal, regal now and no less beautiful in the enveloping fur, explained in animated detail just what she suspected had happened when Jago had come so close to Death.

Raulin listened intently, his eyes never leaving Crystal's face. Jago wondered which motivated Raulin more, concern for his brother or an inability to look away from emerald eyes and ivory skin. The demon sat silently in its corner, its expression impossible to read. Lord Death stood just as silently by the rectangular cut that marked the passage and he kept the dead parading across his face to hide what might otherwise have been revealed. But his eyes, throughout all their many permutations, never moved from the two in the center of the cavern.

Each time he passed the Mother's son, Jago grew more certain he understood both the earlier pain and the anger that followed. Survival in the Empire had consisted for the most part of an intimate knowledge of the pecking order; a skill that translated in the survivors into a finely honed ability to judge their fellow men. To Jago's eyes, Lord Death was deeply, and hopelessly, in love.

Without really knowing why he did it—to protect his brother was no more than an admittedly valid rationalization—he stopped as he carried in the last armload of gear and said in a voice not intended to travel far from where he stood, "Why don't you tell her?"

Lord Death turned and the changing eyes and identical expressions of terror flowed into the features of the auburn-haired man whose amber eyes regarded him coldly. "Tell her what?" he asked in a voice equally quiet.

"Uh . . ."

"Do not presume, mortal. I am fully capable of running my own . . ." A wry smile twisted the full lips. "I am fully capable of running my own . . . life."

"Now let me get this straight." Raulin raised a steaming cup of tea to his mouth. "You talk to Death?"

The four of them, Raulin, Jago, the wizard, and the demon, sat around a small campstove, the red glow of the coals providing more of a focus point than actual warmth. The demon, its captivity explained, sat quietly and pouted. Crystal had refused to let it show off its handiwork, merely informing the brothers that the wall contained the remains of the demon's previous visitors, "and could we please leave it at that." Then she'd smacked its fingers away from the fire. It projected an air of injured innocence which no one paid any attention to.

Jago swallowed a mouthful of hot liquid and nodded.

"And he talks to you?"

Jago nodded again.

"And he's a regular guy? You can see him, touch . . ."

"No," Crystal interupted, a little sadly, "you can't touch him. Nor can he touch you."

"Is he here right now?"

"No." Jago and Crystal spoke together, looked startled, then exchanged shy smiles. Neither knew when the Mother's son had left. One moment he'd been there, the next gone.

Raulin settled his back against the rock wall of the cavern. "How can you be sure?"

Crystal jerked a thumb over her shoulder at the wall of bones. "When the dead are present, I can always see him. Only when there are no dead, can he choose."

"Why?"

She shrugged and Raulin wished the motion had not been covered by the heavy fur. "I don't know. That's just the way it works."

"If he wants you to free the dead, why didn't he stay?" Jago asked. He remembered the thousand voices and their plea. He hadn't needed Crystal's explanation to know what they wanted.

"I think he leaves me to decide without the pressure of our friendship."

Her voice was troubled, as if she suspected a deeper meaning in Lord Death's sudden departure.

Jago considered, for a brief instant, telling her himself, saying, *He loves you, wizard,* but he didn't. Just because the last few weeks of his life had been a bonus, because he really should've died after the brindle attack, it did not mean he wanted to give the *rest* of his life away. So all he said was, "Freeing the dead frees the demon," as if he recognized that as the cause of her trouble.

Crystal sighed. "Yes."

"I am harmless!" protested the demon.

All eyes turned to the wall of bone.

"Well, mostly harmless," it whined. "Oh, please free me. Please . . ."

Jago's hand shot out and grabbed the demon's arm. "Do not howl," he snarled.

The demon looked piqued and easily shook itself free. "Wasn't going to."

Raulin listened to his brother and Crystal talk, sipped his tea, and studied the wall of bones. He couldn't find it in him to blame the demon for the men and women who had died to set that pattern, not even considering that he'd missed being a part of it by only a few hours. If they'd arrived at the cavern before Crystal . . .

He was disappointed that the treasure of the ancient wizard had amounted to nothing more than a strange creature with an appetite for iron. Then his mind slipped back to those moments spent holding Crystal in his arms and he decided the trip hadn't been a total loss. Still, he touched the leather pouch hanging about his neck, they'd had such hopes when they first found that map.

Map!

"Hey!" Jago threw himself out of the way as Raulin leaped up and dashed across the cavern. He twisted and glared at the older man who was running his fingers along the ridges of bone and muttering under his breath. "What do you think you're doing?"

"It's a map, Jago!"

"Yes! Yes!" The demon bounded over to its creation and began patting the wall. "A map! A map!"

"A map?"

"Yes. Look!" Raulin pointed out a triangular wedge of bone that ran diagonally up from the floor, cutting off the lower corner. "This is the mountain range we're in." He touched another pattern. "This is the canyon

we followed to get here, before we started to climb.''
He slapped the wall where a bit of femur jutted from
the mountains. ''This is where we are!''

''Here! Here!'' The demon agreed.

Jago slowly stood and stepped over to the map.
''Then these,'' he said, ''are the mountains they call
the Giant's Spine.''

''Aptly named,'' Raulin added, for they were delineated on the wall in vertebrae.

''And this,'' Jago continued, ignoring him, ''must
be the way . . .''

Both brothers looked up to the top left corner of the wall
where a skull looked back. Barely visible on the yellow-
gray bone was scratched the sigil of the bloody hand.

''. . . to Aryalan's tower,'' Raulin finished.

''Yes! Yes!'' The demon hopped up and down in
excitement, looking even more froglike than it did at
rest. ''The Binding One's hidey hole!'' Then it stopped
jumping and added solemnly. ''But you mustn't go
there. It's dangerous.''

''You should listen to it.'' Crystal still sat by the tiny
stove, bare legs tucked up under the fur. ''Aryalan trapped
it, remember. It knows what it's talking about.''

''Aryalan's long dead,'' Raulin scoffed.

But Jago said softly, ''You knew, didn't you? That
this was a map?''

Crystal nodded.

''And you weren't going to tell us.''

She smiled and rubbed her cheek against the soft
fur of the collar ''No.''

''Why not?'' Raulin returned to her side and
dropped to one knee to better study her face. ''Think
of what we could find there.''

Her gaze flicked past him to the wall of bone.
''Think of what you've found here.''

Raulin dismissed the cavern, the bones, the demon
with a quick wave. ''We're not likely to find its type,''
he nodded at the demon, ''inside the wizard's tower.''

''There will be other dangerous surprises.''

"And that's why you weren't going to tell us about the map? I'm not afraid of the unknown."

I am, she thought, shying away from the dark places Nashawryn had left when she retreated. *I am very afraid of the unknown. Now.* But she kept silent and only looked from Raulin's gray eyes, alight with a fierce joy, to Jago's violet ones. "Now you know the path," she said, "you'll go, won't you, no matter what I say?"

"Yes," Raulin told her.

When she looked to Jago for confirmation he nodded, although she realized he went not for the adventure, or even the possibility of wealth, but because his brother did.

Crystal's head went up and her expression firmed. "I could take it from your minds. I could make you forget the map existed."

Raulin's head went up as well, his jaw tensed and his eyes grew stormy. *Jago was right,* he thought. *Wizards can't be trusted. None of them.* His mouth opened, but Jago spoke first.

"You won't," he said.

"How do you know?" She turned the green of her eyes on him and released enough power so they began to glow. *Let Nashawryn get loose again; she'll burn it from their minds fast enough.*

Jago smiled, a little sadly. "Because I know you."

Crystal sat silent, aghast at what she'd thought. Nashawryn must never get loose again. How could she think . . . and then she felt the laughter and realized she hadn't. Zarsheiy. Stirring up what trouble she could. "I don't even know myself," she murmured.

"Then take my word for it."

Raulin was ashamed at his sudden anger and at the same time mildly amused that he and Jago seemed for an instant to have reversed opinions. He reached out and ran a strand of silver hair between his fingers. It felt cool and soft and finer than silk. "Come with us," he said.

"You asked me that before. At the inn. I said no."

"A lot has changed since then. But even if your answer remains no, we are still going on."

"Yes."

"Yes, you'll come with us, or yes, you know we'll go on anyway."

Crystal could spread herself on the wind and reach Aryalan's tower in hours. Deal with it and destroy it before the brothers even found the trail. But that way moved too close to oblivion even when all was in balance. Now she dared not risk it. She could, as the owl, still beat them to the tower by days. Deal with it and destroy it while they struggled over the mountains. But although the owl had nothing the goddesses could grasp and use, she would have to exist on power and all her power must be used to remain whole. Or what stood for whole these days. And besides, she was lonely.

Lonely. She held back a sigh as she turned the word over in her mind. From the moment the centaurs had taken her from her parents she'd been alone in one way or another. Why, she wondered, her hand creeping up to twist in the fur over her heart, did alone suddenly mean lonely? Perhaps because when she was alone she no longer knew the person she was with. Perhaps the demon had put the word in her mind. Perhaps because there seemed to be an alternative and friendship had become, for the first time since she was eleven, a very real possibility.

"Yes, I'll come with you."

Slowly, Raulin smiled, hearing at least part of her reason for agreeing in her voice.

Jago, who heard the part that Raulin didn't, stepped forward until he could see Crystal's face over his brother's shoulder. "What are you afraid of?" he asked softly.

His return unnoticed, Lord Death raised his head to listen.

Crystal looked down into the depths of the fur—looking into the depths of herself was out of the question—then she sighed, spread her hands, and said simply: "Me." If she traveled with them and their lives also were at risk, they deserved to know.

"There were seven goddesses remaining when the wizards ruled . . ."

She told them all of it, what Tayja had told her and

the background they needed to understand, keeping her voice as emotionless as she could. It was safer that way.

The brothers sat enthralled, barely moving throughout the telling. The demon whimpered twice but otherwise sat still and quiet.

"So you see," she finished, "if I do go with you, you won't be getting a mighty wizard capable of blasting away all opposition. No more snatching you out of danger before the danger really begins. I'll be using most of my power just to stay intact." For the first time in the telling, she met their eyes. "Do you still want me?"

Without looking at Jago, Raulin answered for both of them.

"Yes," he said simply.

"Because you feel sorry for me?" The words slipped out before Crystal could stop them.

"Because we want your company," Raulin told her softly, hearing the fear behind her words. He leered in his best exaggerated manner. "Chaos knows why, but we like you." Then he grew serious. "And I can't deny we could use whatever help you can give."

He would've gone on but Jago, who sat where he could see the rest of the cavern, grabbed his arm and quieted him with a small shake of his head.

"Why didn't you tell me," asked the one true son of the Mother, "when this began?"

Shaking back the silver curtain of her hair, Crystal met Lord Death's eyes. Answering one question, it seemed, led only to others. She shrugged, trying to lessen the importance of her answer for the wrong weight here would lead to questions she knew she couldn't deal with. "I was afraid you wouldn't like me if I wasn't perfect."

Lord Death blinked once or twice in surprise. Of all the possible reasons she might give for shutting him out, for refusing to confide in him, he hadn't expected that. His lips twitched as he thought about it, then he smiled. "You have *never* been perfect," he said.

She returned his smile, partly in response, partly in relief that their friendship seemed back on its old footing, with the awkwardness of the past two meetings buried by that quip. She couldn't know that she had given him hope.

An irrational hope, all things considered, Lord Death acknowledged with an inner sigh.

"Is she talking to *him?*" Raulin hissed.

Jago nodded.

"Is he talking back?"

Jago nodded again.

"I don't think I like this."

"Better get used to it, brother." Jago levered himself to his feet by grasping Raulin's shoulder. His legs had grown stiff from sitting so long in one place while Crystal told her story. "We can't spend the night in here, most of our gear is on the sled. And I don't know about the rest of you, but I'm getting hungry."

On cue, Crystal's stomach grumbled loudly. "Hungry," she agreed, "is definitely the word for it."

Raulin stood and in mirrored moves the brothers each held a hand out to the woman on the ground. Their gazes crossed as each made note of the other's gesture, then locked in near identical glares.

Crystal stared from one to the other in surprise, quickly suppressed the grin threatening to break free—the last time she'd seen those expressions they'd been on the faces of her youngest siblings and had rapidly degenerated to yells of "Can too!" and "Can not!"—and used both offered hands to pull herself up. She supposed it was equally childish of her to feel pleased at being the bone of contention. She didn't care. Perhaps, just perhaps, things were going to work out.

The centaurs, reminded a quiet voice in her mind.

Shall I leave these two alone to be slaughtered? she thought back at it and it stilled.

"Crystal," Lord Death called softly. "My people?"

The demon crept forward and tugged on the edge of the coat. "Free me," it pleaded.

She reached down and touched the demon's head with one pale finger. "Yes." For it had suddenly come to her how she could.

She moved to the center of the cavern and the coat

slid down off her shoulders and to the stone floor. A breeze, an impossible breeze this deep beneath a mountain, fanned her hair into a nimbus of silver light. Green fires blazed up in her eyes and she reached out with her power and drove the green between the red and black that bound the demon.

Those who watched saw the muscles of her back roll and twist and her hands snap up to shoulder height and the knuckles whiten as they closed to fists.

The red and black were weakening and her power became a silver sword to cut the bindings loose.

Her arms went up, the fingers taut, and when she brought them down again, the wall of bone came down too.

"FREE!" No longer gray but an iridescent blur, the demon spun once in place, its arms outstretched, and disappeared.

"FREE!" screamed the dead, and Lord Death vanished too, carrying his children home.

Crystal grabbed the shattered power of the ancient wizard and threw it up in the path of Zarsheiy, the first of the goddesses to attack the weakened shields. Howling with rage, the fire goddess hit the barrier, hit the jagged pieces of red and black and was stopped. It had been a binding power after all.

Well done. The velvet voice of darkness sounded amused and Crystal felt the presences retreat to their own corners once again.

Pleased with her solution, and even more pleased that it had worked, for she hadn't been sure it would, she took a deep breath and relaxed.

"Crystal?"

Jago stepped forward, once again offering her the coat. He kept his eyes carefully on her face but their outer edges crinkled as he said: "For Raulin's sake . . ."

Interlude One

Back in the bright beginning, when the Mother-creator had formed the world from her body and the air about it from her breath, when She had given life to the lesser creatures of the land and air and water, She paused to rest in a grove of silver birch. As She rested, She grew lonely and so called to life the spirit of the tree She sat beneath that She might have company.

And because She stayed for a time in that place, the glory of her spread out into the surrounding land. In the Grove itself, the Peace that was the Mother remained.

When the Age of Wizards ended, a band of Mortals desperately seeking peace were drawn to that land. The Grove became a sacred place. A respectful distance from it, they began to rebuild their lives. They drew boundaries along mountains and rivers and called that which was bounded, Ardhan. These Mortals, the Mother's Youngest, had no way of knowing that the echo of the Mother's presence called to others as well and that they shared their new land with creatures out of legend.

The Elder Races, those created of the Mother's blood, paid little attention to the newcomers. Their lives moved in different ways and only occasionally touched. The Elder Races were few in number and the land was large enough for all. Most of the time. As the years passed, Ardhan gained a reputation as a place where wonders happened.

It was in Ardhan that the Eldest and the Youngest briefly joined.

From Ardhan came the last of the wizards.
In Ardhan, the Council of the Elder Races met.

From his vantage point on the ridge, Doan could see the entire meeting place. Three centaurs. He grunted. Three too many as far as he was concerned. And one, no, two, giants. They sat so still his gaze tended to slide past them for all their size.

"Might as well get on with it," the dwarf muttered to the breezes. They chuckled as they sped away. "Oh, sure," he complained, heading down to level ground, "you can laugh. You don't have to stay."

He dropped the last eight feet, and, mildly disappointed that none of the centaurs shied, started right in. "What I want to know," his hands were on his hips, his chin jutted forward aggressively, and his breath was a plume on the winter air, "is why here? Why not the Grove?"

when we move the water
to
the Grove
the sisters get angry

The thoughts rose up out of the deep pool near which the land-bound Elders had gathered. Although ice clung around the edges, the center, despite the frigid temperature, was clear. Below the surface of the water, pale green and blue bodies wove in and out in a pattern as graceful as it was complicated. The exact number of mer who had answered the Call could not be determined for the waterfolk were never still, but it scarcely mattered for a thought held by one was shared by all.

"And," added the tallest of the centaurs, his coat gleaming like ebony in the early morning sun, "as the Ladies of the Grove cannot leave their trees, little of the outside world concerns them."

"Told you to take a hike did they, C'Tal? Can't say as I blame them."

C'Tal's eyes narrowed and he stared down his nose

at the dwarf. "If you do not wish to be here, why did you choose to answer the call?"

"You think I volunteered? Ha!" Doan hacked and spit into the snow at C'Tal's feet. He disliked centaurs for a number of reasons. Their pomposity, their "Elder-than-thou" attitude, and their lack of anything remotely resembling a sense of humor headed the list, but mostly he disliked them because the Elder Races were supposed to get along and he enjoyed being contrary. "Chaos, no. I had everyone in the caverns begging me to answer so they wouldn't have to risk death by boredom. Now," he shoved his hands behind his broad leather belt, and rocked back on his heels, "what could possibly have got you so twitchy you were willing to associate with the bubble brains."

better bubbles
than stone

C'Tal's tail snapped back and forth in short jerky arcs. A centaur did not "dislike" anyone, but C'Tal certainly disapproved of Doan. Sarcasm and cynicism barred clear thinking. He expected the dwarf's opposition in what was to come. The mer, for all their frivolity, were logical creatures, and he had no doubt he could convince them. The giants, so motionless they appeared more a bit of the earth poking up through the snow than living beings, could decide either way, but C'Tal took comfort in the knowledge that they would at least listen without interrupting.

"We would not have Called had we not thought this to be the gravest of emergencies."

"Too cold for horseflies," Doan mused. "Weevils got into your nosebags?"

quiet Doan
or
we'll be here
all day

C'tal looked smug.

and you, half-horse
speak
we

have places that need us

Irritation visible in his flattened ears, C'Tal crossed his arms over his massive chest, drew his brows down into an impressive frown and announced, "It is the wizard."

"I might have known," Doan sighed. "Every time one of you gets colic you blame it on her." He shook his head. "Why don't you leave the poor kid alone?"

One of C'Tal's companions stepped forward, tossing heavy chestnut hair back out of his eyes. "Surely even you felt the surge of power she called to her use and the breaking of ancient bonds. Are you not curious to discover what she has done?"

Doan smiled unpleasantly. "No, C'Din," he said "I'm not. And you, you four-footed busy . . ."

she has freed

Aryalan's demon

Shocked, the three centaurs and Doan stared down into the water. Even the giants stirred, although they only looked at each other and smiled their slow smiles.

A pale blue body, small enough to fit easily into C'Tal's hand, arced out of the pool, turned once languidly in midair, then disappeared again into the ebb and flow of mer.

the demon's prison had a spring

we

go where water is

"All right," Doan said to the general area, "she freed the demon. So? About time the poor thing got to go home. And yeah, I felt the power surge; it was completely contained. Nothing to do with us."

"That," declared C'tal ponderously, "is not the problem. It merely alerted us to that which we have called the Elder to discuss. She . . ."

"Hold it," the dwarf held up a callused hand. When C'Tal paused, his lips drawn into a thin line, Doan climbed nimbly up the tailings of the ridge he'd followed from the caverns, kicked the snow from a narrow ledge, crossed his legs and sat down. "Talking to you on level ground," he explained sweetly, "gives me a pain in the neck."

"We are aware of herbal remedies," offered the third centaur, a glossy palomino, "that will relieve such pain."

"How about relieving a pain in the ass?"

"Yes," the golden head nodded thoughtfully, "we can ease that also."

"Later," C'Tal bit the word off, his teeth white slabs against the black of his beard, well aware the dwarf was being deliberately irritating. "We believe that when the wizard freed the demon she discovered the location of Aryalan's tower."

"So that's the burr under your blanket." Doan sighed and relaxed. It was just like the centaurs to get upset over something trivial. "I suggested years ago we let her deal with the remaining towers. I said it then and I'll say it now, the poor kid needs something to do. I'm glad she found one on her own."

"She is a danger, the towers are a danger," C'Din pointed out quietly.

"Hold that thought, hayburner," Doan interrupted. "You lot trained her, why not have some trust in your training?"

C'Din shook his head, his forelock falling back down over his eyes. "As you and others have pointed out, we trained the ancient wizards as well." He paused. When no one filled the silence with a reminder of what the ancient wizards had become, he continued. "We feel—now, as we did at your suggestion years ago—that the wizard at the tower is one danger too many. She is already the most powerful being now living. When she reaches the tower and adds the power within to what she already carries, will that not be an undesirable event?"

Doan kept a grip on his temper. C'Din was being very reasonable, for a centaur. And what was worse, he had a valid point. "Why," he growled, "will that be an 'undesirable event'?"

"All power corrupts," C'Tal intoned. "Absolute power corrupts absolutely."

The dwarf's eyes began to glow red and he pulled himself slowly to his feet. The cold of the outside world meant nothing to the Elder, but the chill radiating from Doan caused two of the centaurs to step away and, although he stood his ground, long shivers rippled the skin of C'Tal's back.

stop
cliché becomes cliché
because of truth
power
does
corrupt

The red dimmed but did not die. "I will listen to no more of this. You've got my opinion, not that you'll pay any attention to it. I've stayed at this farce long enough." Doan leaped to the ground, but a huge arm bared his way.

"Wait." The larger of the two giants looked down at him, her face expressionless.

Doan seethed, but until she moved her arm he wasn't going anywhere and he knew it. With ill grace he did the only thing he could. He waited.

"When you called us, C'Tal, what did you intend the Elder to do?" Her voice was strong and deep but softer than her size would lead many to expect. The giants had no need to shout.

C'Tal shrugged. "In some manner, we must prevent the wizard . . ."

"She has a name," Doan snarled.

"Very well." C'Tal's tone made it obvious that he merely humored the dwarf. "We must prevent Crystal from reaching Aryalan's tower."

"No," the giant said.

"No?" chorused all three centaurs.

Doan grinned, his good humor suddenly restored. "You heard her, she said no."

why no

"The remaining towers of the ancient ones *are* a

danger and should be dealt with. The wizard is the only possible solution.''

''That's not what you thought a dozen years ago when we discussed telling her about the towers,'' Doan groused.

Again the giants exchanged their slow smiles.

''We changed our minds,'' said the smaller one.

''So,'' Doan moved to stand before C'Tal, peering up at him through narrowed eyes. ''That's two against sticking our noses in and two for.''

three against
one for
this wizard must be as free to take her own path
as every other creature
we cannot say
this is right
this is
wrong

C'Tal dug at the ground, packing the snow into ice, his ears flat against his head, his companions equally upset. ''So we are to stand by and let the Age of Wizards come again?''

''No.''

Doan turned on the giants, hands on his hips. ''What? Changed your minds again?'' His lip curled and his voice dripped sarcasm but the giants appeared not to notice.

''Power can always be misused, we recognize that . . .''

The centaurs calmed a little.

''. . . so we will watch to see that it is not.''

''You?''

''Me,'' the smaller giant said softly. ''I know the land the tower is in.''

''Not exactly inconspicuous are you?''

''I will offer my help openly.''

''And why should she take it?''

Once more the slow exchange of smiles.

''Will you two stop doing that,'' Doan snarled.

Both giants inclined their heads in a unified apology and Doan rolled his eyes.

"She'll take my help," the smaller continued, "because I have been in the tower."

The silence that followed was so complete that the sound of the mer moving through the water could be clearly heard.

For a change, Doan and the centaurs were in complete accord; his look of incredulity was reproduced in a larger scale on their faces as he demanded: "What in the Mother's name did you do that for?"

The smaller giant looked unperturbed. "I was curious," she explained.

"Aren't you a bit big to get curious?"

The two giants looked down at Doan. Quite a way down, for although the smaller was no more than twelve feet tall, the dwarf barely topped four.

"Aren't you a bit small to take such a tone?" the larger chastised him gently. "We get as curious as any race."

"Not so I've ever noticed."

Two sets of earth-brown eyes twinkled. "You live too fast, dwarf."

what was in

the tower

"A great deal of unpleasantness." The smaller giant sighed. "I did not go all the way in, but from what I saw, Aryalan trusted no one. The way is well trapped."

Doan's eyes narrowed. "And you're willing to go back?"

The larger giant took a deep breath and began to explain again. "The tower must be dealt with. The wizard is the only one who can do it, but the wizard should be watched."

"I am the logical choice to watch the wizard. I will therefore go back," the smaller concluded and spread her hands. "Where is the difficulty?"

C'Tal beamed and bestowed his highest accolade. "An explanation worthy of a centaur." He ignored Doan's snort. "Are we all agreed then?"

we

agree

"And I," said C'Din. The palomino nodded solemnly.

"Doan?"

The dwarf scratched his chin, stared off at the horizon, and finally threw up his hands. "Oh, all right." His brows came down and he glared up at C'Tal. "But not because I think the kid'll misuse anything. I want everyone to understand my position on that."

"You have, as usual," C'Tal said dryly, "made your point of view known."

"Good." He twitched his leather tunic straight. "Remember it." And stomped off.

we

are leaving also

watch well, large ones

"We shall."

And then the pool was empty.

"You have," C'Tal intoned, "our thanks for discovering a solution to the problem. And you will," he continued, "I am sure, not only watch but take steps to ensure there is no abuse of power should such a situation occur."

"We shall."

"Then we also will be departing."

The three centaurs bowed in unison then, still in perfect synchronicity, whirled and galloped away.

The two giants sat quietly while the spray of snow from the centaurs departure settled. Then they sat quietly for a few hours more while the pool iced over and the sun disappeared behind the silver-gray of a winter's sky.

"You didn't tell them why you went only a short way into the tower," said the larger at last.

"No."

"Nor did you tell them that you can't go farther than you did and that if the wizard does, she must go alone."

A curious jay landed on the broad ledge of the smaller giant's shoulder, making a bright patch of blue against the brown. She shrugged carefully so as not to disturb him. "Everyone is happy and I saved much time that would have been spent arguing. The tower must be dealt with. I'll know by then if the wizard must."

"And if she must?"

"I will deal with it. But I see no reason to worry now."

And again they exchanged slow smiles, then sat motionless until the jay grew bored and flew off.

Six

Even with two pulling and one behind, the sleigh seemed to gain in weight on every uphill climb.

And these damn mountains, Jago thought to himself, putting his shoulder against the rear crossbar and shoving, *are more uphill than down!* "Chaos!" the last he cried aloud as his feet lost their purchase and he slammed to his knees on the heavy crust. He reached out to grab for the sleigh then changed his mind as, unbraced, it slid back an inch or two. He heard Crystal gasp and Raulin swear as they took up the extra weight. Moving carefully, for the light cover of dry powder made the crust doubly treacherous and the footholds the two pulling had chopped were out of his reach to either side, he got one foot under him, shifted his balance, fell flat on his back and slid twelve feet back down the mountain to slam up against a granite outcropping.

Kraydak's Empire had not been a pleasant place to grow up in, but some things are better learned in adversity. Jago took full advantage of his education as he cursed the sleigh, the snow, the rock, and then his brother.

"Should you be laughing?" Crystal murmured to Raulin as they carefully backed the sleigh down the mountain. On this footing neither could hold the weight alone so the other could go for the brake and Crystal had promised the brothers that, for her own sake, she would use power only when the problem could not be solved in mortal ways.

"He's okay," Raulin grunted. Leaning back against

the drag of the sleigh had twisted the harness so the straps cut into his armpits. Jago deserved whatever damage he'd done himself for that extra discomfort. "Fortunately, it sounds like he landed on his head."

Jago scrambled out of the way as the sleigh eased up against the rock. When it rested securely, he grabbed one of the handles and gingerly pulled himself to his feet.

As the pressure eased off the straps, Crystal freed herself and hurried around to his side. She wore Jago's spare pants, one of Raulin's shirts, and an old green sweater both of them laid claim to.

"We know it isn't much," Jago had explained when *they'd laid the clothes out for her, "but at least you'll be protected if you lose control again."*

She reached out one hand and lightly touched their offering. Although not enough for warmth—no matter, a wizard, even an unstable one, was not at the mercy of the elements—it was enough to cushion flesh in a way that clothes woven of power could not when the power was no longer there. "I can't shift when I'm so confined," she said slowly. *"If I wear these, I'll be bound to this form."*

"Suits me." Raulin smiled and winked.

His words made the decision easier for her and she wondered if he'd known that when he spoke; wondered if the seemingly careless words actually held care. She dressed and then sculpted herself a pair of soft gray boots from woodsmoke.

"Function follows form," she explained, slipping *them on. "Or at least that's what the centaurs always told me. I could as warmly go barefoot, but this will keep my mind from the task and yours from my feet."*

And both brothers had shuddered at the vision of bare feet on snow.

"Hey, I'm okay," Jago protested as Crystal reached for the strings that tied the heavy fur cap to his head. "I barely felt it." He knew better than to try and push her hands away. Early on, they'd discovered that her physical strength at the very least matched either of theirs. Occasionally, Jago wondered if she held back for fear of doing damage to their tender male egos.

Tossing the hat aside, Crystal probed the back of Jago's skull with gentle fingers. She shook her own head in irritation as he winced and tried to hide it when she found the tender spot.

"Don't worry," she reassured him, although exasperation touched her voice as well. "I use more power than this breathing." Her eyes flared briefly as she healed the bruising and blocked the incipient headache.

"Don't suppose you could do something about the significant lack of grace while you're in there?" Raulin called, sinking down on the front end of the sleigh and not bothering to unhook.

"This from a man who trips over shadows," Jago snorted, jamming his hat back on and securing it. He half-smiled his thanks at Crystal, too tired to get his entire face to cooperate, and pulled his heavy overcoat out from under the loose bindings that secured it. Now that they were no longer working, he was beginning to feel the cold. He yanked Raulin's coat free as well, and threw it at his brother's back. Without turning, or removing the harness, Raulin shrugged into it. It bunched up where the traces connected the harness to the sleigh, but it covered him enough to provide warmth.

All three of them looked up at the twelve feet they'd lost. It seemed like a hundred. The shadow of the mountain turned everything, path, sleigh, spirits, to a bleak and unyielding gray.

"Trouble is," Jago sighed, leaning against the sleigh and scrubbing at his face, "the man following has no traction." He waved at the axes Crystal and Raulin had been using to break through the ice. "He doesn't have his hands free to chip footholds, and that crust is too damn thick to stamp through."

"Trouble is," Raulin echoed, "the man following is a lout."

Jago's violet eyes narrowed. "Crust isn't the only thing that's too damn thick around here."

The underlying good humor, usually present in the brothers' bickering, was noticeably absent. Tempers were short, particularily the more volatile Raulin's. Crystal suspected that only the numbing exhaustion of the past few days had kept things from exploding all over the mountainside. They needed some kind of release from the drag of the sleigh and the constant cold, and, she was forced to admit, the tension her presence caused.

Physical attraction—not quite desire, not yet— stretched between her and Raulin like a bowstring. Explored, it would be easier to live with, but they hadn't had that chance. For the sake of warmth during the bitterly cold nights, the three shared a bed, her wizard's body generating enough heat for them all. If she used power to create privacy, she doubted she'd be able to contain Avreen once they began. If Jago would only take a walk for a couple of hours. . . . But they couldn't ask. Not in the winter. Not in these mountains. And Jago. Healing him was like healing herself, everything just seemed to fall back into place. The bond with him was a comfort—not a torment, not even an itch—and that was a relationship that needed defining as well.

Now this.

She glared back up the mountain.

Three hundred feet, maybe less, and they'd reach the pass and be on level ground for a while.

She kicked at the crust.

And then again.

"I think," she said slowly, "I may have an idea."

Both men turned to look at her, faces blank. Below her feet, the snow began to steam. With a crack, the crust broke and she sank up to her ankles in the softer snow beneath.

"No," they said simultaneously.

"Look," she explained, stepping out of the hole, "it's no more than I do at night when I raise my body temperature. You two pull and I'll push, melting myself a stairway as I go.''

''It might work,'' Raulin said thoughtfully, pushing down his scarf and pulling bits of ice from his mustache.

''No,'' Jago repeated. ''It's too dangerous for you to bleed off power. We can't risk the goddesses getting free.'' He met her eyes. They were the only green they'd seen for the last two days. ''No. We'll think of another way.''

Raulin twisted around and glared but remained silent.

Crystal bit back a sigh. Lately, it seemed she was the only thing they didn't actually fight over. She recognized the stubborn set to Jago's jaw and realized she was just too tired to muster the enthusiasm necessary to change his mind. Let the mountain change it for them, she decided, and pulled herself up on the rock to wait.

So they thought about other ways. Every now and then, one of the brothers would snarl something, the other would growl a negative reply, and silence would fall again. Crystal let them keep it up until she knew they could feel the cold creeping in under their furs and then she said softly, ''There is no other way.''

Raulin muttered an obscenity under his breath, then stood, tossing his coat back to Jago as he did. Jago ducked the heavy fur, letting it fall on the sleigh, slid out of his own, and secured them both. He walked up front and buckled himself into the other harness. Without speaking, in no way acknowledging each other's presence, they began to pull the sleigh away from the rock. When there was enough room, Crystal slipped in behind and began to push.

The first twelve feet went quickly, for only Crystal had to break the crust, and then they slowed as Raulin and Jago began to swing the axes once more. Still, with all three on firm footing, progress was neither as arduous nor as slow as it had been.

Safely in the pass, with the brake shoved deep into the snow, they collapsed.

"I say we make camp here," Raulin panted. "I'm beat."

"Still a couple of hours of day left," Jago argued, getting slowly to his feet. "I'd like to see what's on the other side of the pass."

Moving carefully, Raulin stood as well and began to unlash the gear. "Life is too short," he growled, yanking at a knot, "to waste it by dying of exhaustion."

"And we get little enough daylight to waste it because *you* can't make it get any farther." Jago stretched, leaned against the rock wall of the pass, and crossed his arms. "Getting old, Raulin?"

One step, two, Raulin moved toward his brother. His lips pulled back from his teeth and his hands clenched into fists. *Smart-assed little snot. Had as much of that smug, pompous smile as I can take . . .*

Jago straightened and dropped his weight forward onto the balls of his feet. *Time that arrogant asshole learned he doesn't run my life . . .*

Should I stop them? Crystal wondered. *Perhaps this is the release they need.*

Mortals, snorted Zarsheiy's voice in her head. With Crystal's power turned to heat, the fire goddess stayed close to the barriers that kept her penned. *You'll never understand them.*

Watching Raulin and Jago circling for an opening, Crystal admitted Zarsheiy was probably right.

The tension built until even the mountain seemed aware of it. A deep rumble, felt rather than heard, drew all gazes upward. Another rumble sent one or two tiny white balls dancing down the weight of snow poised above the pass.

"We can't stay here," Crystal said softly, voicing the obvious in case the brothers were too wrapped in anger to realize. "It isn't safe."

The tableau stayed frozen a moment longer, then Raulin spun about and grabbed up a harness.

"Try and keep up," he snarled as he jerked the sleigh into motion.

Jago snatched up the second harness and fell into step. They crossed the three miles of the pass in silence.

Late afternoon sunlight bathed the northwest side of the mountains, giving everything a rosy glow. A long, smooth expanse of pinkish-white snow spread down from the pass for a mile, maybe more, unbroken by rock or tree, and ended in a dark line of forest.

For a long moment the brothers just stood and stared, at the light, at the color, at the lack of gray. From her place behind the sleigh, Crystal saw some of the stiffness fall from their shoulders.

"Forest'd be a good place to spend the night," Raulin observed at last, squinting into the sun. "We'd have lots of wood and a good sized fire for a change."

"Course we'd have to get there before dark," Jago added, kicking at the snow. It was still crusted, though covered by about six inches of powder.

"Angle's a little steep. Stopping could be tricky."

Jago grinned at him. "Worry about that when we get there."

Raulin shrugged and returned the grin, the last few days suddenly forgotten. "Why not."

With a whoop that echoed back from the peaks above them, the brothers yanked off their harnesses and tossed them on the sleigh. While Raulin checked to make sure everything was secure, Jago pulled their coats free. Crystal stood watching, openmouthed.

"What are you doing?" she asked.

"Trust us," Raulin told her, doing up his coat and wrapping his scarf more securely about his head. "You steer?" he asked Jago.

Jago nodded as they pulled the sleigh to the edge of the slope. "Suits me."

Careful not to start things moving too soon, Raulin scrambled up onto the load, settling himself as securely as possible. "Okay, Crystal, come on up."

Crystal began to get the idea. She looked down the

mountain. A steep, straight run into a wall of trees. She looked at Raulin and Jago. They flashed her nearly identical, maniacal grins. *I'm as crazy as they are,* she thought as she climbed on and eased herself down between Raulin's legs. *Release is one thing but this . . .* She leaned back against his chest and felt one arm go around her.

"Hang on," he said into her ear.

All things considered, that seemed like good advice, so she did.

"Okay, Jago, let'er rip!"

The crust that had worked against them all the way up the mountain worked for them now. Jago threw his weight against the crossbar and the sleigh began to move. It picked up speed. Running full out, Jago tightened his grip and yanked himself forward, up onto the backs of the protruding runners.

Faster and faster. The runners roared against the snow.

Crystal squinted into the wind and the stinging load of snow it carried. Pushed back against Raulin's comforting bulk, she realized they were totally at the mercy of the slope. The thought terrified, but was at the same time strangely exhilarating. She stared ahead and tried to remember to breathe.

The slope was not as smooth as it had appeared from the pass.

The sleigh bounced over a hillock. Jago threw his weight in the opposite direction and the airborne runner slammed back onto the snow.

A sudden drop caused Crystal and the sleigh to part company for an instant. She bit back a shriek and hung on tighter. *I should've—ouch—walked!* She thought, as Raulin howled something wordless into the wind.

The sleigh moved off crust and onto granular snow. The roar of the runners softened, but they lost no speed. The forest began to approach very quickly.

Crystal clutched at Raulin's arm. "How do we stop?" she yelled.

A shrug and a wild laugh was the only answer she got.

The forest separated into individual trees.

The sleigh lunged into the air. When it landed, Jago yanked back hard on the brakes and they slowed. A little. Not enough.

This far north, at this time of the year, little or no underbrush filled in the spaces between the trees. The trees still grew too close together to allow the sleigh to pass.

Crystal gathered the power she'd need to stop them before the forest did.

Jago reached forward over the crossbar and slapped Raulin on the left shoulder. Raulin nodded and leaned hard to the right, pulling Crystal over with him. The snow passed as a white blur, distressingly close. As the left runner ran up a ridge, Jago released the left brake and yanked down hard on the right.

"Mother-creator . . ." Crystal felt the sleigh twist beneath her . . .

. . . a strap broke . . .

. . . Raulin's hands on her waist . . .

. . . wind . . .

. . . air . . .

. . . cold . . .

. . . and the sudden shock of impact.

White. All she could see was white. Slowly, checking to make sure everything still worked, Crystal pulled her face out of the snowbank and turned. The sleigh lay on its side, half its contents fanned out over the snow. Raulin, she realized, had tossed her free. Raulin, who now roared with laughter and clapped his brother on the shoulder in congratulations. They'd dumped the sleigh on purpose! And they knew they would have to dump it right from the beginning! Her eyes narrowed as she dug snow out of her ears. Why those two . . .

The first snowball took Raulin just above the elbow. The second clipped Jago on the thigh. The third hit the edge of the runner now up in the air and sprayed wet white powder over both of them.

They turned, startled, and two lovely large handfuls caught both of them in the face.

"Oh, so that's the way it's going to be, is it?" Raulin yelled, scraping his face clean. He ducked another missile, scooped up a double fistful of snow and began returning fire.

Crystal twisted nimbly out of the way. "You'll have to do better than that," she taunted, tossing her hair back behind her shoulders. She bent to pick up more snow and Jago, who'd crept around the other end of the sleigh, scored a direct hit.

For the next little while the air was white as snowballs flew thick and fast. Sometimes two against one—and not always the same two—and sometimes all of them for themselves, but it soon became obvious that Crystal got hit far less often than the other two.

"I think," Jago shouted to his brother, currently an ally sharing the dubious shelter behind the sleigh, "she cheats."

"Does she now . . ." Raulin drawled. A snowball chose that moment to curve around their barrier and smack him in the side of the head. "Well, cheaters," he grinned, "never prosper." He jerked a thumb up and Jago nodded. Together they swarmed over the sleigh. Raulin hit her high. Jago hit her low.

Howling with laughter, in a tangle of arms and legs and great fur coats and flying silver hair, they rolled the last twenty feet to the forest and thudded up against the trunk of a young pine. The tree rocked, shook, and dumped its entire load of snow on their heads.

Lord Death stood quietly and watched the camp take shape just inside the shelter of the forest. Although he could not have been seen, he kept to shadow. It suited his mood.

"I am tired of watching," he said softly to the wind. It whirled about him, unable to offer comfort, and a clump of snow blew from a branch above. He held out his hand and the snow passed through it, in no way affected by his presence.

"I am tired of watching," he said again, his eyes on the silver-haired woman by the fire. "But I don't know what else I can do."

"What I want to know," Jago unwound the copper wire securing the end of one braid, "is how you got to be such a deadly aim with a snowball."

Crystal smiled and poked at the fire. Behind the shields Zarsheiy stirred and the blaze flared up, but as the fire goddess seemed content to merely vent her frustration, Crystal ignored her. "The centaurs," she explained. "They live on the great plains. No hills but lots of snow. They seemed to think it would improve my coordination."

"Seems like too much fun for a centaur to approve of."

"They'll approve of anything, as long as there's a lesson in it."

Jago snorted and shook his head. Free of the braids, his hair fell to his waist in a rippling golden mass. "Doesn't sound like much of a childhood," he said, beginning to comb it.

The wizard shrugged. "It wasn't so bad."

"I suppose. Still, it sounds . . . HEY!" He whirled and swung at his brother's legs, but Raulin had already backed out of reach. "He's jealous," Jago told Crystal, rubbing his head where Raulin had plucked out a hair. "Just because he'd losing his . . ."

"Ha!" Raulin stepped over the log they were using as a bench and dropped down onto it. He reached for the blackened metal teapot and poured himself a cup. "Your vanity is going to get your ass in trouble someday. Should've had that whole mess chopped off years ago."

"Mess?" Jago turned, his hair glowing gold in the firelight, the wooden comb pointing at Raulin's face. "I'll cut my hair when you get rid of that growth on your upper lip."

"I'll see you in Chaos first."

"More than likely."

Their words held the cadence of a litany and Crystal relaxed, savoring the heat of the fire, the sweet strength of the tea, and the comfort of companionship. Just for an instant, she thought she saw something move in the darkness under the trees. She dropped her gaze into her mug, losing the image in its contents. The darkness was Nashawryn's realm and she had no intention of loosing that dread goddess again.

Out under the trees, Lord Death sighed. Once, she would have looked for him, but she didn't need him now. Still, she was happy. He'd never heard her laugh the way she had that afternoon. Wasn't that what he wanted? Wasn't it?

Raulin settled his forearms on his knees and watched his brother and the wizard. They looked, he thought, like the sun and the moon come down to share his fire. He had a sudden vision of the two of them entwined, great lengths of gold and silver hair wrapping about them and the rush of desire that accompanied it left him momentarily weak. As though aware of his thoughts, Jago turned to look at him and Raulin raised his mug in a slow and silent toast. Jago grinned, raised both brows, and returned to freeing a tangle. Coincidence, Raulin decided. Although the love between them was the strongest and best thing in both their lives, it had never expressed itself as mind-reading. Not even when they'd been children and could've used it. . . .

With his attention apparently on his hair, Jago managed to keep both Crystal and his brother within sight. He had a sudden urge to shout, "Would you two get it over with so I can figure out where I fit in!" but he held his peace. Would talking to Raulin do any good? He doubted it; his brother never welcomed interference in his love life—Jago smiled at memories—as much as he'd always needed it. . . .

Crystal stared into the fire, acutely conscious of the man to either side of her. They were so much the same in so many ways and yet she reacted completely differently to each. She wished she'd learned more about men in her twelve years of wandering. Twelve years.

The fire danced with visions of the battle on the Tage Plateau, with the pyramids of bodies Kraydak had built across half the world. Kraydak and his armies. Kraydak's Horde. The men of the Empire.

"Raulin, how old are you?" she asked softly, because she daren't ask the other question, the question that naturally followed her line of thought.

Raulin sighed. "Thirty-seven. Jago is thirty-three."

"Then you were . . ."

"Part of Kraydak's armies?" He shifted, snagged the pot, and poured more tea. He'd wondered, off and on, how long it would take her to make that connection. "I was. Jago wasn't."

She turned over a number of responses in her mind, sure of how she felt but unsure of how to express it. Jago broke into the silence before she got the chance.

"Does it matter?" His voice was flat. "He didn't have a choice, Crystal. When they took you, you went. Or you died. They never came for me. That's the only difference. He didn't fight for anything he believed in. He only fought to stay alive. When you destroyed Kraydak, you freed Raulin as much as you freed countries under Kraydak's yoke. Does that make him the enemy now?" His face remained expressionless as he stared at her, but in his heart he prayed for her to say no, to not tear down the delicate friendship that had begun to grow among the three of them.

Crystal raised her head and Jago fell into the brilliant green of her eyes.

You've always hurt for him, haven't you?

He felt the question, knew it hadn't been spoken aloud. He felt her take his answer. Across the bond that stretched between them, across the bond woven of bits and pieces pulled from both their lives, he felt her say: *I hurt for all of them.*

He felt her pain and knew she meant every life that Kraydak had touched.

And he felt how it cut and tore when they wouldn't let her help but ran in fear and suspicion because she came of the same race Kraydak did. Felt her despair and burned with shame that he had considered even for an instant she would forget who the real enemy had been.

Then he again sat beside the fire, looking into a crystal tear that ran down the curve of an ivory cheek. His face grew hot and he tried to turn away, but she laid a hand along his cheek and stopped him.

"We carry the pain," she said softly, "because it is all that we can do."

The why, made up for both of guilt and doubt and caring, they didn't have to speak of.

A second tear joined the first. "I never realized before that I wasn't carrying it alone."

Jago turned his head, not taking his eyes from her, and softly kissed the palm that held him. She smiled, a little tremulously, and drew the hand away to wipe the tears dry with the place his lips had touched.

The bond between them strengthened, for only one thing was stronger than pain shared for love's sake and that was love shared for the same reason.

Raulin watched the only two people in the world who meant anything to him, and nodded. They'd worked it out. He wasn't sure how and he didn't care. He could leave it there, but though he knew what her answer would be, he needed her to tell him as well.

"Am I the enemy, Crystal?" he asked.

She turned to face him, pushing her hair back off her face as she moved, the warmth of her smile reaching across the distance. "You never were."

There had been only one enemy in that war and Crystal knew that better than anyone. But he still released a breath he didn't remember holding as her words dissolved a bitter doubt he hadn't known he had. He returned her smile with an equal warmth and then tried to calm his pulse when she flushed and looked away. He wondered how Jago would feel about looking for more firewood.

Off in the distance, a wolf howled, the lonely sound filling the night and giving all three a chance to regain a little composure. Raulin threw another log on the fire, Jago began rebraiding his hair, and Crystal began to sing.

It started as a formless kind of a hum, an outlet for the emotions that threatened to overflow. She stared off at nothing as the music began to form patterns and then the pattern evolved into a song. It was an old song, from before the Age of Wizards, a ballad of how the last of the air elementals fell in love with a mortal woman.

Jago's fingers began to move to the rhythm of the song. He remembered the last time he'd heard it; his mother sitting in their one comfortable chair with her old worn mandolin in her lap, Raulin sprawled on the hearth replacing the leather strapping around the handle of his dagger—replacing it with a strip torn from one of *his* vests if Jago remembered correctly. That had been about the last night they'd shared as a family. Soon after, Raulin had been taken and he'd been gone barely a month when their mother had died. The mandolin had been sold to pay for her pyre. He smiled as he wound off the braid, holding only the memory of that last night, letting the others go.

The centaurs had taught Crystal to sing as a means of focusing her power. She went one step beyond on her own.

Raulin's jaw dropped as, in the air over the camp, the song came to life. In a tiny patch of clear blue sky, Laur-anthonel swooped and dove and raced the wind. His hair was the color of sunshine, his eyes a storm-cloud gray. From the stunned expression on his brother's face, Raulin assumed Jago saw the same. An arm's reach away from the reality of woodsmoke and trampled snow, Laur-anthonel exalted in his freedom as the song named him more than mortal and less than god; he ruled the winds, no one ruled him. For once more aware of the wizard than the woman, Raulin relaxed and let the music take him.

Crystal sang on, oblivious to anything but the song. The goddesses, with no weakness to give them opening and no calling to their aspects, remained quiet.

Enthralled, Jago stared as the tiny image of the Lord of Air passed over the lands of men, heard singing and stopped to listen—little knowing that he heard his doom as well.

As the song changed, so did the vision; the blue sky of Laur-anthonel's domain replaced by a tower room in a stone keep where the King of Valen's youngest daughter sat at her loom and sang. The shuttle flicked in and out as, with Crystal's voice, Kara poured out her heart, weaving her hopes and dreams into the music. Ten thousand years later, in the air over the camp in the mountains, Laur-anthonel lost his heart again. He paused at her window, and she, feeling the breeze, turned and met his gaze. They exchanged a look so piercingly impassioned that Crystal fell silent, fearing the music might shatter it, and for an instant the image, and that look, hung in the air alone.

Kara found her tongue before the Lord of Air, and Crystal sang of her sudden love for this man who had come in answer to her dreams. She let her own undefined yearning seep into the music, lending Kara's words a sweet poignancy. In the pause between verses, as she drew a breath to continue, a strong rich baritone took up Laur-anthonel's response.

At first, Crystal thought the breezes sang with her, for they often did, and then she realized, shocked, that it was Raulin. She whirled to face him, the image in the air fading as her attention moved from it. Still singing Laur-anthonel's pledge of eternal devotion, Raulin raised an arm and indicated the barely visible lovers. They firmed as Crystal let the music take her up again.

Laur-anthonel, Jago was certain, had never behaved in such a way before for he could see the image of the Lord of Air take on his brother's mannerisms. And his brother's strengths. And, as the courtship progressed, his brother's feelings. He wondered if he should be watching such an outpouring of emotion, decided the music excused him, and knew that, right or wrong, he couldn't leave before the last note faded.

Free to sing Kara's part alone, Crystal found herself involved as she'd never been before. Her heart nearly broke with Kara's anguish at what she thought was love's betrayal and her spirit soared along with her voice as love proved true in the end. She forgot Jago listened, forgot everything outside the music, and sang to Raulin only; her yearning no longer undefined.

When Kara and her love were joined at last, the lines between the passion of the song and the passion of the singers blurred. Their joy rose into the night clear and strong, and then, as though they had rehearsed it, both voices fell to barely above a whisper as they spoke their vows to love.

Never before, Jago thought as the final vow gave way to silence, Raulin's voice wrapped around the core of silver that was Crystal. *And never again.* An intensity like that happened once in a lifetime and he thanked the Mother that he'd been allowed to hear it.

As the crackling of the fire and the movement of the trees surrounding the camp began to fill the quiet, Raulin, never taking his eyes from Crystal's face, held out his hand. Silently, for all that was necessary had been said, Crystal laid hers in it. He pulled her into his arms and bent his head to hers . . .

Jago shook himself free of the spell and for his own sake, for he knew they had forgotten his existence, went for a walk in the woods . . .

. . . where he discovered he had not been the music's only audience.

"What can I give her to stand with that?" Lord Death demanded. "How . . ." He buried his face in his hands and gave a long shuddering sigh. When he looked up his face showed red from the pressure of his fingers. "I can't even touch her, you know."

Jago nodded. "I know." Without thinking, he held out his hand.

Lord Death stared at it until he drew it back, and then, with only a small bit of the pain still in his face, he left Jago alone in the night.

Behind him, from the circle of firelight, Jago heard another song rise, the oldest song of all, and was glad Lord Death had at least been spared hearing it.

Seven

A motionless silhouette against the winter's sky, the giant faced into the wind and read the news from it. The weather would hold, and that was all to the good. Giants seldom worried about weather, able by both sheer bulk and temperament to wait out the fiercest storm, but she wanted to remain on schedule. Both her pace and her path were carefully planned. She would meet up with the wizard and her companions close enough to the tower to be of obvious assistance.

A breeze ruffled her close-cropped brown curls and she smiled at the information it volunteered. It seemed that at the moment the young wizard had little interest in ruling the world and had found a more pleasant pastime.

And I wish her joy of it, she thought, picking a careful way down the steep and icy trail, *for the Mother knows she's had little enough joy in her life until now.*

According to the demon's map, Aryalan's tower lay north and west of the forest. As the sleigh could not be maneuvered through the trees, the way due north was closed. Therefore, they moved west for three days, skirting the edge of the woods until the forest dropped down into a valley which angled almost exactly in the direction they needed to go.

"This," Raulin declared upon seeing it, "was on old frog-face's wall."

As Raulin remembered their path in greater detail than either Jago or Crystal, and as the valley offered shelter and obvious signs of game, they descended into it, still following the forest.

Jago watched Raulin's and Crystal's backs and grinned. They weren't holding hands, but they might as well have been; he doubted he could slip a dagger blade between their shoulders. Separated by the sleigh and the length of the traces, he couldn't hear what they said, but he had a pretty good idea they weren't whispering lovers' platitudes. For starters, he didn't think Raulin knew any.

As though aware of his thoughts, Crystal raised her voice, ". . . because it's a woman's song and when you change the lyrics so that a man can sing it you change the meaning!"

Raulin's reply was pitched too low to carry back to his brother but Crystal's response of "I am not being sexist!" filled in the words. They disagreed without the tentativeness of most new lovers and through that Jago recognized the depth of their feelings. It sounded remarkable similar to the way he and Raulin argued and they'd had over thirty years together.

To his surprise, he felt no jealousy at this closeness. Not of Crystal for coming between him and his brother. Not of Raulin for monopolizing the only woman they would likely meet for some time. Crystal hadn't come between them; while they hadn't exactly grown closer, the rising tension was gone. And Raulin, he knew, did not demand that Crystal remain exclusively with him. Their mother had raised them to believe in a woman's choice, and the brothers had shared bed-partners before. Somehow, though, Jago couldn't see himself with Crystal. It had nothing to do with his mistrust of wizards; he'd lost that back in the demon's cave and in a short time she'd become almost as important to him as Raulin. That was it. She felt like the sister he'd never had.

He watched her reach up to tug on Raulin's mustache and nodded sagely. Yes, like a sister. His sister and his brother and . . . He shook his head and left that line of thought dangling. Taking the analogy too far dropped him into murky waters indeed. Enough that they found pleasure in each other and that he in no way felt excluded from their company because of it.

Besides, the gear had never been in such good repair. Now he went over it for at least an hour each night before retiring to the shelter the three of them still shared.

Crystal found Raulin both an enthusiastic and a considerate lover, as straightforward and uncomplicated in bed as out of it. She thanked the Mother-creator that Jago approved of their relationship and treated the inevitable silliness with amused tolerance. Two things disturbed her. Avreen had made no attempts at freedom in spite of the amount of energy directed toward her aspect. For that matter, none of the goddesses made their presence felt during her nights with Raulin, almost as if something blocked them out . . .

I've seen more fire in wet wood.

. . . although Zarsheiy made a number of sarcastic comments during the day.

She wasn't complaining, lovemaking had never felt so, well, so complete, but Avreen's silence puzzled her. The second thing that disturbed her was the continuing absence of Lord Death. Not for years had he gone so long without appearing. In spite of the companionship of both men, she missed him. He was, after all, her oldest friend.

Raulin had decided early in life that women and men were not intended to understand each other. He therefore refused to analyze the experience during those few times when they seemed to. He stuck to that principle now. Lovemaking with Crystal lifted him to the heights every night. He cherished it, he enjoyed it, he didn't worry about it. Fortune beckoned, and he traveled to it with a beautiful woman by his side and his brother at his back. What more could any man ask for?

* * *

Their first morning in the valley, they crossed rabbit spore three times, and once a huge buck, his head held high under a majestic spread of antlers, regarded them somberly for an instant before spinning and bounding away.

"Snares tonight," Raulin declared, rubbing his hands in anticipation, "and meat tomorrow!"

Crystal laughed, suddenly looking wild and fey. "Meat tonight, I think."

Doan sprawled in the curve of a giant stone foreleg, his brow furrowed in thought. He often came to the Dragon's Cavern when he had a particularly knotty problem to work out and wanted to be uninterrupted. His brother dwarves had developed the habit of avoiding the cavern when the dragon had been alive—not from fear; a large dragon in a confined space in warm weather smelled impossibly unpleasant—and now, although the dragon curled about the center pillar had returned to stone, the habit remained.

"I could," he said, "let the giant handle it." He twisted into another position and drummed his fingers against his thigh. It bothered him that the giants considered Aryalan's tower enough of a danger to get involved. The notion that Crystal herself might *be* a danger rather than *in* danger, he discarded completely. He admitted, reluctantly, that the centaurs might have reason for paranoia, considering how the last wizards they trained had turned out. He also admitted, more reluctantly still, that this wizard was an image of the Eldest, of Milthra, the Lady of the Grove, and that might, perhaps, be influencing his thinking.

Snarling at nothing in particular, he swung down to the ground.

"Only one way to be sure," he informed the dragon, slapping it affectionately on its sandstone nose. He hitched up his pants and went to collect his weapons from the forge.

"Heading off again?" asked a brother, glancing up

from his anvil where a vaguely axehead-shaped piece of iron glowed red hot.

Doan pulled his favorite sword off a wall where a large number of weapons hung. It annoyed him that so few of them ever got used. It annoyed him even more that no one paid attention to his complaints. "You got a problem with that, Drik?"

"Nope." The smith swung his hammer and the iron sprayed sparks. "Just curious. This trip got anything to do with the Call?"

"Might."

"I thought the Council decided to let the giants handle it."

"Yeah, well you know what they say," Doan buckled on the swordbelt and settled the familiar weight across his back, "if you want a thing done right, do it yourself."

"Figure you'll need your sword?"

"What do you think, slag brain?" Grumbling beneath his breath that anything in Aryalan's tower would be a welcome change, he picked up a dagger and stomped from the room.

"Pleasure talking to you too, Doan," Drik called after him, shook his head, and returned to work.

The huge white owl opened its talons, releasing the hare it carried into Raulin's arms. Raulin staggered a little under the weight of the dead animal, then shifted his grip and held it out by the ears.

"Fresh meat!" he exclaimed.

"So I see." Jago set a pot of snow on the fire to melt. "Are you going to clean it or do we spend all night looking at it?"

Raulin tossed him the carcass. "You do it. You need the practice."

"I'll do it," Jago agreed, pulling out his knife and laying the hare on a patch of clean snow, "because *you* are inept." He slit the belly and scooped out the entrails. "You want these, Crystal?"

She stepped into the firelight and bent to pick up

her clothes. "Not now thanks, I just ate. Maybe later."

"You know I consider you my heart's delight," Raulin said, watching her dress with deep enjoyment, "but that's disgusting."

Crystal pulled the sweater over her head, her expression thoughtful. Lord Death had said much the same the night things between them had fallen apart so badly. Was he still angry with her? She hadn't seen him since . . . since the demon's cave, weeks ago. Uncertain whether anything could go wrong with the one true son of the Mother, she still began to grow uneasy at his absence.

"Crystal?" Raulin gently lifted her chin. "Please don't look worried. I didn't mean it."

She managed a smile, pushing her concern for Lord Death back out of sight. "It's okay." She snaked her arms under his open overcoat and around his waist. "When I'm not in feathers I find it pretty disgusting too." Leaning forward, she kissed him hard and when her mouth was free again, added: "I try not to think about it." Which, she suddenly remembered, releasing Raulin to pull on her boots, was exactly what she'd said to Lord Death. All the concern came tumbling back.

Best make up your mind, Zarsheiy taunted. *The quick or the dead.*

What? Usually Crystal ignored her, but usually the goddess' jibes made sense.

Poor child, don't you know your own mind? False sympathy dripped from the thought.

That's hardly surprising, Crystal gave a mental snort, *since I've squatters in most of it*. Her hair, she realized as she straightened, curtained her face from Raulin's view so she carefully schooled her features before it fell back and he grew upset again. For reasons unknown, it didn't seem right discussing Lord Death with Raulin. Maybe if she had some time alone with Jago . . .

"That tickles," she said lightly, as he traced a finger along the edge of her left ear.

He grinned and winked. "You know, I've never kissed a bird before."

"A number of birdbrains," Jago put in, skewering the cleaned hare and setting it over the fire. He shielded himself with the teapot as Raulin took a quick step in his direction. "Hurt the cook and the cook burns dinner!"

"As you're just as likely to burn it without my help that's not much of a threat. I'll . . ."

They never heard just what Raulin planned as an anthem of wolf howls drowned out his next words. The three froze as the chorus climbed up the scale, then faded.

"Great bloody Chaos," Jago breathed, trying to wet his lips with a tongue gone dry.

"Great bloody Chaos' balls," Raulin expanded, swallowing convulsively. "Both of them." He drew a long shuddering breath and added, "In a sling."

Crystal clutched at a wandering breeze. "They have us surrounded . . ." She twisted, seemed to reach for something neither brother could see, and threw up her hands in disgust. "There's more, but it won't tell me."

She seemed frustrated rather than afraid, so the brothers took their cue from her. They began to breathe almost normally again. Raulin continued to stare into the darkness, but Jago sank down to tend the fire.

"Think the meat attracted them?" Raulin asked, trying to forget that howl despite the chills still running up and down his back.

"Perhaps." Crystal tossed her head. She stepped toward the trees, then back, then twisted her hair with her hands. "But there's lots of game around here. They can't be hungry enough to approach the fire."

"Well, they haven't yet," Jago offered, pouring the snow, now transformed to boiling water, into the teapot, dumping it, tossing in a handful of herbs and refilling the pot.

Suddenly, golden eyes glowed just outside the ring of light and then just as suddenly disappeared.

"And then again," he continued, his voice steady but the hand that set the pot back on the coals shaking visibly, "who wants first watch?"

"Wolves do not attack people." Crystal pronounced each word clearly and calmly, but whether she spoke to convince herself, the brothers, or the wolves, not even she was sure.

"Maybe they don't," Raulin admitted, his head jerking back and forth as he tried to watch all directions at once. He pulled off his mitts and wiped his now sweaty palms. "But they don't act like this either. Jago, you take first watch. Crystal second. I'll take last."

Not even Crystal's wizard-sight saw the wolves again that night, but they continued to make themselves heard. No golden eyes broke the darkness, but howls shivered through the silence, time after time. Crystal wove a net of power about the shelter, blocking the noise so the two within could get some sleep.

Nashawryn stirred each time the wolves called.

Sitting alone on second watch, she fed wood to the fire and power to the barriers that held the dark goddess confined.

At dawn, the howling stopped. Daggers drawn, while Crystal stood by ready to help if necessary, Raulin and Jago slipped into the woods and separated, each circling half the camp. Just before they completed the circle, following tracks now deserted by their makers, Jago dropped to one knee and beckoned to Raulin. "Come take a look at this."

Raulin came, looked over Jago's shoulder, and whistled through his teeth. "Big bugger," he said, carefully noncommittal.

"Big bugger? That's it? Look at the depth of that print!" Jago put his fist against the snow and pushed. "This stuff's damp under the trees; it compacts. This wolf's gotta weigh more than it should."

"I hate to break it to you, junior, but that's not our

biggest problem. There's a track as large on the other side of camp that wasn't made by any wolf.''

Jago stood, brushing snow off his pants, his eyes beginning to look a little wild. "Then what?''

"Looks like a cat.''

"That big?''

"Uh-huh.''

"You know what I think?''

"Uh-huh. You think you should've stayed home and found honest work.''

"How did you know?''

Raulin drapped an arm around his brother's shoulders. "It's what you always think when our ass is in the fire.''

"Do we tell Crystal?''

"Only if you intend on living to an honored old age.''

"Good point.''

They took one more look at the oversized print, at the whole line of oversized prints, and headed back to camp.

When told, Crystal looked thoughtful.

"What is it?'' Raulin asked, buckling himself into the harness.

"I don't . . .'' She shook her head and bent to pick up the other trace. "I've got the feeling I'm forgetting something very important. Something someone once told me.''

"Oh, that's very definite.'' Raulin watcher her shrug the harness on, leered, and reached out a hand. "Let me help you settle that strap.''

Crystal grinned, the thoughtful look vanished, and she slapped his hand away from her breast. "Is that all you ever think of?''

"Yes!'' Jago called from his position behind the sleigh. "It's all he's thought of since he turned thirteen. Now, can we get going before our visitors return for breakfast?''

One silver brow rose. "Thirteen?''

Raulin threw his weight forward, straightening out

his trace with an audible snap. "So what're we going to do, just hang around here all day? Let's go."

Except that the way was easier than any they'd traveled for some time, the morning passed no differently than others they'd shared. The quiet of a world muffled in snow soothed ragged emotions and, gradually, night terrors faded. They made good time, pausing only once to rest, and covered nearly ten miles.

"Hey!" Crystal yelled at the brother's backs. "Let's stop for lunch, I'm starved."

". . . and a huge conservatory . . ." Raulin spread his arms, deep in his favorite topic of conversation; spending the gold he knew they'd find at the tower.

"What do you want a conservatory for?"

"For plants . . ."

"I know that's what it's for, you uncultured boob, I just couldn't figure out why you'd want one."

"Guys! Food?" Crystal tried again as Raulin swung, Jago ducked, and neither heard her. She sighed, they'd never hear her now. A strong tug and the metal prongs of both brakes dug deep into the snow. The sleigh stopped cold and she used just enough power to ensure it couldn't move farther.

Raulin, being heavier, kept his balance. Jago's feet took a step his body couldn't complete, his arms windmilled, and he sat down.

"Oaf," Raulin said fondly and extended a hand to help him up.

Back on his feet, Jago turned to face Crystal, who shrugged, and smiled.

"It got your attention," she pointed out. "Let's eat."

Jago's stomach chose that moment to loudly express its agreement. His mouth, open to deliver a blistering retort to Crystal, closed. He unbuckled his harness. "Well, I guess that's my vote. Raulin?"

The older man squinted into the sunlight then along the direction they had to go. "We're making such good time . . ."

"We won't get anywhere if we faint from hunger."

"True enough." He tossed his harness on top of his brother's. "I'll be back in a minute."

As he walked into a nearby copse of trees he heard Jago say, "You notice how he only has to go when there's work to do?" Distance cut Crystal's reply down to a musical murmur. Raulin grinned, the sound reminding him of murmurs into his chest, inarticulate expression of contentment. He swung behind a scruffy jackpine.

Crack!

The grin vanished and he froze, the image of giant tracks in his mind's eye. The hair on the back of his neck lifted and he felt himself watched. In the silence he could hear the tree's needles rub together, a faint *shirk shirk* that now seemed sinister. He managed to do what he had to—the sound was not repeated—then backed slowly out of the trees.

Branches, he knew, often cracked in the cold. He really wished it was cold enough for that to be a valid explanation.

Crystal looked up from the small blaze that heated the ever-present teapot, and frowned. "Raulin, are you all right?"

Jago snorted and tossed his brother a hunk of left-over rabbit. "Probably left it out too long and it froze."

"Something was in those trees with me." He kept his voice matter-of-fact; no sense in causing panic by frothing at the mouth.

Crystal stood to kick snow over the fire, but Raulin stopped her.

"We still have to eat. And the fire's a weapon if we need it."

Acknowledgment at last!

Shut up, Zarsheiy!

Conversation was strained and no one felt the urge to linger over tea.

They hadn't traveled more than a couple of miles when Jago held up his hand for a halt. "Raulin," he called without turning, "did you by chance *see* what joined you in the trees at lunch."

"No. Heard something. Why?"

"Because something is pacing us, something big and black. I've caught sight of it a couple of times now."

"Last night's visitor?"

"Could be."

Crystal's eyes flared as she tried to see through rock and trees and get a good look at their companion. Finally she gave up. "Wolves hunt at night."

"It isn't hunting, just following."

"Well, if it decides to move in . . ." Raulin unstrapped an oilskin bundle and laid it carefully on the snow. Squatting, he cut free the lengths of tarred rope that held it closed. As he opened it and lifted free what it contained, his expression was bleak. The crossbow was a soldier's weapon, easy to manufacture, easy to use. Raulin had been a soldier. He'd hoped he'd never have to be one again. Memories of men and women screaming and dying stirred. With an effort, he pushed them back.

"Are you sure . . ." Jago began, recognizing his brother's discomfort, knowing the source.

"Yes." He stood, slinging the deerskin quiver over one shoulder, and shoved the oilskin on the sleigh where the weight of his pack would hold it securely. Letting the head of the bow fall forward, he hooked the heavy bowstring with the cocking lever and shoved the toe of one boot into the iron bracing ring. A hard pull and the string snapped safely behind the trigger.

"Loading it too?"

"An unloaded bow is a fancy club." He heard the armsmaster's voice in that and his lips curled into a mixture of a snarl and a smile. He slipped a quarrel into position and laid the bow carefully on top of the load, the head pointed toward the trees at the left, the stock inches from where his hands rested on the crossbar of the sleigh.

He looked up and met Crystal's eyes; met not unearthly power, only concern and a question. So he smiled, a real smile this time, and answered it.

"I'm okay."

She nodded and reached out her hand. Although the length of the sleigh separated her palm and his face, he felt her stroke his cheek, leaving a residue of warmth and comfort behind.

"If you don't watch that," his smile quirked up into a grin and he waggled his brows suggestively, "I'll start howling myself."

The geography of the valley limited the sleigh to two directions; forward the way they'd been going, following a river course now buried under half a winter's accumulation of snow, or back the way they'd come. They went on. Crystal and Jago each kept one eye on their path and one eye on the trees and scrub that lined their path. Raulin followed blindly, trying to watch both sides of the trail at once.

As though aware it had been spotted, the creature pacing them took less care to remain unnoticed. They heard it on occasion, the crack and crash of a heavy body forcing its way through the brush, and once or twice saw sumac sway and shake off its load of snow as something unseen pushed past.

The sun sank lower in the sky, the trees began to thin as the forest they'd followed for so long began to end, and they reached a place where the slope to the valley's edge ran clear.

"Higher ground might not be a bad idea," Jago suggested as they paused to consider their next move.

"Maybe," Raulin agreed, "but that slope'll . . . Chaos!"

A huge black wolf stood in the clearing. Teeth bared, it growled.

It stepped forward and the growl grew louder.

Raulin's hand dropped down to the crossbow, rested a moment on the stock, and lifted back to the sleigh when the wolf moved no closer. Unless it attacked, he wouldn't fire. He wasn't sure he could. "Let's move it," he said quietly, throwing his weight against the crossbar and almost running the sleigh up the back of Jago's legs. "Just keep it smooth and quiet and I think we'll be all right."

As the wolf and the path from the valley fell behind, Raulin felt cold fingers brush against his spine. He knew those golden eyes continued to watch and he kept his own locked on the silver sway of Crystal's hair, fighting the urge to turn and walk backward, keeping the enemy in sight. *Enemy,* he snorted to himself. *Try to think of it as a big dog. You'll be happier.*

A flash of black among the trees to the left and they knew they were accompanied still.

"There!" Crystal called, and pointed.

A smaller gray wolf sped across a clearing on the right and disappeared into cover.

"Two," Raulin grunted.

From the left a howl, and from behind an answer. And then another. And then another. And then the valley filled with sound. As the last echo died away the sun slipped below the valley's edge and suddenly, although true night was still hours away, shadows ruled.

"Run!" Raulin barked, catching up the crossbow and ramming his shoulder against the sleigh. "We're too out in the open to fight."

So they ran. With wolves to either side and wolves behind. Jago floundered on a patch of soft snow and almost fell, but Crystal grabbed his arm and yanked him back onto his feet. Forced off the river's path, they scrambled up hills, heading due north into the rougher going of the mountains.

Why don't they attack? Crystal wondered. *What are they waiting for?* Sleek shapes, just on the edge of her vision, kept pace but came no closer. The power needed to protect Raulin and Jago would weaken the shields and free the goddesses. She could only hope that in leaving Zarsheiy would do more damage to her enemies than to her friends.

Ahead of them waited a jumble of rock and a cliff-face that rose eight to ten feet out of the mountain.

"The cliff," Raulin panted. "Get our backs against it!"

With the end in sight, they managed another burst of speed.

The front curve of the right runner caught under a rock and the sleigh slewed to a stop. The leather straps dug into Crystal's breasts as dead weight caught up to her and she plummeted to one knee, gasping, all the air forced out of her lungs. Jago's runner kept moving, spinning sleigh and Jago to the right, whipping both feet out from under him. Raulin's chin slammed into the crossbar and he bit his tongue. His eyes filled at the impact but he stumbled forward, half blind, grabbed Jago, and pulled him to his feet.

"Crystal!" He yelled. "The harnesses!"

A flash of green and the harnesses split.

Raulin pushed his brother on ahead and turned back to help Crystal.

"The cliff, it's our only chance!"

Plunging forward, they almost crashed into Jago who had stopped and stood staring at their intended refuge. "I think not," he said quietly. Raulin and Crystal rocked to a halt beside him.

The black wolf stood on the cliff top. Its teeth gleamed white even in the dusk and its open mouth made it look almost as if it laughed. Then it leaped.

Raulin raised the crossbow and pulled the trigger.

The wolf's scream, when the quarrel drove into its haunch, sounded like nothing out of an animal's throat and when the body hit the ground almost at Raulin's feet, a young man snarled up at them—a young man with thick black hair that grew to a peak in the front and down to the center of his back like a mane, with fierce golden eyes, with very white teeth, and with a crossbow quarrel through one muscular thigh. As they watched, he warped and changed until the great black wolf crouched and worried at the arrow. A little blood matted the fur, but the shaft blocked most of the bleeding.

Jago's mouth worked, but no sound came out. Even

Raulin seemed to have nothing to say. And Crystal finally remembered what had nagged at her all day.

Morning council in the Queen's pavilion the day after Halda had fallen to Kraydak's Horde; Kly, the Duke of Lorn's daughter, had tried to reassure Mikhail that his sister, Halda's Queen, still lived. "The mountains have hundreds of caverns and passageways, milord," she had said. "The wer have used them for generations."

"Wer," she repeated aloud. "He's wer."

"Good guess, wizard. Jason, come here."

Still snarling, the wolf rose and trotted past them on three legs, the uneven gait detracting not a bit from his strength. Their gazes never left him and they turned like puppets following his direction.

Four wolves, two mountain cats, and a man stood between them and the sleigh. Jason, apparently ignoring the arrow, went to stand at the man's side, his injured leg tucked up, paw resting inches above the snow.

The man was naked and shivered slightly in the cold. In his hands he carried a rod almost two feet long crafted of amethyst wrapped in bronze wire. His hair grew like Jason's, proclaiming him kin, and his smile was feral and most unpleasant.

"We don't like wizards on our land."

Kly's voice came out of the past again. *"The wer hate the wizards with an intensity hard to imagine. The names of the wizards are curses to them."*

The rod came up, its bronze tip pointed at Crystal.

Her thoughts ran out like water; the harder she tried to hold them the faster they moved. The void that remained wrapped her in warmth and comfort. Her vision fogged. She swayed, felt Raulin's arms go around her, felt herself slide to the ground. She heard Raulin's roar from a distance, heard an answering roar from one of the great cats, and saw a ginger colored blur go past. Her head refused to turn, so she watched the snow instead of the fight, deprived of the energy to care.

The fight finished before Jago had a chance to help. The great cat returned to its position on one flank of the group and Jago looked down to where Raulin sprawled on the ground. He appeared winded more than hurt. The cat's front paws had slammed into his chest but done no real damage.

"We give only one warning, mortal. Move toward us again and you die."

Jago forced his breathing to calm. Forced reason to win out over anger. "What do you want?" His voice sounded almost normal and only he knew what it took to keep it that way.

"The wizard." The wei spat the word into the air.

Raulin struggled to his feet and tried to surge forward but Jago grabbed his arm and held him back. "Stop it, Raulin," he commanded. "You can't help her if you get killed."

The man's upper lip lifted to reveal his teeth and his eyes narrowed.

"You can't help her. You are no match for Hela alone," the ginger cat looked smug, "and we bind the wizard's power."

So that's what happened, Crystal thought muzzily. She wondered vaguely if he bound the goddesses as well, but it really didn't matter much.

A gray-brown wolf, almost matching Jason in size, flowed into his manshape. "I will take her, Eli, as Jason is injured."

Eli nodded, handing over the rod. "Hela, Gel, watch the mortals." Then he returned to fur.

As the man and both great cats approached, Jago kept his hand on Raulin's arm, not for restraint, but for knowledge; Raulin was the fighter. When Raulin's arm tensed, he flung himself forward, hand grabbing for his dagger, seeing Raulin do the same only much less quietly.

Gel met him in mid-leap. A forepaw hit Jago's head with the force of a club, driving him to the ground. His head rang. His vision exploded into orange and yellow lights. He couldn't see or hear, so he slashed out blindly at the musky smell. Claws ripped through his mitten and into his hand. He lost his grip on the dagger and barely felt the pain when another blow to his head plunged him into darkness.

Raulin rolled as he dove forward, coming up under the cat's attack, driving both feet into Hela's chest and throwing her to the ground. Then he had his arms full of claws and teeth. His dagger went flying. Bringing her back legs up, Hela kicked, shredding his clothes. Raulin screamed as the claws tore into skin. He lost his grip on her jaw. Her teeth closed on his throat.

"Not good, not good." The giant shook her head at the news the breeze had brought. She would have to hurry.

Eight

"You're lucky the inner pack wanted you alive, wizard."

Alive. Crystal caught hold of the word and used it to drag herself a little way out of the pain. She tried to open her eyes, but even so delicate an action was beyond her. Her arms dangled in air, her face bounced against bare skin, something hard dug into her stomach. She forced the information together. Carried over a shoulder.

The shoulder dipped and she dropped onto rock.

New pain and old pain reinforced almost washed her away once more, but she hung grimly onto awareness.

"Cap her," husked a distant voice.

Again she tried to open her eyes. The lids trembled but wouldn't rise.

Rough hands yanked her into a sitting position. Ribs ground together. She whimpered and power flowed sluggishly, responding to the hurt. A smooth band, cold but too heavy to be metal, settled down around her head. Another of the same stuff curved under her chin and snicked into the first band just in front of each ear. She jerked at the sound; very loud, very sharp, and somehow very final.

The hands released her and she collapsed, the band chiming musically as it slammed against the stone. Her throat spasmed as she fought for air, sucking it through her half open mouth. No air got through the ruin of her nose. She tasted blood.

Slowly, very slowly, power began to smooth the jagged edges. Her breathing eased and her body relaxed enough to allow healing. She lay on her side, knees up, arms pressed tight against her chest, and tried to remember.

What had happened to Raulin and Jago? The wer, she remembered, and the rod, and the binding, but there her memories ended. Once over the gap, her thoughts seemed clear enough. Had the binding worn off? To test it she would have to reach for her power . . .

No. Best let the power continue repairing the damage her body had taken. It would do that without her interference and she didn't know what would happen if she attempted control. She was a little afraid to try.

The wer, the rod, the binding . . . and what then?

Beginning softly, an eerie harmonic discord rose in volume to bone shaking intensity. Not the wolves, this was a scream not a song. Shoulders hunched against the sound, Crystal brought her hands up and rubbed at her eyes. She had to see. Something sealed her lids shut. The upper layer crumbled under her touch. Most of the lower, gummy and warm, scrubbed away. Her lashes matted and stuck, but she managed to force her eyes open.

Blood. Smeared across her palms. She touched one eye again and the fingers came away red. Her blood then. Better than the alternative.

The undulating cry went on. And on. And on.

What had happened to Raulin and Jago?

Gathering her returning strength, she placed both bloody palms against the rock and pushed. Ignoring the protest of her body, she managed to almost sit up.

She lay against the wall of a large, roughly circular cavern. Flickering torches, jammed into random niches in the stone, barely lit the space. In the center of the cavern, a number of the great cats surrounded a flat topped boulder. Muzzles lifted, the cats wailed. On the boulder were two black . . . things.

Crystal remembered.

The wer had hoisted her up and bent to sling her over one shoulder, moving her line of sight to include, for the first time since she'd fallen under the rod, Raulin and Jago. She saw the cats attack. She saw the brothers go down. She heard Raulin scream. That had penetrated the mists sifting through her mind. Still outwardly blank, still bound by the rod, deep within her head she'd raged and torn at the walls of her prison.

Something gave.

The cats had burned.

And not with an external flame that could be doused but from inside, with goddess fire. The cats had screamed and thrashed as they died, torment flicking them through change after change. The wolves had circled and snarled but found nothing to do until Jason had flowed into his manshape, hobbled forward to where Crystal lay limp and exulting and had beaten the wizard senseless.

In the cavern, the cats fell silent and began to move away. Two changed and lifted the bodies from the boulder. One followed his kin, the other approached Crystal, the charred remains held tenderly against his chest. A body-length away he stopped and stared down at her with topaz eyes.

"You killed my mate," he said.

Crystal refused to let his grief throw her into guilt. Straightening as much as she could, she stared back at him. "She was killing mine."

He hissed and spat, then turned his back on her and walked from the cavern.

Carefully, Crystal leaned back, easing her weight off her arms and letting the wall support her. She stretched out her legs, the movement hurting less than she'd anticipated. The worst of the pain seemed over, but the healing went on and would for some time. She saw that her feet were bare, and rubbed her cheek against the sweater's shoulder. The brothers lived, for their places within her were still filled, but they were also injured and she had no idea how badly.

If they die because of you, she vowed silently to the wer, *you shall see what wizardry is capable of.*

* * *

"Mortal, wake! You cannot die if I refuse to take you!"

Jago stirred and regretted it. He opened his eyes and shut them instantly. The moonlight seemed to burn holes in his brain.

"You try my patience, mortal!"

Squinting, although the action hurt his head, Jago managed to focus on an auburn-haired man, whose amber eyes flashed with anger.

"Lord . . ." He swallowed and tried again. "Lord Death?"

"Jago?" Raulin's face pushed into his line of vision. He didn't look right somehow. "Jago, wake up!"

"S'what he said."

"Who?"

"Lord Death."

"You're not dead!"

Jago pulled in a shuddering breath. "I know. Hurts too much." He figured out what bothered him about Raulin; the skin of his face seemed almost gray. "You don't look too good."

Raulin's mouth twisted. "You should see the other guy."

Jago rolled himself up on one elbow. The world spun, the insides of his head with it, and he spewed all over the snow. He felt Raulin's arm around his shoulders and when his guts stopped heaving, his brother lowered him gently back down.

"You think you can lie quietly for a few minutes?"

The stars began to whirl. "I don't think I've got a choice." He refused to close his eyes, and concentrated on making the stars behave. Somewhere over to the left, he heard Raulin banging things together loudly. Very loudly. Much too loudly. The sound bounced about the inside of his skull setting the stars, which had just begun to calm down, jigging once more. He wondered where Lord Death had gotten to and . . .

"Crystal!"

"Take it easy. Let's try sitting again, I brought a

pack for you to lean on.'' As he spoke, Raulin eased his brother up, very slowly, until he reclined against the pack.

Jago clenched his teeth against the nausea and sucked in lungful after lungful of cold air. His head stopped spinning and settled into a steady, tormenting throb. Answered by a sharper throbbing . . . He raised his right hand and looked at a mangled ruin.

The throbbing turned to the brindle's roar, teeth dug into his legs and . . . No! He got control of himself, although his legs continued to ache in memory. He met Raulin's worried eyes, Raulin who no doubt suspected what he was thinking, and searched for something to say that would ease that look of strain.

''I guess,'' he said at last, ''I won't be playing the harp any more.''

''You can't play the harp,'' Raulin said gruffly.

''Then I guess I won't be playing it any less.''

Raulin's relieved smile was all Jago could've asked for and he managed a small one of his own.

''Here,'' Raulin wrapped the fingers of Jago's good hand around a warm mug, ''drink this while I bandage.''

Jago took a cautious sip, recognized the bitter brew as a painkiller from their emergency kit, and relaxed.

When Raulin saw Jago actually drinking the potion, he turned his attention to the mangled hand. The great cat's claws had ripped through skin, and flesh, and hooked down into the tendons. Several of the small bones had been displaced and one knuckle barely remained attached. Shreds of tissue were white with frostbite for the hand had lain half buried in snow. Miraculously, most major blood vessels seemed intact. Ignoring Jago's groans, Raulin rebuilt what he could and wrapped the whole tightly in clean linen. It was a better field dressing than any he'd had time to do during the war. He appreciated the irony that experience gained in such wholesale slaughter had twice now come to Jago's aid. Not that this in any way compared to the brindle.

"You know," he said, tying off the end, "when your head starts working again, this is going to hurt like Chaos."

"It already does."

"Good."

"Good?"

"If it can hurt, it can heal. Can you move your fingers?"

The fingers moved a little although Jago turned gray with pain during the attempt.

"What happened?" he asked, just managing to keep the scream from breaking through.

Raulin laid Jago's hand gently in his lap. "Well, it's my guess, they didn't have Crystal bound as tightly as they thought 'cause when we went down those cats started to burn. Think you can stand? Your clothes get wet from sitting in melting snow and you're going to be a lot worse off."

Jago remembered not to nod. "Yeah. I think so."

With an arm around Raulin's shoulder, Jago got slowly to his feet and stood swaying until the world steadied, then the two of them made their way over to the sleigh.

"Probably a good thing you'd already gone out," Raulin continued, "because the smell of those cats burning . . . Anyway, I flopped over and played dead." His voice grew grim and much colder than the winter night. "I could still hear what they did to Crystal."

"She lives."

Jago turned to face Lord Death who walked at his other side. "I know." The bond between Crystal and himself had not broken.

"They dragged her off. I saw where they entered the mountain." Raulin had either not heard his brother or had assumed the words were directed to him. "And we're going after her as soon as you're steady on your feet."

"The two of us against a mountain full of wer?"

Jago asked as they reached the sleigh and Raulin released him.

"Yeah."

"Should be interesting."

The smiles they exchanged came from a lifetime of standing together. Some things got done regardless of the odds; this was one of them.

Raulin brushed the clinging snow off his brother's back and helped him into his huge fur overcoat. Jago, who'd just begun to notice a creeping chill, sighed thankfully and sank down on the front of the sleigh.

He watched Raulin strip their gear to bare essentials, his grip on the world not yet strong enough to help. "What about you?"

Raulin snorted and pulled his scarf down off his throat. Almost invisible in the beard stubble were four punctures, two on each side of his windpipe. "Teeth had hardly touched," he said, "when the cat started to burn and lost interest. I got off light."

"Only because he ignores the rest of the damage."

"He what!"

Lord Death nodded and Jago whirled on Raulin who stared at his brother, completely confused by the sudden outburst.

"Open your coat!"

"Why?"

"Just do it!"

Raulin sighed and slowly unhooked the fasteners. Under his coat, the clothing he'd been wearing hung in tatters. Under his clothing, eight angry, red lines marked where Hela's claws had torn through to skin.

"Only scratches, I swear." He tried to close the coat, but Jago glared it back open.

"Get me the emergency kit."

"Look . . ."

"Get it!"

He got it, then stood almost still as, one-handed, Jago pulled bits of cloth from the cuts, all at least a quarter inch deep and most already looking pink and inflamed. Two started bleeding sluggishly again as the scab holding the remains of Raulin's shirt inside the wound came free.

"Cat scratches," Lord Death said, as Jago reached for the roll of linen, "often become infected. You'd better disinfect those."

Jago nodded thoughtfully and reached instead for the bottle of raw alcohol.

"Now hold it, what're you going to do with that?"

"What do you think?" Jago asked, pouring some of the liquid on a cloth balanced on his knee. "That mess has to be cleaned."

"Not with that stuff, it doesn't." Raulin backed away, but Jago grabbed a corner of his coat.

"Knock me over," he warned, "and I'll have a relapse."

Raulin sullenly stopped moving.

Jago flipped the coat open again and wiped at the scoring with the alcohol laden cloth. "Stop squirming. Cat scratches often become infected."

"Says . . . CHAOS! . . . who?"

"Lord Death."

"When did he become a . . . DAMMIT JAGO! . . . healer?"

"I am the Great Healer," said Lord Death quietly. "Mortals come to me when all other healers have failed."

"What did he say?" Raulin could tell by Jago's expression that the Mother's son had answered the question himself.

"He's expounding philosophy. If you'd stop dancing away, this'd go faster and we could start after Crystal."

Raulin growled an inarticulate curse but stood motionless while Jago finished.

Lord Death watched Jago's ministrations with a number of emotions warring in his breast. He needed Raulin reasonably healthy to rescue Crystal, but he resented the time spent on healing when every moment Crystal stayed with the wer put her in greater danger. He hated the thought that these mortals could attack the wer without his help and he could do little without theirs. And a very small part of him enjoyed Raulin's pain.

A linen bandage soon covered Raulin from armpits to waist. Although exposed flesh rippled with goose-bumps, he only shrugged his coat closed. Putting on freezing cold clothes underneath it would do more harm than good at this point. A fire would draw the wer. The small campstove threw heat only to the cooking surface; not enough to warm clothing.

"I'll be okay," he answered Jago's silent question, bending to complete the packs. "The coat's warm enough for fighting."

Jago nodded, there not being much else he could do, and in a little while Raulin helped him into his pack. He tried to ignore Lord Death whose patience appeared to be growing short.

"He won't need that," Lord Death snapped as Raulin settled his own pack and loaded the crossbow.

"Why not?" Jago asked, waving Raulin quiet.

"Because I will lead you to Crystal on paths the wer do not walk."

"You?"

"What's he saying?" Raulin demanded.

"He says you don't need the crossbow. That he'll lead us to Crystal on paths the wer don't walk."

"He will?" Raulin turned over the idea. Lord Death could see the wer, but the wer couldn't see him. Jago could follow his direction and he, Raulin, could follow Jago. "It might work." He unloaded the bow and hung it from his pack by the quiver, out of the way but near to hand. His brow furrowed. "Ask him if . . ."

"He can hear *you,*" Jago interrupted.

"Yeah, well . . ." Raulin straightened and spoke where Jago pointed. "If you can get in and out of there without being seen, why do you need us?"

"Tell your brother," Lord Death said to Jago, "that I cannot carry Crystal if it comes to that." He paused and fought to keep anything at all from showing on his face or in his voice as he added, "He can."

* * *

Crystal sat alone in the cavern for what seemed a very long time. She ran her fingers lightly over the band on her head and decided it was the same material as the rod. It fit snugly, almost as if it had been made for her head. It was a power binding of some kind, of that she was certain. Tentatively she reached in and directed the healing that still went on. Her power responded.

Cautiously, she manipulated and tested and discovered that everything appeared to be under her control. Her shields had remained up and not even Zarsheiy was missing. That surprised her, for there had been nothing containing the fire goddess when the cats had burned. Nor could she understand why Zarsheiy stayed so silent; this situation should've called forth scathing remarks.

She's sulking.

Crystal recognized Tayja's voice.

The link between you and her and Avreen was so strong that she found herself back behind the barriers before she could even think of freedom.

Avreen worked with me?

Of course, child, you've given her ample reason to stay.

Crystal felt herself flush. Raulin. She sighed and wondered if Raulin realized they had more of an audience each night than Jago, who patiently killed time by the fire. She touched the places the brothers held in her heart, knew they continued to live, and reached out with her power to call them.

Pain.

Screaming and writhing, she clutched at her head. Hot knives drove into her brain. A vise tightened and crushed. Then, as suddenly as it began, it stopped.

"So you have discovered what the cap can do."

Gasping, she scrambled back into a sitting position, her fingers tearing at the bands.

The old wer who stood over her smiled. "You cannot remove it," he said, "and if you try to use power against it, or to augment your strength, or in any way it finds your actions aggressive," he shrugged, "you now know what will happen. The wizards," his lips curled back in a snarl of pure hate, "built their devices of torment well." He flicked a hoary nail against the cap. "With this they could keep their fellows captive, healthy, whole, and helpless. You cannot use your powers to escape."

Hoarse from screaming, Crystal rasped, "They made this to use on each other?"

He spread his hands. "Who else has power to trap? As the wizards grew more powerful, their only adversaries were each other. Did you not destroy the only other one of your kind?"

"That was different!"

"He is still dead."

"I'm not like other wizards!"

"I see no difference."

Crystal worked her weight up the wall until she stood looking down at him. Small things hurt, but even her nose had begun to function again. She could smell the heavy animal scent of both the caverns and the wer who faced her. Basically, she was whole. For now. "Why," she asked with dignity, "am I alive?"

"Now? Specifically?" He slid his hands beneath the loose poncho he wore, a piece of clothing easy to slip out of in wolf form. His smile showed a broken tooth and dripped with malice. "We've waited many generations to catch a wizard. To visit on you some of the torment your kind laid on us. When we escaped during the Doom, we stole what toys we could. One brought you low. One you wear."

"But I had nothing to do with your creation . . ."

"It doesn't matter!" He spat the words. "You are wizard!"

For an instant a craggy gray wolf stood before her, its lean and hollow flanks jutting from the poncho. Pale eyes blazed with rage. Then the old man stood there again, breathing heavily through his nose, obviously fighting to keep his emotions under control.

"It's been thousands of years," Crystal said, shaken, "why do you still hate wizards so?"

"You see," he snarled, "but you do not understand." He turned and began to walk across the cavern. "Follow. I will make you understand. And then you will begin to pay."

The wolf on guard at the entrance to the wers' tunnels reclined, head on paws, half asleep. Young and complacent, sure the wer were the only predators in the valley, the attack took him by surprise. In the brief struggle, he flicked into his manshape and Jago slammed him behind the ear with his dagger hilt. As he fell, he became wolf again.

"We can't tie him," Jago pointed out, grabbing him by the forelegs and dragging him away. "If he changes, the rope will slice his hands off."

"Do you care?" Raulin asked, remembering the sounds of heavy feet and fists pounding against Crystal.

"He's just a kid . . ."

Raulin sighed. "Yeah, I guess."

They blocked the tunnel, hoping more to slow the guard than to stop him entirely.

"What if he doesn't try to follow and just goes for help."

"This is the only way into the valley from the mountain," Lord Death explained, eyeing the rock pile impatiently. "If he goes for help, it will take him some time and accomplish the same thing as far as we are concerned."

They advanced into the mountain, their eyes adapting in the darkness enough to pick out the darker shadows that marked companions. Moving as quietly as they could, Raulin followed Jago who followed Lord Death who made no noise at all.

Not a great deal of time had passed when Jago flattened against the rock. Raulin mirrored the move a second later. They'd come to a fork, one branch black and deserted, the other lit—although the torches burned so far apart they gave a twilight effect at best. No sounds came from the inhabited passage but given the freshness of the torches, wer could not be far.

Lord Death walked forward, passed the torch, and disappeared into the gloom.

The brothers waited. And waited.

Raulin wrinkled his nose against the overpowering odor of pine. He picked a crushed needle out of his mustache and fought the urge to sneeze. *Not many walking pine trees in these parts* he'd pointed out when Lord Death had suggested they hide their scent.

And there are no mortals at all, Lord Death had pointed out in turn. *The wer will react less to the smell of pine than the smell of meat.*

Meat. Raulin hadn't wanted to ask.

Jago started as Lord Death stepped out of air in front of him. The movement jarred his hand and he bit back a curse.

"I suggest you keep it quieter," Lord Death warned. "We are reaching the inhabited sections of the mountain and must go carefully. Come, this section is safe."

They passed the first torch and came to a small cave angling back into the rock. Faintly, over the smell of pine clotting their noses, came the musky scent of cat. The brothers froze.

Lord Death, no longer sensing them following, stopped, turned, and glared. "I said it was safe. They will not wake for some time, I have touched their dreams."

His mouth close to Raulin's ear, Jago repeated Lord Death's words.

As they moved on, Raulin shook his head. *Dreams touched by Death,* he thought. *Nice.*

The old wer led Crystal to a small cavern spilling soft lamplight into the tunnel; a higher level of technology than any she'd yet seen. Jason's wolfshape lay across the door, not on guard for his attention was turned within. When he caught their scent, he whirled, rising into manshape with the move. Gray paste covered his arrow wound.

"What are you doing here, wizard?" he growled.

"I brought her, Jason."

"Why?"

"To show her why we hate."

A whimper from the cavern and Jason's hands clenched into fists. His golden eyes filled with fury. "Show herrrr." The last came out more growl than word as the great black wolf trembled with the effort not to attack.

Another whimper spun him back into the cavern.

"Go." The old wer pointed and Crystal stepped forward.

The cavern, the size of a large bedchamber, held a low table and a stool, rough shelves cut into the rock walls and filled with carvings of wer in all their shapes, and a large box bed, heaped high with furs. The lamp sat on the table, close by the bed. An ancient woman knelt by the box and crooned, soft and comforting, too low to be heard more than a few feet away. The young woman on the bed was obviously in labor.

"In the early months," the old wer said softly in Crystal's ear, "the mother's changing does no harm, but after the wolf is ready to be born she must stay in womanshape to carry the mortal half to term. If she changes, the child and usually the mother as well dies. This is the torment the wizards gave us; strong emotion sets off the change outside of our control. Surprise, anger . . ." He paused and the woman on the bed whimpered again as a contraction rippled her swollen belly. ". . . pain."

"Then why . . ."

"Our lives are long and in wolfshape the urge to mate is very strong. Although wer did not ask to be created, neither do wer wish to die. Do you wonder why we hate you?"

"The cats . . ."

"Are more indolent by nature so their time is a little

less hard. They have three males for every female. We have five.''

Even as Crystal recognized the singsong cadence of the crooning, she saw the trance it was meant to maintain fail.

''Jason?'' The young woman's eyes tried to focus as the pain pulled her out of her hypnotic state.

He poked his nose into her hand and she clutched at it, then stroked the cheek of a worried young man.

To Crystal's wizard sight the fingers of the hand seemed shorter than they should and the russet hair grew too thickly across the back.

''No!'' she cried aloud, heard an answering cry within, felt the shattering of a goddess bond, and began to move.

The Eldest of the Elder Races had a part in Crystal's making and with Milthra's strength she met Jason's charge and hurled him aside.

When she reached the bed she was already singing, throwing power into her voice regardless of what the cap would do. She rested one hand on the woman's head and the other on her stomach and sang her an easing of pain. The change, barely a heartbeat begun, stopped. The fingers grew longer, the hair less. Then Crystal went deeper, wizard and goddess acting as one, touched the core of the wer, found the flaw, and healed it.

The cry of a newborn blended for a moment with her song, then it continued alone.

When Crystal raised her head, wer jammed the door, drawn by the use of power.

''What . . .'' The old wer spread his hands searching for the words.

Crystal swayed, the place where her power had been was an aching void. The fire, the repairing of herself, and now this; she had nothing more to give. ''I healed her. She controls her changes now.''

''How? The cap . . .''

''The cap works to prevent escape.'' Her head throbbed and the places beneath the cap felt bruised.

It had reacted to the power, but it hadn't tried to stop her.

"Why?"

Crystal looked at the girl-child sucking lustily on her mother's breast, squirming as her father licked her clean. "I am not like other wizards," she told him, and tumbled into the void.

Lord Death stopped, head cocked as though he listened. "Lives. A number of them," he said suddenly, waving Jago toward one of the small caves. "Hide there until I return for you."

Jago pulled Raulin through the arched doorway, a small portion of his mind noting that it could never have been naturally carved. "Someone's coming," he hissed in explanation. "Hide."

They pressed up against the wall where the angle was too sharp for them to be seen from the passage, packs pushed hard into the rock. They heard the questioning cries of puzzled cats first, and then the soft thud of pads running on stone. The sounds grew louder, filled their ears, then faded.

Raulin relaxed his grip on his dagger, silently released the breath he'd been holding, and sagged against the wall. The wounds under his bandages ached. He stretched, trying to remain flexible but knowing he was stiffening up. He felt Jago still tensed beside him.

"What is it?" he leaned over to whisper.

A nervous smile glimmered briefly. "I started thinking about all the rock piled up above us."

Raulin bit back a laugh. "With all the things we have to worry about . . ." After the strange half-light of the tunnels his eyes adjusted quickly to the greater gloom of the cave. He saw the sweat sheen Jago's face and touched his brother's arm. "These mountains have stood for thousands of years, they'll last a few hours more."

Jago nodded. He plucked at the sling holding his injured hand immobile against his chest, and forced his thoughts away from the great weight of stone they moved under. *Crystal needs you. Think of Crystal.* From deep in his mind came a wisp of song. He sighed and the knots in his muscles eased.

"Hey." Raulin leaned over one of the shadowy bundles that almost filled the cave. "Tanned hides."

Intrigued, Jago moved beside him. The corner of hide felt butter soft between his fingers. "Trade goods?" he guessed.

Raulin shrugged. "Makes sense."

"The danger has passed. Come."

"He's back?" Raulin asked, reading Jago's reaction.

"Yeah." Jago tried to calm his pounding heart as he rose and turned. Lord Death stood in the entrance, the light from the passage igniting copper strands in his hair. He cast no shadow into the cave.

"Things have changed," said the Mother's son, his expression unreadable. "We must hurry."

"I can't decide; are you brave or stupid? I mean, considering that you expected the cap to fry your brains."

Crystal tried to focus. Browns and blues swam in front of her and finally arranged themselves into a young girl with wild chestnut curls and cornflower eyes. She didn't look much like one of the wer.

The girl grinned.

Pale greens swirled about in soothing patterns and Crystal realized where she was. "I'm not awake."

"Out cold," agreed the girl. "Your power is slowly rebuilding but for now, you're stuck here."

Crystal's stomach spasmed. "I'm starving."

"You surprised? You better hope they feed you soon or, even after you regain consciousness, you'll be mush for days." The girl spun about. "The others can't get this high in your head with no power to use, but I go where I want."

"Are you trying to get free?"

"Maybe. Maybe not."

"You're Eegri." she smiled, despite the hunger, as one long lashed lid dropped in a saucy wink.

"Maybe. Maybe not."

"You weren't the one who . . ."

"Don't be ridiculous," Eegri snorted, "I don't do babies." Then she looked thoughtful. "Not after the initial gamble. No, you broke Sholah loose with that stunt, shattering the remaining matrix. Geta's still sulking, but the rest of us are rummaging about quite separately. So," she drew her legs up and sat cross-legged on nothing, "answer my question. Brave or stupid?"

Crystal considered it for a moment, weaving a strand of hair through her fingers. "I guess," she said at last, "you could say I took a chance."

Eegri stared at her, then burst into peals of laughter. "I like you, wizard!" Her smile fell on Crystal like a benediction and a delicious smell filled the air. "You got lucky. They're feeding you."

Her mouth flooding with saliva, Crystal felt herself pulled back to consciousness. "Did you do that?" she asked the fading goddess of chance.

Eegri's smile hung on an instant longer. "Maybe. Maybe not."

Crystal opened her eyes to see the ancient woman who had knelt by the birth bed. In age-twisted hands, she held a large clay bowl filled with heavy porridge. Her gray eyes, while not kind, were at least neutral.

"You saved my granddaughter and her child," she explained. "Eat."

She backed quickly away as Crystal grabbed up the bowl and began shoving handfuls of the warm food into her mouth. Then, recovering, the wer admonished sharply, "Eat slower. You'll choke." Male voices from the passage admonished her in turn, but she snarled them into silence as she left.

Crystal felt the rumble of moving rock, and ignored it, concentrating on the food. The porridge only just took the edge off her hunger, but its weight was a comfort in her stomach, and when the bowl had been licked clean she felt able to look around. She was in a small cave, about eight feet square, and a single torch was jammed into a crack by the door—by the blocked door. She got up, put her palms against the stone, and pushed. As she expected, nothing happened.

"I am going to get my strength back," she muttered, sitting back down, "and then I am leaving. Cap or no cap."

Lord Death sped down the passageway, Raulin and Jago keeping up with difficulty. "Soon we'll come to a short passage that leads to the central cavern. Cross the passage quickly and quietly. The wer meet to decide Crystal's fate."

"Meet where?" Raulin wanted to know when Jago had echoed the information.

"Where do you think," Lord Death said coldly without turning.

"In the central cavern," Jago translated.

"Wonderful," Raulin muttered and reached behind him for his crossbow.

The passage was indeed short. Crossing it, quickly and quietly as instructed, the brothers could clearly hear the debate going on in the cavern.

". . . healed Beth, we let her go."

"And who will heal my daughter when her time comes? No! We keep the wizard chained to do our bidding as her kind once kept us!"

"Wizards are the pain givers. Kill her!"

"She healed Beth!"

"But why?"

"Wizards can't be trusted, her reasons . . ."

The voices faded in the distance. They ran about a hundred meters along secondary passageways until Lord Death stopped before a roughly circular boulder pushed tight against the rock wall. "She's behind this."

Raulin shook his head, put his shoulder against the

curve, and pushed. The boulder rocked. He bent and studied the floor. "Grooved," he said, standing. "Can't be moved from the inside, but the two of us should manage fine. Jago."

With a sound like half the mountain falling, the huge stone rolled out of the way.

Raulin straighted up and took a deep breath through gritted teeth. He waited until the pain smoothed out of his face, then ducked into the cave, his eyes half closed as though afraid of what he'd find.

Jago leaned a moment longer against the stone. *Lucky they're arguing too hard to hear that,* he thought, following his brother through the opening. *We won't get a chance like it again.*

Raulin had caught Crystal up in his arms, ignoring his injuries as he pressed her against his chest, and covered her face with kisses. "I knew you were alive. I knew it." But the shadows in his eyes said he'd had his doubts.

Crystal's fingers danced over every bit of Raulin she could reach.

He touched the cap and his expression hardened. "Is that what they hold you with?"

She drew his hand away, not allowing him to see how his tugging at the band sent slivers of pain into her head.

"We've got to get out of here," Jago said softly. She turned to face him then and he felt her joy, less demonstrative than her response to Raulin, but just as deep.

"You're both injured. I have no power . . ."

"It doesn't matter," Jago told her, wishing he could wipe the helplessness from her voice, "we have no time either. Come on."

The three of them stepped back out into the passageway and Crystal froze.

"You've come back."

Lord Death smiled hesitantly at her. "I couldn't leave you in the hands of your enemies."

"But . . ." She looked from Raulin to Jago.

"I brought them to you." When she stepped toward him, the smile vanished, and he turned away, feeling too exposed with Jago watching. "Now, I will take you out."

Crystal quickly hid the hurt but not before Jago saw it and vowed to have a word or two with the Mother's son.

They traveled as quickly as they could, tossing caution aside with all the wer accounted for in council. The air freshened, the light changed subtly, and at last they could see the silver of moonlight on snow.

"It's still the middle of the night," Crystal marveled, sagging against Raulin with a sigh. "It feels like it should be days later."

"Well, we've cut days off our time," Jago told them peering out into the night. "We've come out on the opposite side of the mountain."

Just then the faintest of howls drifted up along their trail.

"I think," said Raulin, propelling them out of the mountain, "you've been missed."

They fought their way down the icy slope, almost blinded by the sudden brightness. The howls grew louder. Four legs move much faster than two, especially with injuries and a long night beginning to take their toll.

"Leave me and save yourselves!" Crystal cried as a sharp edge cut into her bootless feet. She stumbled and fell to her knees.

"None of that," Raulin snapped, pulling her up. "We stay together, all of us."

As they ran, his arm tight about her waist, she left a bloody trail on the ice.

Jago tripped on a hidden branch and reached out to steady himself on an oddly shaped outcroppping. His fingers clutched at cloth.

"Gaaa . . ."

"Gently, mortal, I will not hurt you." The giant picked up Raulin and Crystal who had careened into an outstreched arm, and drew all three of them against the shelter of her body. "You are safe. There is no longer any need to hurry."

And then the wer were upon them.

Nine

Crystal buried her face against the giant's warm side and refused to think about the wer howling around them. Her power had dropped to such a level that her bare feet actually throbbed with cold. Raulin and Jago were both wounded and she could do nothing for them. Hunger tied knots in her stomach. Her head hurt. One more thing and she'd break down and cry. She'd deal with the wer later.

Raulin enfolded Crystal protectively in his arms. The giant still held them loosely and he felt as if they'd reached a safe harbor. Let the wer slaver and growl, he was certain that the giant could take care of them.

Jago sagged and whimpered as his weight fell forward on the ruin of his hand. A gentle grip lifted him and settled him comfortably against a massive thigh and a soft touch along his back eased the pain. He saw his brother and Crystal safe against the giant's other side, thanked the Mother-creator for their good fortune, and relaxed.

The wer circled, two dozen wolves and half that number again of cats. They moved constantly, a seething wall of eyes and fangs gleaming in the moonlight, with here and there a pale flash of skin quickly clothed again in fur.

The giant sat patiently, held their prey, and waited.

Finally Eli padded out of the pack and shifted to his manshape.

"You have something that belongs to us, Elder," he called.

"Yes," she said, her slow, pleasant voice neither

acknowledging the wer as a threat nor threatening them in turn, "I believe I do. You may come in and remove it from the wizard's head and we shall be on our way."

Eli looked puzzled, then he caught sight of the cap lying deeply purple against the silver of Crystal's hair. "Not that toy," he snarled. "The wizard."

"But she can't *belong* to you. One person can't own another. If I remember correctly, that's what your people cried out to the wizards who tried to own you."

"She is a wizard!" Eli almost screamed it. "The wizards kept us in torment. Created us so we would always exist in torment!" His emotions overcame him. He flowed back into wolfshape and raised his muzzle to the moon. The pack joined in.

The giant waited silently until the echoes of the howl finished bouncing back off the mountains, then said, "What you say is true, but as this wizard had nothing to do with that and is in fact younger than a number of you I fail to see your point."

Another wolf rose to two legs and growled, "We could take her."

"You could try," corrected the giant gently. "I wouldn't advise it." A quiet certainty radiated with the words, lapping over the wer, calming them. When most had stilled, she raised her voice, just a little. "I am taking these children to my camp. You may spend the night outside in the dark and the cold watching if you wish, but we will still be there in the morning. If you have anything else to say, you may say it then."

"We can't just let the wizard go," wailed a man-shape of one of the cats.

"I *said*, we will be *there* in the morning."

He opened his mouth, closed it, snapped back to fur, and began vigorously washing a hind leg.

"Can you mortals walk?"

It took the brothers a second to realize that she was speaking to them.

Raulin's chest burned with lines of fire, but he nodded. "Yes, I can."

"Me too," Jago straightened, taking elaborate care

not to jar his hand. He was beginning to have fond memories of the mauling he'd taken from the brindle, at least he'd been out through most of that.

"Then follow in my footsteps," she said, standing and scooping a semiconscious Crystal up in her arms. "I will always take the easiest path. Don't worry," she added comfortingly, ignoring the wer who scrambled out of her way, "it isn't far."

They looked at each other, they looked at the wer—who appeared more confused than aggressive—and they did as they were told. Her huge footsteps were easy enough to follow, even in the uncertain moonlight. Jago estimated her height at close to twelve feet and at most only four of that was leg. As tall as she was, she actually looked taller sitting down.

It isn't far can be a dubious statement when uttered by a giant, but she led them only a short way down the mountain to where she'd set up her camp within a small copse of trees. In the center of the clearing a fire burned, and on the embers at the edge of the fire, just beginning to steam, sat a teapot.

Jago started. It looked like their teapot; but theirs had been left with the sleigh on the other side of the mountain. Except—his eyes bulged a bit—wasn't that their sleigh drawn up on the far side of the fire? And that shelter . . .

"Uh, Raulin . . ."

"Yeah. I see, I see."

The giant laid Crystal gently down on the sleigh, turned, saw the brothers' bewilderment, and smiled. "The breezes told me where to find your equipment, so I brought it with me when I came. Now," she squatted by the teapot and filled three enamel mugs, "drink this and shortly you may sleep."

Raulin stuck his nose over the mug she'd handed him, and sniffed. The painkiller from the emergency kit and something else. He took a cautious sip. Raspberries?

"Doesn't taste like goat-piss anymore," Jago muttered.

"No reason why it should," pointed out the giant, leaving Crystal, who after a number of mouthfuls was managing on her own. "I can do nothing for your hand," she told Jago sadly. "It is beyond my skill. But in the morning . . ."

He nodded. "Crystal can take care of it." That thought had kept him from screaming hysterics or black despair all night.

"But you," she advanced on Raulin, "you, I can soothe." She flipped open his coat and had the old bandages unwrapped before he had time for more than a single yelp. Clicking her tongue at the flaming red lines, she fished a flat metal container from a pocket, and spread the ointment it contained over the wounds. Even before she finished they looked less angry. She cocooned him in fresh linen, and pulled one of his spare shirts, warm and soft, over his head. Lifting the empty mugs from two sets of lax fingers, she pushed the brothers toward the shelter.

"The wizard will join you when she's had something to eat," she admonished as they hesitated. "Sleep."

"Well, I'm not going to argue with her," Raulin muttered, dropping to his knees and crawling inside.

Jago half turned, gave a small bow in the giant's direction, and followed.

"Now," she loomed over Crystal, "first we will remove this ugly piece of work." Her large hands circled the cap and she added, "I'm sorry, child, but this may hurt." Then she pulled.

Crystal's back arched and she tried not to cry out as, with a crack that seemed to shatter her skull, the band broke. Panting, she collapsed back on the sleigh as the giant methodically snapped the polished amethyst into tiny pieces. "Please," she said, when she thought she could control her voice, "I need food."

"Yes, of course you do." The giant placed a large biscuit in Crystal's hand.

Crystal took a tentative bite, sighed, and crammed

the rest into her mouth. When she finished swallowing, the giant handed her another.

"I haven't had these since the centaurs," she said through a mouthful of crumbs. The taste conjured up wild runs across the plains; the thunder of hooves pounding against the ground, the smells of centaur and upturned sod blending and becoming one, her hair blowing into a tangled cloud as she clung to a broad back and rode down the wind. She could feel strength seeping back. "I could never get enough of them."

"I think you've had enough at present," the giant chuckled. "Just one of those horse-cakes could keep your teachers fed for a whole day. They may, as the dwarves assert, be pompous and pedantic," she said, sliding her arms under the wizard and carrying her over to the shelter, "but they can cook."

Crystal yawned, suddenly more tired than she'd been since her battles with Kraydak. "Have you a name," she asked.

"I have a number of names. Today, I am Balaniki Sokoji."

"Sokoji," Crystal repeated, crawling inside. "Pretty. I like it." She snuggled down between the brothers and fell asleep with Raulin's arms about her and Jago's breath warm on the back of her neck.

"Good morning, Sokoji."

"Good morning, Crystal, wizard. How do you feel?"

"I have less power back than I expected to," she shrugged, "but I had more power to replace than I'm used to." She stretched and smiled. "I guess I feel fine."

"Good." Sokoji bent over the fire and stirred the porridge that bubbled and steamed. "Come and eat and you'll feel better still."

Crystal, her feet healed during the night, glided forward an inch above the snow. She reached out, caught a plume of woodsmoke rising lazily on the still morning air and from it formed herself new boots.

"It would be more practical," observed the giant, "to visit a cobbler."

"It would," Crystal agreed, accepting a huge portion of the oatmeal and nodding her thanks. "But by the time I realized that, there were no cobblers around." As she ate, she told the giant everything; the first time she'd heard the voices in her head, the healing of Jago, her fight with Lord Death when Zarsheiy nearly broke free, the demon, agreeing to accompany the brothers to Aryalan's tower, and the wer. She didn't know why, exactly, but she felt Sokoji should know.

Sokoji sat immobile while Crystal spoke. Much of the story, she knew. The goddesses, however, she would have to think on. *They* were an aspect even the centaurs had not considered.

"Crystal?"

She turned to see Raulin crawling out of the shelter, his bandages brilliant white in the morning sun.

When he spotted her and saw that she was all right, his worried expression vanished. "I woke up and you weren't there . . ." he said, spreading his hands. He reached back inside for more clothing, but Crystal stopped him before he could put it on.

"Wait," she said, wrapping warmth about him. "I want to look at your chest."

"It doesn't even hurt anymore," Raulin began, going to her side. He noticed the giant sitting motionless on the other side of the fire. "Is she okay?"

"She's fine," Crystal assured him, undoing the dressing. "Her name is Sokoji and she's thinking. Lift your arms."

He did. "She looks like she froze during the night."

"The centaurs once took me to visit a giant. She sat like that the entire two days we stayed. Apparently she'd been thinking for almost six years."

"What about?"

"No one knew."

The eight parallel lines on Raulin's chest no longer looked dangerous. Although the cuts themselves had not healed, the flesh around them appeared healthy and firm. Crystal set her fingertips just under the collarbone where they began and, humming softly, traced each line. The wounds glowed briefly green and vanished. Then her hands moved a little lower.

"Crystal! We're not alone!"

"Prude."

"Whoops! Excuse me if I'm interrupting."

Raulin flushed deep red and pulled the heavy undershirt, still clutched in one fist, over his head.

Jago tossed him a shirt and sweater, grinning broadly. "I noticed you hadn't got dressed this morning. Guess now I know why."

"You don't know anything, you little . . ." Raulin stopped in mid diatribe, his eyes widening. "Your hand!"

Both Jago's hands were whole.

"That's two I owe you," he said softly to Crystal, his eyes bright with emotion. "Thank you."

"I have less power than I expected to." And she had no memory of healing Jago. As it healed her when she needed it, whether she directed it or not, her power had also healed him, using the life-bond between them.

"Come and eat," she said, suddenly unsure of what this closeness would demand of her. "Power alone can only do so much."

As the brothers ate under Sokoji's unwinking stare—Jago having been reassured as Raulin had been—Crystal spotted movement in the trees and went thankfully to meet it.

Raulin rose in protest but Jago dragged him back, mouthing the words "Lord Death." He'd sensed Crystal's discomfort, knew it had something to do with him and Raulin, and wished, not for the first time, that Lord Death had a more corporeal form. As much as he had grown to love the wizard, Jago suspected that her kind could never be happy with mere mortals.

They stood silently for a moment, Crystal gazing down at the branch in her hands and stroking the needles, and Lord Death staring off at nothing, then they both bcgan to speak at once.

"Please, go ahead."

She hesitated but realized he would not speak until she did. "I missed you," she said at last. "What kept you away?"

"Would you have me sit at night and keep company with them?" Even to his own ears, he sounded bitter.

"Why not? You've sat with me in mortal company before."

But I meant more to you than the company then, he thought to himself. *Ironic isn't it that someday those two will die and be mine and you I can never have.* All he said aloud was, "No."

"Have I upset you somehow, I . . ."

Her distress at his refusal showed in both face and voice and while he cursed himself for hurting her, he also marveled that he could. "Two mortals, a giant, and a wizard make a crowded campsite." That to lighten the *no*. And then he took a chance. "But if you want me, step away from the fire and call."

"And you'll come?"

"If you call me," he reiterated, meeting her eyes, wondering why he put himself in such a position, "I will always come." *What if she never called? What if she did?*

Crystal heard a deeper meaning beneath his words and knew she could probably force it out. But did she want to? Was it something that could survive being dragged out and totally revealed between them?

Not yet, murmured a voice.

Idiot, snapped another.

"You must do something about the wer," said Lord Death, not totally unaware of the turmoil he'd caused and pulling away from it for his own sake.

"What?" The sudden change of subject caught Crystal off balance.

"You cannot leave them as they are when you can heal them."

"The changes?"

"Yes. You can right a very great wrong." Young women and infants, faces feral and in great pain, flickered across his features.

She shook her head, hiding behind a curtain of silver hair until he wore his own face again.

"I am Death, Crystal, and often I seem cruel, but these have been robbed of even a chance at life. I am not as cruel as that. Too many come to me too young."

She thought of the power it would take to heal so many, how her shields would weaken. She thought of the goddesses breaking free. She opened her mouth to say she couldn't, looked at Lord Death and knew he expected her to say she would. Although he had seen the excesses of the ancient wizards, he had never, she realized suddenly, expected her to follow their path. *Free my people*, were the first words he'd ever said to her. She would not have *Heal the wer* be the last.

"I will heal them," she said and felt that his smile of approval well rewarded her for the risk.

When Crystal returned to the campsite, Raulin and Jago sat nervously watching the giant who, as far as Crystal could see, hadn't moved.

"I have to speak to the wer," she said.

"Are you crazy?" asked Raulin, standing and striding over to her. He took hold of both her shoulders and gave her a little shake. "You barely escaped from them with your life. Go near them and they'll zap you with that rod again."

"They won't dare, not while Sokoji is with us."

"In case you hadn't noticed, Sokoji is not with us."

"I am only thinking, mortal, I am not dead."

Crystal suppressed a smile as Raulin paled. She gently patted his cheek and whispered, "Don't worry, they're used to it." Sliding out from under his hands, she crossed the camp until she stood at the giant's knee. "I need to speak with the pack. Will you come with me?"

Sokoji nodded. "I will."

Crystal raised her voice slightly, turning her head so

she faced the trees beyond the giant. "Then I will speak with the pack, the entire pack, when the sun has moved a handspan in the sky. They will speak with me because they remember what I did for Beth. The Elder will see that we both, the pack and I, are no threat to each other."

A shadow separated itself from the shadows of the forest and moved off toward the mountain.

"I knew it," Raulin muttered, still a little rattled by the giant's sudden return to awareness. "I knew we were being watched."

One handspan of the sun later, Crystal stepped out of the trees and faced the wer, the giant on her right and the brothers on her left.

"You can't leave us behind, Crystal," Jago had said quietly. And he was correct. She couldn't.

The wolves had grouped in the center of the slope, the cats in their regular flanking position to each side. Of the sixty-two wer assembled, all but two walked on four legs. A young woman stood at the back of the pack, warmly dressed in leather and fur, holding a squirming bundle in her arms. It had to be Beth. A great black wolf wove about her legs, every now and then whining and sticking his nose in the bundle.

"You will not, of course, be using that," Sokoji called out.

Crystal followed her gaze and saw the amethyst rod between the forepaws of a wolf she thought she recognized as Eli.

"We will not use it if we are not attacked," Beth replied, settling the baby more securely in her arms, "but we must be able to defend ourselves, Elder."

Sokoji looked unconvinced. "I would prefer it with one less likely to use it."

Beth shrugged. "Eli is hunt-leader."

"It doesn't matter, Sokoji." Although she spoke to the giant, Crystal's voice carried up the mountain. "I'll give him no reason to think his people under attack."

"And if he uses it anyway, I'll rip his tail out and

strangle him with it," Raulin muttered, not at all comfortable standing so exposed before the wer.

Crystal ignored him and continued. "I have only one thing to say. If you wish it, I will remove from the women the flaw of the ancient wizards and heal them all as I healed Beth, a gift they will pass on to their daughters."

The silence on the mountain was so complete the sun could almost be heard moving across the sky. For different reasons, Raulin and Jago were as shocked as the wer. Only Sokoji seemed unaffected.

Then one of the cats changed and a tawny-haired woman with eyes as green as Crystal's asked suspiciously, "Why only the women, wizard?"

"That is *my* flaw. I am sorry, but I have nothing in me to touch the men."

"No!" An old man crouched on the mountainside. "Each generation we grow more stable, some of the younger ones are able to walk with mortals and keep them unaware of what they are. We don't take anything from wizards!"

"Some? Two! Two only!"

"Each generation we grow fewer!"

Bodies shifted out of wolf and cat all over the pack, ignoring the cold in the need for a voice.

"What good is it, if she cannot change the men?"

"It's women who die!" screamed a girl, barely in her teens. The male wolf beside her bared his teeth and growled. She slipped into wolfshape, rolled on her back and exposed her throat, but before he could close his teeth on the soft fur Jason threw himself between them and cuffed the male away.

"She's right," Jason snarled, taking on his manshape but looking no less furious, "it is the women who die. This is their choice. Not ours."

"But what of us," whined the male, shifting only long enough to form the words and not rising off his belly.

"It is too soon to tell, but I think," Jason looked back at Beth and his features softened as he met her smile, "when the women have control, it will help us remain calm."

"And what do you want for this great gift, wizard?" Eli stood, the rod dangling from his fingers.

Crystal's face hardened.

"I want you to ask me. Come to the camp when you've reached a decision."

Then she turned on her heel and headed back into the trees.

The brothers held their peace until they reached the camp but only just.

"Crystal, you are out of your mind! They almost killed you and you want to help them?" Raulin stomped about, one hand twisting at his mustache, the other waving in the air. "Put yourself at risk for *them?*"

"*They* are women and children, Raulin." She explained about the random changes and what that meant to childbirth. Her shoulders squared. "I can't allow such suffering to continue when I could banish it."

"And if the goddesses break free while your power is elsewhere?" Jago asked quietly.

"Sholah, I know, is with me in this."

We cannot leave them as they are, agreed the goddess, although only Crystal could hear her.

"And the rest'll shatter you into nothing!" added Raulin, still driven to stomp around the clearing by the force of his emotions.

"I'll take that chance."

"No." Lord Death's quiet tone carried a finality just bordering on the melodramatic.

"Listen, Crystal," Raulin began. Sokoji laid a massive hand on his shoulder.

"Gently, mortal, let the Mother's son have his say. He seems to agree with you."

"What? Is he here?" Raulin glared up at the giant. "And you can see him too? Oh, great." He threw himself down on the sleigh beside his brother. "Well, maybe he can talk her out of sacrificing herself."

"Maybe he can," Jago murmured, watching Crystal, watching Lord Death.

"I didn't realize what I asked of you," Lord Death told her, his eyes locked on her face.

"I'm ashamed you had to ask." Crystal flushed. "For all my talk, I am more like the ancient wizards than I suspected."

"You needn't do this to prove yourself to me."

She smiled. "I'm not. I'm proving myself to me."

He nodded slowly and she saw he understood. Something blazed for a moment in his eyes, something that caused her heart to pound and then both it and Lord Death were gone.

Raulin got to his feet and Jago, knowing his brother was neither as brash nor as insensitive as he pretended, wondered what he would say, even having seen only Crystal's side of that conversation.

But, concern the single emotion in his voice, Raulin only said, "Can't it wait? Just until you get the goddesses under control?"

"And if I never do? Should I let more innocents die because I'm afraid to take a risk?" She cupped her hands, letting them fill with sunlight, then wove a garland out of glowing golden strands. With a disdainful toss of her head, she let it dissolve. "Do I spend the rest of my life using only enough power to do pretty tricks? I am the only one who can help them. They need me."

"We need you, Crystal."

"No," she corrected gently, "you want me and as wondrous as that is, it isn't the same thing. If I turn my back on the wer, I am no better than the wizards who created them, denying the responsibility of my power."

He lifted her hand to her lips. "Then I will stand with you and do what I can to help."

Jago rose and took her other hand between both of his. "I also," he told her.

Crystal's lower lip trembled and she blinked rapidly.

"Idiot," Raulin said tenderly, and drew her into his arms.

The centaurs wrought better than they will ever believe, Sokoji thought. *And I hope I am there when this wizard-child comes to believe it herself.*

Later that day, while Crystal and the giant were deep in discussion, Jago went to his brother and demanded an explanation.

Raulin looked up from the harness he mended—Crystal's method of releasing the buckles had turned them into slag—and raised both brows. "An explanation of what?" he asked.

"Don't give me that, brother, you've never been good at hiding what you feel. Why no response to Crystal's conversation with Lord Death?"

"I gave her the only response I had."

Jago snorted.

Raulin sighed. "Look, Jago, you're a complicated man, I'm not. I'm her lover and her friend, but I've never fooled myself that I'm her love. In a lot of ways, you're closer to her than I am." He shrugged and reached for his dagger. The metal wouldn't pry free, he'd have to cut the leather. "As for this morning, well, I don't see as it changes anything. I'll share her bed for as long as she'll have me and when it's over, I'll thank the Mother-creator that I knew her."

"I thought you loved her . . ."

"Of course I do. So do you. And she loves us both." He grinned and winked. "Although in different ways. But there's too much to her for just you and me. We couldn't hold her and we shouldn't try to. Close your mouth now, and pass me the repair kit."

Jago did as he was bid and then picked up the other harness. "I guess I underestimated you," he said, turning the straps over in his hands.

"I guess you did," Raulin agreed. "You forgot, I've got hidden depths." He looked smug. "It's why I always get the girls."

"They feel sorry for you," corrected Jago, ducking a wild backhand, and more relieved than he could say that when Crystal finally found her own heart she wouldn't be breaking Raulin's.

That evening, just before the sky grew dark enough for stars, the wer came with their answer. Only Beth, Jason, and their daughter actually entered the camp, but it didn't take wizard-sight to spot the rest out under the trees.

Her head high, Beth ignored everyone but Crystal. She walked across the clearing as if she owned it. The baby rode in a sling across her chest and she kept one arm curled protectively around it. The other arm hung by her side, hand resting on Jason's head. She stopped in front of the wizard and gray eyes looked fearlessly into green.

Raulin stepped up to stand behind Crystal's right shoulder, facing the great black wolf.

Jason growled.

Raulin growled back.

From that moment on, they ignored each other.

"Have you come to a decision?" Crystal asked, trying desperately not to laugh.

"We have." Beth's mouth twitched as well. She took a deep breath to steady herself, during which time Crystal also gained control. "Will you heal us, wizard?" she asked simply.

Crystal nodded. "I will."

"There are three other packs . . ."

"Them too."

"They can be here in a quartermoon."

"Then in a quartermoon, no female wer will be at the mercy of the changes again. I will heal all of you then."

The sling wriggled and a tiny fist fell free to flail in the air, turning to a tiny paw as it waved.

"Get down, Jason," Beth admonished as his nose got in her way. She tucked the arm in safely, and looked back to Crystal. "Thank you," she said. *For my life and my daughter's, not what you may, or may not, do in a quartermoon*. Then she turned and they walked away from the camp.

* * *

During the week of waiting, Crystal spent a lot of time with Sokoji. The giant's presence calmed the goddesses, lessening the constant struggle to keep them confined. They discussed the healing and once Crystal went into the trees and told the startled sentry she needed to talk with a woman who knew how wer children learned to change.

Beth's grandmother answered the summons, her womanshape so wrapped in leather and fur she could barely walk. She eased herself down by the fire and accepted the offered mug of tea.

"Yes, it'd be damned uncomfortable to change, dressed like this," she said in answer to Crystal's startled expression, "but at my age emotions know their place." Her face creased as she thought of two babies born dead. "Now it no longer matters, I change when I want. You got any honey for this tea?"

"I'm sorry," Jago told her, "we're out."

"I'm sorry too. Tea without honey is an abomination." She sipped, made a face, and decided the warmth made up for the taste. "You wanted to know how the children change?"

As Crystal had suspected, the random changes were necessary in the young, giving the parents a way to teach with stimuli, a sudden cuff snapping the child into the desired form. Only with the female's first heat, did it become dangerous.

Raulin and Jago occupied themselves with butchering a young buck Eli and his hunters dragged into the camp.

"We don't want you hunting on our land," the wer snarled, "and anything you intend to waste, return to us."

"Very gracious," muttered Raulin.

"Very," Jago agreed.

But they were careful to return what they couldn't use to the pack.

The weather held, cold and clear, and the quarter-moon passed.

* * *

Crystal stood, silver and ivory in the moonlight, surrounded by wer. Of the three hundred gathered, less than one hundred were female; Beth and Jason's daughter the only child.

"Is this all of you?" she asked, when they had settled into place and the only movement was the slap of tails on snow.

"No." A young woman stood shivering in the cold. "My sister has reached the time of no changes and could not travel." She looked as though she wanted to add something, then shook her head and flowed back into wolfshape.

So few, Crystal thought sadly. If only she had done this sooner. If only they had come to her, asked for her help—but they were too blinded by hate to consider it. As far as the wer were concerned, the wizards were the pain givers and her defeat of Kraydak did not erase the fact that she was a wizard. She sighed, grieving for all the lost ones, then reached for her power and began to sing. Her hair fanned out around her, the moonlight dancing down each strand.

The wer pricked up their ears and waited.

Crystal's eyes began to glow a deep summer's green as she poured power into her voice. She felt Sholah join her, merge with her, and the song changed as the goddess' wisdom gave it form. As it spread, radiating outward, Crystal spread herself with it, becoming a part of the power, becoming, in a way, both the singer and the song.

For an instant, the females listening heard not with their ears but with their hearts, and during that instant Crystal's power touched them and remade the fatal flaw.

The power built until the air thrummed with it and still Crystal sang.

The song changed again. Crystal began to reach. *All* the females of the wer had been her promise, not all but one.

The wer were forced to avert their eyes, so brightly did she reflect the moonlight.

From the sister, she picked up the blood tie and followed it back over the mountains. Back. Back. Her power stretched, thinned; she began to pull from the barriers. There! The thought patterns of the wer were unmistakable. She touched the woman gently. The barriers wavered. She could feel Zarsheiy waiting for them to fall.

The woman started, perhaps sensing the wizard's touch, and the change began.

Crystal stopped the change, held it, and reached fo: power to complete the healing.

The barriers fell.

FREE! Zarshiey surged forward.

And slammed into a wall of darkness.

The wer are mine. Nashawryn's cold voice filled Crystal's head, cutting through Zarsheiy's screams of frustration. *Feared by mortals, hunters in the night; I give them my protection. Finish what you have begun, wizard, I stand by you.*

Crystal reached again for power and found, even still linked with Sholah, that no power remained for her to tap, it was all tied up in the other goddesses. The other goddesses . . .

Keeping a careful hold on the change, Crystal slid into the woman's mind searching for the love she held for the child she carried.

Clever, murmured Avreen, and gave up the portion of power she controlled.

The song finished.

Crystal let her body pull her home.

Ten

From where Lord Death stood, the figures grouped around the sleigh were tiny. Even Sokoji appeared no more than two or three inches high. He watched the giant reach down and lift the sleigh over a rocky ledge and frowned. She was the reason he watched from so far away. Unlike Crystal and the mortal, who could see him only if he wished it—although if one did, they both did—the Elder Races, so close in creation to the Mother, could see him whether he liked it or not. And he did not like it, for Sokoji always drew his presence to Crystal's attention. Which meant he had to appear to her as well. . . .

Which meant they talked. . . .

And every conversation seemed to skirt dangerous topics; his feelings, her feelings, their feelings. And every conversation had Jago and the giant listening in, drawing conclusions, trying to bring into the open that which he preferred to have remain hidden.

So now he took the coward's way and watched from a distance.

Crystal laughed at something Jago said, and Lord Death ground his teeth. Once, he remembered with a bitter smile, he'd encouraged her to spend time with mortals. Had, in fact, given her Jago's life and with it Raulin's gratitude. And now, Jago gave her the companionship she used to share with him, and Raulin . . . He looked down at his hands. Raulin gave her the one thing he never could. Even Sokoji placed one more life between them; another living creature, to listen and to help.

"If it was just the two of us again," he murmured at the wizard's distant figure. He could tell her then. If when he finished speaking she didn't have another pair of arms to turn to that were not his nor ever could be.

He no longer wondered what madness had directed him when he said he would answer her call. He had named it the night she'd risked everything and healed the wer because he had asked her to.

"I am Death," he told a passing breeze. *And I am in love. And it hurts.* He sighed and shook his head. "This is your doing, father," he added aloud. The one true son of the Mother had been fathered by Chaos but never throughout the millennia since his birth had he felt so chaotic.

In midafternoon, between one moment and the next, the world turned gray and almost all the light vanished. Close objects took on a sharp-edged clarity and distant ones disappeared into a merging of snow and sky. For an instant, everything fell completely still, waiting, then the wind came up in strong and random gusts that whipped Crystal's hair about and threatened to knock the mortals off their feet.

"There," Sokoji pointed. "The best I think we have time to find."

There, was a small triangular cut in the mountain, about ten feet deep and almost that across its open end. It offered protection on three sides from the coming storm.

"I think you're right," Raulin agreed, squinting against a sudden flurry of snow. "Let's move, people."

They secured the sleigh across the open end, for only by wizardry could they have fit it inside. By the time they'd wrestled up the shelter, anchoring it firmly within the mountain, the world had turned white and the air was solid with snow.

"Will you be all right out here?" Crystal yelled at Sokoji above the shriek of the wind.

"Of course I will, child." The giant folded her legs and settled herself comfortably against the rock wall. She pulled a hat out of her pocket and tugged it on. It looked like a bright red bird's nest overturned on her head. "I shall sit here and think." Brushing the already accumulated snow off her lap, she linked her hands and stilled.

Crystal reached out and patted the giant's knee affectionately.

"Hey, come on!" Raulin grabbed Crystal's shoulders and spun her about. "Get inside before you get buried. Or lost."

"Lost?" They took the three steps across the cut, from the giant to the shelter, together. "How could I get lost?"

"Storms are tricky." He pushed her to her knees and held open the outer flap. "Get turned around and the next thing you know you wander off and freeze to death."

Crystal smiled, shook her head, and crawled inside, Raulin close behind. Before he ducked in, he noted that the sleigh, at the very edge of the windbreak provided by the mountain, had become a shapeless white blob and the giant, although as much out of the storm as possible, could barely be seen.

Because they'd brought in most of their gear, the usually snug shelter could only be described as cramped.

"How about cozy?" Crystal asked, when Raulin did just that after contorting himself around various bundles and into a sitting position.

Raulin only growled and tried to discover what was poking him in the back. Enough soft, silver light came from Crystal's hair for him to see her pulling their teapot out of a pack.

She tossed it in his lap. "Fill this with snow, would you, please."

He did, and even though he carefully snaked his arm out between the two flaps, a small eddy of snow found the opening and danced inside. Crystal clicked her tongue and danced it back out.

She slid against Jago, set the full teapot Raulin handed her in front of her on the floor, muttered something at it, and dumped a package of tea in the now boiling water.

"Should you be using your power like that?" asked Jago, twisting around and digging out the mugs.

Crystal ducked his elbow and caught the teapot before it could spill. "I can't see as it'll hurt. Zarshiey seems happier when her aspect is being used; it's when she gets bored that she tries to make a run for it."

And she hates *being talked about as if she isn't there.*

Then maybe she shouldn't listen, Crystal responded to the goddess' complaint.

By rearranging a number of the packs, and intertwining two or three legs, they managed to achieve positions where they could both drink their tea and be reasonably happy doing it. Body heat had warmed the shelter to a satisfying temperature, so damp outer coats were removed and piled against the entrance as an added protection from drafts. Crystal had muted the sound of the storm and, although an occasional gust shook the felt and canvas walls, in their island of comfort and safety, it had become vaguely unreal.

They ate a small meal—more for something to do than from hunger.

"We need more room," groused Raulin as they finished, stretching out long legs and almost kicking Jago in the stomach.

You'd have more room if you'd lie down, Avreen suggested. *And more still if you . . .*

Shut up, Avreen! But she passed on the suggestion, minus the corollary, to the brothers.

Raulin added the corollary on his own and, with a deep sigh, Jago offered to go sit in the storm until they finished.

Crystal smacked them both.

The amount of squirming necessary to spread out the bedrolls with three adults taking up the space where the bedrolls had to go was impressive but, with only a minor bit of wizardry, they were finally spread.

"I don't know about the rest of you," panted Jago, pulling off his jacket and folding it into a pillow, "but that exhausted me." He collapsed backward, then bounced up again quickly, apologizing for nearly crushing Crystal's elbow.

She only smiled and snuggled her back against Raulin's front, head pillowed on his forearm. Her eyes began to close. Jago lay down more carefully the second time, bending where necessary to fit. Because of the packs, the three of them were close. Very close.

"I hate to disillusion you, Raulin," Jago said dryly, "but that's my wrist you're stroking."

Eventually—being trapped in a small shelter by a storm having limited their options—they all fell asleep, tangled in and around each other like puppies.

Raulin woke, and lay quietly in the darkness listening to Crystal and Jago breathe. He wondered if the storm still raged and decided it didn't matter one way or another—he *had* to go outside. Slowly and carefully, he slid out of Crystal's arms, unwinding a strand of silken hair from around his throat. She murmured in her sleep, but didn't wake. Easing his feet into his boots, he laced them loosely, then pulled his overcoat from the pile of fur by the door—the loops that closed his were cord, Jago's closed with leather—contorted himself into it and backed out into the night.

By both kicking the snow away and compacting it with his body, Raulin got free of the shelter, made sure both flaps had closed securely behind him, and stood. As his head rose above the level of the tent, the wind, snow-laden, struck him full in the face. The storm did, indeed, still rage. And it was cold. Raulin quickly fastened his coat and tried to bury his ears in the collar. He'd come out with neither hat nor mittens. Just to be on the safe side, he bent and tightened his boot laces. By the time he finished, his fingers were already growing stiff.

He plunged around the shelter and began to make his way the length of it to where the sleigh marked the edge of the cut. After the wizard-created warmth inside, the night air felt like knives in his lungs and he was positive the interior of his nose had frozen. Had the wind not been making such a noise, he was sure he'd be able to hear the nose hairs crackling.

"Lucky I'm not going to be out here long," he muttered, stumbling into a drift that reached his thighs. "Any sensible wizard," he added, plowing forward, "would have built her tower farther south."

His foot hit something hard and he tripped, falling against the object and burying his arms up to the elbows.

Righting himself, he shook the snow from his sleeves. "Well, it seems I've found the sleigh." He followed the angle to where the lower, front end butted up against rock, clambered over, and out of the cut.

A solid wall of snow slammed into him and, if not for the rock wall at his back, it would have swept him up and away. Eyes closed against the wind, Raulin kept one hand on the mountain and staggered five paces from the camp.

"Far enough," he decided, and did what he had to. When he finished, he reached out again to use the mountain as his guide. It seemed to have moved. He knew he hadn't. He stepped forward, arms outstretched, expecting to punch his hands into rock. Nothing. His hands were numb with cold, but he thought they should be able to feel a mountain. He took another step. Still nothing. He squinted in the direction he knew he had to go. All he could see was storm. All he could see in *any* direction was storm.

"Okay," he drew his hands up into his sleeves as far as they would go, "let's just stop and think about this for a moment." Closing his eyes again, for they certainly weren't any help, he took two deliberate steps backward. "Okay, now I turn to the left and go five paces which will take me back to the . . ." He bent and flailed around. Nothing. No sleigh.

"All right," he fought to keep his breathing steady; panic would help the storm, not him. "All right, I could've angled off a little. I turn left again and keep going straight. I'll eventually hit either the sleigh or the mountain."

Eventually didn't happen in six steps, or seven, or eight.

When he tried to open his eyes, he found the lashes had frozen.

"CRYSTAL!"

His scream only added to the wailing of the storm. Crystal and Jago slept on.

"All right, all right, I'm coming!" Doan stomped out into the storm and stood solidly against the wind. The voice that had imperiously roused him out of sleep had quieted and the Chaos-born storm blocked his sight. His eyes glowed red and a shadowy figure became visible about five body lengths away. He stepped toward it and it moved back.

"Don't play your games with me, Mother's son," he grunted, for only Lord Death could walk unhindered through a blizzard, "I am not in the mood." But he followed anyway, curiosity growing with every step, until the shadow stopped beside a body half buried in the snow. Doan's brow furrowed. The body didn't seem to have a head. He grabbed it and flipped it over. The coat had been pulled up in a turtle attempt at warmth. The man within still lived and he seemed vaguely familiar. Doan searched his memory for a name.

Raulin. That was it. One of the mortals whom the breezes had reported traveling with Crystal. His mouth twitched as he remembered the stories the breezes told. Their descriptions appeared fairly accurate, although Doan couldn't understand the continuous jokes about the man's mustache. When it wasn't frozen solid it was probably quite respectable. But what was he doing out alone in the storm?

And why had Lord Death come to him?

The dwarf bent and hoisted Raulin up on his shoulders. The weight gave him no trouble, but he cursed a little at the length. *Ah well*, he thought, *it can't hurt bits of him to drag. Snow's soft.*

He paused before starting back and cocked his head at the shadow lingering at the edge of sight. "Why didn't you wake Crystal?" he asked.

The shadow that was Lord Death vanished into the storm.

Thinking deeply, Doan carried Raulin to safety.

Once inside, he stripped the heavy outer coat off his burden and checked exposed skin for frostbite. Ears, the end of the nose, a patch on each cheek, and fingertips, he decided, all of them superficial although the ears were a close thing. He tucked Raulin's hands up in his own armpits, and carefully began to warm the mortal's face. Only the ears still showed white when Raulin finally opened his eyes.

I've been found! was Raulin's first jubilant thought. *Who or what is that?* was the second. Thick red-brown hair, eyes the same color deep-set under heavy brows, flat cheekbones, a pronounced nose, and a mustache that made his own look scanty made up the face which bent over him, concern and irritation showing about equally.

"Mom?" he asked for lack of anything better to say.

Doan laughed.

Raulin noted that the irritation disappeared with the laughter although the man remained ugly—he took another look—and short. "You're a dwarf."

"You have a problem with that?"

Raulin thought of Crystal, Sokoji, a mountain full of wer, and the one-sided conversations his brother had with Lord Death. "No."

"Good. Name's Doan. You're Raulin. Can you sit?"

"I think so." He did and got his first good look around. Blocks of snow arched up over his head, high enough for the dwarf to stand straight. He lay on a low platform; made, he realized, of furs thrown over snow not cut away to form the walls and ceiling. A small campstove, much like his and Jago's, burned and kept the place, if not warm, at least comfortable. "Where am I? What is this?"

"Snowhouse," Doan explained, busy at his pack. "I built it when I sensed the storm coming."

"You built this?"

"You think it grew here?" He turned and handed Raulin a small stone flask. "Here, take a sip of this and you'll feel more the thing."

Raulin looked at it and decided it was the kind of container that could hold only one liquid.

"Ah, alcohol and frostbite don't mix."

"You arguing with me, mortal?"

No, Raulin decided, he wasn't. He accepted the flask, pulled free the stopper and took a cautious sip. The top of his head blew off. Or at least it *felt* like the top of his head blew off. He swallowed again. Someone wrote a name in fire along his spine. The third mouthful turned to edged steel in his throat and cut all the way down. He returned the flask.

"Thank you," he said, surprised at how normal his voice sounded. "I feel much better now." And he probably would, the moment the world stopped bouncing. He definitely no longer felt cold.

Doan nodded, took a healthy swallow himself and stowed the flask away. "Centaurs brew it. They get a few snorts of this stuff in them and they become almost bearable. Now," he shoved his hands behind his belt and rocked back on his heels, "what in Chaos were you doing out in that weather?"

"I was writing my name in the snow."

Doan grinned. "About what I figured. Took one step too far and . . . You know, you're one damned lucky mortal."

"I know," Raulin agreed, shuddering. When he'd fallen that last time, he'd been sure he wouldn't be getting up again. His last thoughts, after he'd cursed the Chaos-born storm with every bit of profanity he knew, had been equally of Crystal and Jago; his one consolation that they would probably find consolation in each other.

"You have any idea why the Mother's son came to me instead of Crystal when he wanted your ass pulled out of the storm?" The tone was only just conversational.

Raulin thought about it for a moment. "Yeah. I can hazard a guess."

"You gonna tell me? Remembering, of course, who pulled your ass out of the storm."

"It's not my story to tell."

"Bullshit. You're in this story up to your eyeballs. Tell."

"He's in love."

"The Mother's son in love? With Crystal?" Doan laughed. Suddenly, Lord Death's actions made sense. Of a sort. "And it confuses him."

"That'd be my guess. I don't imagine love is a usual emotion for Lord Death."

"Is this common knowledge?"

Raulin shrugged. "Everyone seems to know but Crystal." He paused and matched Doan's grin. "And possibly Lord Death."

"Why haven't you told her?"

He shrugged again. "Because I'm not sure how she feels about him and until I am, I'm not going to mess up how she feels about me."

Doan's eyes twinkled and he clapped Raulin on the shoulder, knocking him into the wall. "I like you," he said, "you think like a dwarf. Come on, let's get you back before the wizard wakes up and brings the mountain down looking for you."

"Okay," Raulin slid to the edge of the platform and began pulling on his coat. "But I've no idea where back is."

"No matter. I do. Dwarves don't get lost. Ever." Doan shrugged into his own heavy fur. "When we get outside, keep both hands on my shoulders and I'll anchor you. We'll move fast enough so you won't freeze up again."

Raulin nodded, then reached out and touched Doan gently on the arm. "Thank you," he said.

Doan snorted. "Thank Crystal. I'd save a hundred mortals if it saved her one tear." His gaze grew distant and strangely sad. "And this doesn't make up for the one I couldn't save."

Outside Doan's snowhouse, the storm had eased a little and by the time they reached the camp, the wind had died. It continued to snow, but softly, the flakes large and gentle.

Raulin turned to thank the dwarf again, but Doan had disappeared and the line of footprints stretching back into the night was filling rapidly. Suddenly, he was exhausted and, barely able to raise his legs, he climbed over the sleigh. He floundered through the drifts to the shelter's entrance and tossing armloads of snow away, dropped to his knees and crawled inside, shedding the snowy overcoat like a skin.

The warm air smelled like sweat and wet fur and safety.

Shifting Crystal's legs, he made enough room to pull off his boots and then he stretched out at her side. She grumbled a little because he was cold, but he whispered reassurances in her ear and she sank back into a deeper sleep. Seconds later, holding Crystal close and with one hand cupped around his brother's shoulder, Raulin joined her.

When Raulin next opened his eyes, Crystal and Jago were discussing shoving snow down his pants to wake him. "Is it morning?" he muttered, rising up on his elbows.

"It is." Crystal bent forward and kissed him briskly. "Jago's been out and the storm's over."

Raulin fell back and tried to drag Crystal with him. When she didn't budge, he yawned instead. "How come Jago never has to get up in the night anymore?" he wondered, remembering his near disaster, what had caused it, and how long it had been since Jago had woken him up by crawling over him to get to the door.

Jago shrugged. "Strength of character?"

In much the way it healed him, your power takes care of these things as he sleeps. Sholah sounded amused.

"What?" the brothers asked in unison as Crystal suddenly grinned.

She passed on Sholah's explanation and Raulin threw up his hands.

"Figures. Some guys get all the luck." He meant to tell them then, about the storm and his rescue and Doan, but Jago threw him his coat and the story got lost in the scramble out of the shelter.

Sokoji looked like a massive snow drift, angled up against the mountain.

"Is she okay under there?" Jago reached out and pushed a mitten-print into the unbroken expanse of white.

"I think so. The Elder Races don't worry much about the weather."

Raulin opened his mouth to tell them of the shelter made from blocks of snow, but the emerald of Crystal's eyes grew momentarily brighter and she called the giant's name. In the flurry of Sokoji's awakening—the cut looked for a moment as if the storm had returned—the story got lost again.

During breakfast, he almost mentioned it, reminded of the centaurs' brew by a burning mouthful of too hot tea, but Jago asked him something about the day's route and the story wandered off once more.

He never did tell what happened. He never quite knew why.

"Saving the life of a mortal," Lord Death buried his face in his hands, "I don't believe I did that." In memory, he saw Crystal laughing with Raulin, Crystal holding Raulin, Crystal and Raulin. He groaned. He knew, had Raulin died, Crystal would not have blamed him. But he knew also that every time she looked at him afterward, she'd be looking for Raulin's face, torn between wanting and not wanting to see it on the face of Death.

If only he could touch her. If only he knew how she really felt. Sometimes it seemed her manner held more than friendship and sometimes it seemed not to hold even that.

"Why isn't it this complicated for mortals?" he wondered. He remembered the goddess of love blessing the couples who knelt before her altars, blithely interfering in the lives of her worshipers. Thousands of years ago that had been, and things had certainly not been as simple since. The Mother's son looked down at the shelter where Crystal lay wrapped in Raulin's arms. It would take Avreen to straighten out this tangle, he suspected.

Avreen.

Crystal carried the goddesses within her.

And wasn't sleep a small piece of the oblivion that came with Death?

He would have to be very careful he touched only the part of Crystal that was Avreen, but if he succeeded it would be worth the risk.

The ripe greens of summer swirled around him and Lord Death allowed himself a smile of triumph. He had managed to slip deep into Crystal's sleeping mind, safely past the guardians that would have alerted her to his presence.

"Avreen," he called softly, afraid that if he hesitated in what he'd come to do, he'd lose his nerve. "Avreen, I need you."

"No need to tell me *that*, Mother's son." A throaty chuckle thrummed in the air behind him. "Your yearning is a blazing beacon to me."

Lord Death turned, or perhaps the place turned around him, he couldn't be sure. His jaw dropped and he froze.

Avreen smiled a lazy sort of a smile and pushed silver hair back off her face with a long fingered ivory hand. Thickly lashed lids half closed over emerald eyes. "What did you expect?" she asked, her voice low and teasing. "I wear the face of love and each sees in me what they most desire."

It had taken Lord Death only a second to realize it wasn't Crystal before him, Avreen was more . . . more knowing than Crystal could ever be. Forcing himself to really look at the goddess, he saw physical differences as well. Avreen's features were Crystal's ripened; fuller, lusher, inviting just by existing. He found the effect disturbing.

He wondered what, or who, Crystal saw when she looked on Avreen. He wondered, but he didn't ask.

"What is it you want from me, Mother's son?"

"I thought you knew." How could she not know, appearing as she had?

The goddess smiled again and even Lord Death felt the power of it. He gave thanks he had been created more than mortal for he doubted a mortal man could survive Avreen's personal attention.

"The rules state you must petition me. I cannot act without it," she told him. "Although I warn you before you speak," she added dryly, "my range of influence is not great at this time."

"I want . . ." He paused. If he said it, especially here, to her, he made it real. He gathered up his courage. "I want Crystal to love me." The words came out louder than he intended and barely under control.

"And you want me to . . ." Avreen prompted.

"Well, to make her. Love me."

"Are you sure that's what you want?"

"Of course." He tried to bury the confusion. "I'm here."

"Ah."

"You can, can't you?"

"Yes." The goddess' eyes crinkled at the corners and she looked as if she thought about a very pleasant secret. "But why should I?"

"Why?" Lord Death waved his hands about in short jerky motions. *Why?* "Well, because . . ." *Because I love her.* He knew that was the answer Avreen wanted.

He couldn't say it. He could barely admit it to himself, he couldn't say it aloud. "Just because. Will you do it?"

"Will she do what?"

Again the voice behind him. Not throaty this time, not low and seductive, but clear and sharp. Ringing. Like a silver bell struck with a silver hammer. He didn't want to turn, but he did. They were, after all, in her mind.

"Crystal." He carefully kept all emotion from his voice as he said her name.

Crystal stood and stared at Lord Death, one hand working in the loose fabric of her tunic front. He was no construct of her imagination, no dream—not this time. She took a step toward him, brows drawn down in puzzlement. "What are you doing here?"

He didn't have a reason he could tell her, so he remained silent.

"Will Avreen do what?"

He shook his head.

"How did you get here?" Crystal heard her voice rising. Why wouldn't he speak? What did he hide?"

"Death and sleep are cousins of a sort," he said, grateful for a question he could finally answer. He felt like a bug, pinned under the hurt in Crystal's eyes. "As I am the one, I can work with the other."

"So you dropped in for a visit?"

He winced at the sarcasm and countered with a question of his own. "How did you know I was here? I kept far away from the Crystal part of you."

"You took a chance." She looked momentarily exasperated, but not, he thought, at him. "You lost."

"Maybe." The disembodied voice teetered on the edge of laughter. "Maybe not."

Lord Death recognized the source of Crystal's exasperation. He had dealt with the goddess of chance in the past. "Lady Eegri." He inclined his head. "Why have you interfered?"

"Have I interfered?" She popped into sight and gave

him a saucy wink. "I thought I helped. *She* says you lost the toss, not me." Then only her giggle remained.

For an instant the wizard and the Mother's son were in complete accord as they exchanged a puzzled glance and shook their heads. Mortals had formed the other goddesses out of aspects of the Mother's creation but Eegri, they had called out of themselves.

"So, Crystal, shall I leave you two alone to talk?"

Avreen's words brought Crystal's anger rushing back. She'd trusted Lord Death, had thought him her friend; yet he snuck into her mind like a thief and refused to explain his presence when caught. Friends didn't act like that. What could he be doing? Her head went up and her eyes began to glow.

"I am no more susceptible to your power than you are to mine, wizard." Lord Death began to grow angry as well. How dare she think she had to force him. How dare she try!

The glow faded but the eyes remained hard. "Then why are you here?"

"Can't you trust me?"

Had he spoken more gently Crystal would have responded differently, she knew, because she did trust him. But it sounded like a challenge and she would not be challenged when he was in the wrong.

"The last who so snuck under my defenses was Kraydak."

"Do you compare me to him, then?"

"I do not. Your actions speak for themselves."

That hurt. More so, Lord Death admitted, because it was true. He had done pretty much exactly what Kraydak had done. For other reasons, perhaps, but that could be no excuse. *What am I doing here?* he asked himself, suddenly aghast at what he had been about to do.

"Crystal, I . . ."

"No." Her voice threatened to break and she got it firmly back under control. How could he? "No excuses."

"If you'd only listen . . ."

"Oh, so that's it, you don't think I listen to you."
Guilt sharpened her voice; she hadn't been listening
to him. As soon as Raulin and Jago had come into her
life, she'd all but abandoned the friendship with Lord
Death and the realization she could do such a thing
twisted like a knife. "You think I should just drop
everything and come to your beck and call?"

"My beck and call? When have I ever called you?"
Lord Death began to grow angry again. It was easiest.
If I called, asked his heart, too terrified of the answer
to trust the words to his mouth, *would you come?*

Crystal responded to his anger. Of all the emotions
beating at her, anger, at least, she understood. "What
are you doing in my mind?" And her hair swirled
forward to hide the question in her eyes. *Why haven't
you ever called me?* She'd needed him so much in the
past, but he'd never once shown he needed her.

"I am Death!" It was the last cry of a drowning
man. "I go where I choose."

"Tell me why you sought out Avreen!"

"Why should I?"

"Because I . . ."

"What?" He made it a taunt.

"Because I said so!" Crystal almost screamed it.

"Hah!"

Eyes blazing, she stepped forward, placed both
hands against his chest and pushed.

Lord Death fell backward and stared up at her from
where he lay. He could feel the pressure of her hands,
her touch. He wet dry lips and watched her hand reach
out again, the way a bird would watch a snake. She
would not touch in anger this time, he could see that
in her face. And he saw as well, a fear as great as his.

The warmth of her hand caressed his cheek and the
hand itself would do so in an instant.

He panicked and threw himself from Crystal's mind.

Avreen's laughter followed his flight.

Interlude Two

After the Mother-creator had formed the world, and walked upon it, and given it life, and after she had shaped the Elder Races, Chaos came out of the void and lay with her and She bore him a son. Their son was Death and from that moment onward, all things created began to die.

So terrible was this aspect that Chaos had bestowed upon his son, it was easy to forget Death was also his Mother's child and that nothing died without contributing to life.

"I hope you're still taking care of business while you're moping around, 'cause things'll sure be in a damned mess if you aren't."

"Go away, dwarf," Lord Death growled, without turning his head. "I want to be alone."

"Oh. Alone." Doan swung out of his pack and leaned it against the wind-scoured rock. Then he clambered up and sat beside the Mother's son. "Tough."

Lord Death sighed, considered going elsewhere—he had a world to choose from, after all—and stayed where he was. It just didn't seem worth the bother. He turned to face the dwarf, allowing the newly dead to parade across his face. Doan grunted—it might have been satisfaction, Lord Death neither knew nor cared—and he let his features fall back into those of the auburn-haired, amber-eyed young man.

They sat in silence for a while, staring into the purple distance.

They sat in silence for a while longer.

"All right!" Lord Death exclaimed at last, throwing up his hands, unable to stand it any more. "What do you want?"

"Me?" Doan shifted his sword so the scabbard strap didn't bind. "I don't want anything. No, I just thought that if you maybe needed to talk to someone . . ."

"I could talk to you?"

Red fires began to glow in Doan's eyes. "You got a problem with that?"

"You're a dwarf!"

"Yeah. So?"

Lord Death's voice got a little shrill as he pointed out the obvious. "You don't even *have* females!"

The red fires faded and Doan grinned. "Oh. Is that the problem." He scratched at the back of his neck and settled into a more comfortable position. "I spent a lot of time with mortals over the years and some women don't care how short a man is, long as everything works."

"But if you don't have female dwarves, how . . . I mean it can't be an urge natural to your kind." *And I can't believe I'm discussing this,* Lord Death added to himself.

"Well, it's kind of an acquired taste." Doan thought about it a minute. "Like eating pickled eggs." His grin broadened into a smile. " 'Course I can't recall any of my brothers having a fondness for pickled eggs either."

"Look, this is fascinating," Lord Death desperately wanted to cut off any reminiscences, he didn't think he could handle them, not in his current state of mind, "but I don't need to talk to anyone!"

"No? 'Course, saving mortals isn't exactly normal behavior for you . . ."

Lord Death whirled on him, lips drawn back. "What do *you* know about normal behavior for me?" he snarled.

Doan remained unimpressed by both the snarl and the implied threat. "You seem to forget, I was around long before the Mother-creator presented you to the world."

"And that gives you the right to judge me?"

"No. But it gives me some grounds for pointing out that you're acting like an ass."

And Doan sat alone on the rock. He smiled and

leaned back, soaking up as much warmth as he could from the winter sun. His breathing began to deepen and his eyes began to close and at first he thought the soft voice belonged to a breeze. When he realized whose it was, spotting a bowed head from the corner of one eye, he allowed himself an inward—and smug—pat on the back, but showed no outward sign.

". . . but I guess I started to love her when she faced Kraydak in his own tower, knowing that if she lost not even I could take her from Kraydak's grip. Kraydak had a habit of holding on to my people; he drew power from the dead trapped in his walls and I can't bear to think of what he would have done to her. But she won and I asked the dragon to take her home. I remember that it asked me why, and I said I didn't know. I didn't, then. Or I wouldn't admit it.

"I began to watch her. Curiosity about this lastborn wizard, I thought at the time. Do you know what she went through trying to lift Kraydak's yoke from the Empire? People would run from her in fear, or fall on their faces in terror, or worse still, try to squirm their way into her favor so she would toss them scraps as Kraydak had done. They only saw the wizard, not the child who so desperately wanted to help. She wasn't even twenty when it began. Do you remember what it was like to be that young?"

"Huh? Me?"

Lord Death ignored the interruption and continued in the same quiet, almost singsong tone, but Doan, jolted out of somnolence by the question, saw that the angle of Death's cheek had softened and he looked barely out of his teens. "The young die as well as the old, so I know what it's like at that age. How everything cuts, how easy it is to take up the guilt of something you didn't do. Not even the shields the centaurs had given her could stop all the hurting."

"Shields?" Doan snorted, unable to contain himself. "What shields?"

"Duty and responsibility can be a shield as well as a shackle, dwarf. They've kept her from the path of the ancient ones and, for a while, they were all that kept her sane. Crystal had been created for one purpose and one purpose only, and no one gave a thought to how she'd feel when that was finished, knowing the world held no place for her. Although I'd give anything to stop it, I'm not surprised she's being torn apart. I'm surprised she's lasted so long.

"Anyway, after she defeated Kraydak, I spent a lot of time watching her. And when I saw how lonely she'd become, I started talking to her, getting to know her. I told myself that the mortal part of her heritage made her my responsibility and so I kept my mind open for other mortals who were worthy of her." He gave a short bark of bitter laughter. "And we can see how well that worked out." His voice grew melancholy. "We're unique, Crystal and I. We belong together. I love her so much I can't think of anything else."

"So tell her."

"I can't. Not now."

"You're going to let a mortal stand in your way?"

"No, it's not that . . ."

Doan narrowed his eyes. Was the Mother's son blushing? "What have you done?" he asked, trying not to smile.

Lord Death sat quietly for a moment then the words came out in a rush. "I asked Avreen to make Crystal love me."

"And Crystal found out?"

"Yes."

"Hmm," Doan nodded his head slowly, "I can see how that might put a sword through a relationship. Why didn't you start by asking Avreen what Crystal's feelings were?"

"What?"

Doan sighed. "Read my lips, Mother's son; Crystal's feelings. Why didn't you ask Avreen what they were?"

Lord Death was definitely blushing. "I didn't want to know," he mumbled. "I wanted to be sure."

"I am somehow sadly disappointed," Doan remarked to the world in general, "to find the Mother's son, a divine and immortal being, acting like a mortal youth whose balls have just dropped."

"Well, I've never been in love before!"

"That's not much of an excuse."

"If you'd ever been in love . . ."

"I was in love once." The uneasy silence this time was Doan's as he remembered Milthra, the Lady of the Grove, and all the long years he'd guarded her child, because that was the only thing she could take from him. "And I suppose," he admitted at last, "it's led me to do some stupid things. But," he added, just in case Lord Death should get ideas, "nothing as stupid as that. Asked Avreen to make her love you, indeed. And am I to understand when Crystal discovered you mucking about in her head you didn't throw yourself on her mercy and declare your undying," Doan snorted, "as it were, love?"

"Not exactly. We fought."

"Brilliant."

'She started it!" Lord Death rested his fingers against his chest where the touch of Crystal's hands still burned. And she'd finished it as well. "What can I do?"

"Stop worrying about what she feels, and tell her what you feel."

"I can't."

"It's the only way to untie the knot you've got yourself in." Doan's voice was matter-of-fact but not uncaring. "It's the only way to untie the knot you've got her in. Give her a chance."

Lord Death looked desperate. "I don't know how," he whispered, and vanished.

Doan shook his head, suddenly understanding. "No, you wouldn't, would you. You're Death and Death is a surety. There's nothing sure about love." He got to his feet and stretched the kinks out of his legs. Then he faced the place where Lord Death had been.

"You know how," he said, "but you're afraid."

And he thought he heard the breeze sob, "Yes."

Eleven

But why won't you tell me what he wanted?

Because it's none of your concern.

None of my concern? What are you talking about, you're a part of ME!

"Crystal, are you all right?" Raulin grabbed her arm as she stumbled and swung her around to face him. He gave her a little shake for her eyes were unfocused and she'd clearly not been watching the trail.

"Huh? Oh, sorry." Crystal freed enough of her attention from her argument with Avreen to smile sheepishly at Raulin. "I was just, well . . ."

"Talking to yourself?" he finished, maintaining his hold on her shoulders.

She winced a little at his choice of words, for despite what she'd just screamed at Avreen, she didn't consider the goddesses to be a part of her any longer; at least not a part of the *her* that mattered.

"Hey, is everything okay up there?" Jago called from his position at the back of the sleigh. He pushed his snow goggles up on his forehead and peered at Raulin, trying to read his expression. All morning he'd been getting the feeling that Crystal was upset and he hoped it wasn't about something Raulin had done. "Do you guys need to take a break?"

"Crystal?" Raulin asked softly.

"No," she shook her head and her hair made a dance of the motion. "I'm all right, really."

Raulin tightened his fingers for an instant, then let her go, half-turning to face his brother. "We're okay."

Jago looked openly skeptical.

Raulin sighed. "Crystal just lost sight of the trail and tripped."

"You sure?"

"What?" Raulin spread his arms. "You think I tripped her?"

"Wouldn't be the first time." Jago ducked the snowball Raulin lobbed at him and added in a loud aside to Sokoji, "Some guys will do anything to get a woman in their arms."

Sokoji looked interested. "Really?" she asked Raulin.

Raulin flushed a deep red and threw himself forward into the harness. "If we're not taking a break," he muttered, "let's go." He tried to ignore Jago explaining mortal relationships to the giant. Out of the corner of his eye he saw Crystal smile. He knew her hearing was better than his, so he assumed she was listening to his brother. He didn't see the smile freeze and her eyes grow distracted again.

He wanted something to do with me, didn't he?

I'm not going to tell you. Avreen's voice was irritatingly smug. *The Mother's son asked a boon of the goddess. I don't betray those confidences.*

You'd betray anything that suited you, Zarsheiy snorted.

The wizard does have a point, Tayja's voice, the voice of reason joined in. *You are, as much as any of us, a part of her.*

Avreen laughed. *Only because I choose to be.*

Ha!

I could leave any time I wanted to.

HA! Zarsheiy said again, louder.

I stay because I choose to.

Maybe, murmured a quiet voice. *Maybe not.*

You know nothing. But the words lacked their previous conviction.

Stop it! All of you! Crystal put power into the command and the quarreling goddesses fell silent, but behind the deepest barrier, darkness stirred.

Careful, little wizard, Nashawryn sounded amused.

Force our sister to tell you what she knows and you may have to face things you have no desire to.

"Crystal, what is it?"

Raulin's anxious concern snapped her back to the surface. She took a deep breath and motioned for him to keep walking.

"It's nothing, really."

He looked into her eyes and nodded but wasn't reassured. "It's nothing now," he allowed, "but a moment ago you seemed terrified. What frightened you?"

Crystal's brow furrowed. What had frightened her? She wasn't sure so she gave him the easy answer, hoping he'd dig no further. "Nashawryn."

"Oh." He bent and dragged a protruding branch out of the snow, tossing it clear of the sleigh's path. "Oh," he said again.

"Don't worry," Crystal snagged his hand and brought it to her lips, "she can't get through the barriers." She paused, muttered something unintelligible, and pulled off his mitten.

Raulin laughed, his uneasiness pushed aside by the disgusted way she held the mitten between two fingers and then completely buried by the soft touch of her lips on the back of his hand.

She peered up at him through her lashes and he felt his heart begin to beat faster.

"What do you think you're doing?" he asked, mesmerized by the tip of her tongue as it made a circuit of her mouth.

"I'm using you to chase the bogie-goddess away."

He clutched at his chest with his free hand, and said, "I feel so cheap." With a sudden twist of his fingers, he had his harness undone.

Crystal's eyes widened as he unhooked hers as well and in practically the same motion scooped her up in his arms. She hurriedly adjusted her weight as his snowshoes sank a little deeper in the fine powder.

Moving as quickly as the snowshoes allowed, Raulin carried her off the trail, murmuring into her hair,

"She's a pretty powerful goddess. It'll take more than a little hand kissing to chase her away."

"But you'll freeze," Crystal laughed, settling herself more comfortably.

Raulin kissed her on the nose. "You're a wizard, think of something."

"Hey!" Jago yelled. "Where do you two think you're going?"

"Never mind," Raulin called back, neither lessening his pace nor turning his head. "Start lunch."

"You could make better time," Sokoji observed as Raulin and Crystal disappeared behind a boulder, "if those two were not together on the harnesses."

"And if my brother could get a grip on his libido," Jago grumbled, pulling out the campstove and the teapot. But he wasn't really angry, for he could feel the easing of the tensions Crystal had been under all morning.

After lunch, Sokoji stood, stretched, and pointed almost due north, toward a mountain that looked as if its upper third had been sheared off. "That is the way you must go," she said, "if you wish to reach Aryalan's tower. Tonight we can be at the pass and tomorrow cross into her valley."

"Not that I'm saying you're wrong, Elder, but according to frog-face's map, we should be heading for the highest peak in the range." Raulin came and stood beside the giant, waving his arm in the direction they'd been traveling. "And the highest mountain in the range is that one there."

"Yes," Sokoji agreed, "now it is. But the demon had not been to the tower for many years, not since before the Doom. The mountain you point to did not exist then. Aryalan drew it out of the earth to stop the dragon, and this mountain . . ." The giant sighed and shook her head as she gazed at the jutting angles of rock that still looked raw even after more than a thousand years. "We called it the Mighty One, and it became as you see it now during the battle."

"Are you sure?" Raulin sounded skeptical.

"Mortal, giants are never unsure. It is a skill we have. And besides, when last I went to the tower, that is the route I took."

"Yeah, a thousand years ago . . ."

Sokoji turned to face him. "No, six winters ago."

"You were at the tower six winters ago?" Jago moved to stand by Raulin and stared up at the giant. "Why didn't you tell us this before?"

"Didn't I?" Her forehead wrinkled as she recalled all the words she'd spoken to the brothers. "Oh. I didn't. How odd. Never mind, I shall tell you of it now." She waved a massive hand toward the sleigh. "Perhaps if we could travel while I speak . . . We have little enough daylight this far north to waste any and it will mean we need not hurry later on."

Raulin and Jago exchanged glances so identically put out that Sokoji smiled. "I have not been keeping knowledge from you. I was quite sure I'd told you."

"I thought you said giants were never unsure," Raulin reminded her.

"I did," Sokoji agreed placidly. "But I did not say we were never mistaken."

There was a long moment of silence, then Jago started to laugh. Raulin glowered for a moment more then, unable to keep the corners of his mouth from twitching back, joined him. Soon they were bent double and swiping at the tears leaking from their eyes.

Staring at them in fascination, Sokoji walked over to where Crystal leaned against the high back of the sleigh. "Are they hysterical?" she asked.

"No. They're mortals." Crystal smiled at the two men who were still laughing but were beginning to regain control. "They tend to be a bit extreme."

The giant cocked one eyebrow in the wizard's direction. "So I noticed this morning."

Crystal had the grace to blush.

When they moved out, the brothers wore the harnesses while Crystal followed behind, the positions shaking down with an even mix of teasing and threats between Raulin and Jago. Sokoji walked by the front of the sleigh where the mortals could hear her unassisted and where she could use her strength to ease the path.

Although Crystal could've heard a leaf fall back in the Sacred Grove in Ardhan, she missed the start of the giant's story absorbed in watching Raulin and Jago walk. They looked like a cross between bears and ducks in their heavy fur coats and snowshoes. She grinned and gave thanks she had no need for the awkward footgear—her feet sank only as far as she allowed them to—then gave her attention to Sokoji's words.

". . . and when the storm calmed, the winds told me that the door had been uncovered. I thought on it for some time . . ."

"One year or two?" Raulin asked, unable to help himself.

"Three. Mortals did not come that way, so I had no need to make a hasty decision. In the end, I admit curiosity alone drew me to the tower for watching would have been sufficient; there was no need to explore. Of old, the tower sat in the midst of a lake, perfectly round and created by Aryalan. Lilies bloomed on its surface, swans glided majestically about, and regardless of the season in the lands surrounding it, the lake remained in perpetual high summer. The tower appeared to be a summerhouse, in the old eastern style, very ornate but not overly large. It rested on an island as perfectly round as the lake. The summerhouse was merely the entrance way, the island itself was the tower."

As Sokoji spoke, her listeners saw the red tiled roofs curving over black lacquer walls, breathed deeply of the exotic flowers, heard the music that played softly from dawn to dusk.

"The Doom destroyed all that, of course, and eventually the wizard as well. Winter, so long denied, moved quickly in to cover both lake and island with ice and snow. When I came at last to view what the storm had uncovered, only memory told me such beauty had ever been.''

Jago sighed and Raulin turned to look at him in surprise.

"You grew up in Kraydak's Empire, Jago. You know how evil the ancient wizards were. How can you be sorry Aryalan's tower got trashed?''

"Beauty is neither good nor evil, brother, it just is.''

"Well, this was beauty no longer,'' Sokoji continued as Raulin sputtered. "The lilies, the swans, and the flowers had long since died and of the summerhouse only a single room remained whole. The residue of power echoed strongly and I felt it recognize me as an intruder.''

"Trapped,'' Raulin declared, stepping on the edge of his own snowshoe and almost tripping himself in his excitement.

"Yes,'' the giant agreed, reaching out a hand to steady him. "But as I said, only the residue of power remained and it was not enough to hold one of the Elder.'' Her voice took on a faint shading of pain. "Although it came closer than I care to remember. In the room's floor is a trapdoor and if you seek treasure you need go no farther, for it is made of ebony and ruby. Enough wealth to enjoy ease the rest of your days.''

"What? In the gatehouse?'' Raulin asked incredulously while Jago looked relieved.

"The ancient wizards were fond of gaudy display.''

Crystal remembered the gold-lined room in Kraydak's tower and wondered what his halls had been like when he was at the height of his power.

"Sokoji,'' she called. "Did you not lift the door?''

"What difference does it make?'' Jago broke in before Sokoji had a chance to answer, praying Crystal hadn't put ideas into Raulin's head. "We won't need to go into the tower itself.''

Raulin, who had a pretty good idea of his brother's thoughts, caught Crystal's eye and winked. "I'm kind of curious myself," he said blandly. Jago whirled on him, mouth open to deliver a blistering lecture on irresponsibility, when he added, "Not that we'll be entering ourselves. Will we, Jago?"

Jago sputtered in his turn and Raulin punched him gently on the arm.

"Don't worry, little brother, I intend to get rich, not dead."

Sokoji shook her head. Mortals, it would take much thought to understand them, she decided. "Do not think the gatehouse is without dangers," she warned. "Less dangerous than the tower does not mean safe, but, yes, I lifted the door. Below it, a massive staircase spiraled down for a distance over twice my height. It, too, had been trapped but the ancient destruction had fortunately rendered all but one inoperative. That one . . ." She sighed and began again. "That one gave me a small amount of trouble, but in the end I overcame it."

"Why do I get the feeling we don't want to know what went on?"

Sokoji looked down at Raulin, her brown eyes serious. "It doesn't matter. I will tell you no more than I have." She chewed on the edge of her lip—something the others had never seen her do—made a visible effort to banish the memory, and continued. "At the bottom of the stairs there stood another door. I didn't open it although I had paid the price."

"Why not?" Jago asked gently.

"I couldn't pass," she said simply. "In both height and width, it had been built too small."

They traveled in silence after that; Raulin's thoughts on treasure and the battle that would come before he held it, Crystal's moving beyond the second door, and Jago wondering what could be so bad that the giant could not, would not, speak of it.

The next morning they got their first good look at the pass into Aryalan's valley.

"Forget it," Raulin declared emphatically. "There has to be another way."

"Not without going many miles. Another month of traveling perhaps. What's wrong with this path?"

"It's too . . ." Raulin waved his hands about and Jago finished it for him.

"High."

"Yes?"

Jago gripped Raulin's shoulder. "My brother," he explained, "hasn't much of a head for heights. Nor," he added, taking another look at the pass, "are either of us related to goats."

From where they stood they could see the ledge they had to follow dwindling into almost nothing as it curved around the mountain.

"Look, why don't we just follow the gorge," suggested Raulin. "It's going in the right direction. It's an easy walk. When it ends, *then* we can take to the ledge."

Sokoji shook her head. "The gorge ends in a cliff, thirty of your body lengths or more high. If you wish to enter the valley, this is the only way."

Crystal caught both Raulin's hands in hers. "It has to be wider than it appears," she said gently, "or Sokoji would not be able to use it." Her eyes began to glow and she allowed him to sink a little way into their emerald depths. "I would never let you fall." The glow dimmed.

He returned the pressure of her fingers and said, "My heart believes you; I'll see what I can do to convince my feet."

Working quickly, for Sokoji was vague about the length of the pass and none of them wanted to be caught on the ledge after dark, they stripped the sleigh of everything they could carry. Even considering the size of the packs, looming like great misshapen growths on the brother's backs, that seemed a distressingly small amount when compared to what remained on the sleigh.

"It's not as bad as it looks," Jago reassured Crystal

after she pointed this out. He settled the rope holding the bedrolls into a more comfortable position on her shoulders. "We always figured we'd have to leave the sleigh at some point. With you and Sokoji helping out, we're taking more than we planned on."

"You planned on being without the shelter?" She shivered in sympathy, warming the fingers he held out to her—knots and lashings needed freedom from mittens.

"It's only for one night," Raulin reminded her. "The next night we'll be in the gatehouse—Sokoji promises it's safe—and the night after, we'll be back at the sleigh. Provided, of course, we haven't all dashed our brains out falling off the mountain."

"Land on your head, you'll bounce."

"I'd land on yours given half a chance."

Jago reached over and chucked him under the chin. "Glad to see you've regained your sunny disposition."

Raulin growled something uncomplimentary and shook his fist at the younger man, but Crystal saw the tightness leave his face for the first time since he'd seen the pass.

Slipping a small bag of oatmeal into her pocket—a pocket Jago was certain already held the teapot—Sokoji shook her head at their bickering and asked, "Are you ready then?"

"As ready as we'll ever be," Raulin sighed.

Crystal and Jago nodded.

The giant turned and led the way up the blasted slope of the Mighty One.

Great chunks of pinkish granite made a straight line impossible, so they wove a serpentine path around and over the destruction, often traveling at an angle where hands were needed as much as feet.

"I don't think," Raulin panted as they rested about halfway between the sleigh and the rock ledge they were aiming for, "I have ever been so tired. This pack weighs two hundred pounds."

"Old and out of shape," gasped Jago, pulling off his hat and fanning himself with the end of one braid.

He let a mitten dangle from its string and scratched vigorously at his beard; sweat was running into it and it itched. Maybe it would've been a better idea to let Crystal remove it as she had Raulin's. . . .

"Are your legs sore?" Crystal asked, squatting beside Raulin and studying him with a worried frown. She laid a hand on his thigh and he covered it with one of his.

"Crystal, we've been walking up and down mountains for weeks now. My legs are like rock." He groaned without opening his eyes. "My back, however, is killing me. Thank you," he added as it suddenly stopped. "Now, if you could just transport us to the tower . . ."

"I could make your packs lighter."

"We discussed this already. You use your power for necessities only. Lightening our packs is no necessity." He heaved himself to his feet. His undershirt—living up to its name under four further layers of clothing plus the great fur overcoat—was soaking wet and sticking to his back. Drops of sweat trickled down his sides, and, adding a new sensation to the discomfort, a freezing wind kept trying to sneak into his sleeves, finding the smallest of spaces between mittens and cuffs. "On your feet, junior, we're wasting daylight."

Jago sighed, put his hat on, and tried to stand. The pack remained where it was and, because he was securely attached, so did Jago. "You could quit laughing and help," he pointed out when he'd stopped flailing.

Sokoji reached down and lifted him easily to his feet, her face grave. "Turtles," she said helpfully, "have much the same problem."

"Thank you." He glared at Raulin, daring him to say a word and put out a hand to steady himself. "Chaos!" The corner of granite he'd grabbed had sliced into his outer mitten, almost going through the heavy sheepskin. He studied the slash and then the rock. "That thing's got an edge like a knife," he marveled.

Raulin ran a cautious thumb along it and stuck the

thumb in his mouth when it proved not to be cautious enough.

Jago grinned at him. "All right, don't take my word for it . . ." He glanced down as his mitt flared green, but an equal flare in Crystal's eyes decided him against commenting on the necessity of the power use.

"You'd think these edges would've worn smooth by now," Raulin said reflectively. "It's been a long time."

Sokoji's eyes lifted to the shattered peak. "The mountain remembers," she said softly.

"Are you saying this mountain thinks?" asked Raulin.

"It remembers. The mountains are the bones of the Mother."

"Why don't I find that reassuring?" he muttered as they began to climb again.

The ledge was wider than it appeared from the ground and for a little while it edged a slope not much steeper than the one they'd just come up.

Raulin kept his mind on his feet and his gaze firmly locked on Sokoji's broad back. He tried not to notice as the angle of the slope dropped away until the only word for it became cliff. He reminded himself that on level ground he had walked a path much narrower than the width they had here.

Sokoji stopped suddenly and he bumped against her. "Give me the rope," she said.

Jago took the coil off his shoulder and passed it up to the giant who tied one end about her waist and handed the rest back to Raulin.

"Keep about my body length of slack between us," she instructed. "Then tie it securely and give it to your brother so he can do the same."

"Why so much slack?" Raulin asked, trying to keep his thoughts off all the possible reasons for the rope.

"If you fall, the slack gives those next to you time to anchor themselves." She caught the look on his face and patted his shoulder with a comforting but heavy hand. "You need not continue. At this point we can still easily turn and go back."

"At this point? Does that mean we can't turn later on?"

"Yes."

"I had to ask."

"Could be worse," Jago murmured behind him. "We could be in the snowshoes."

Raulin closed his eyes and leaned against the mountainside, noting absently as he did that it rose up as perpendicular on the right as it fell away on the other side. He heard his brother say they could turn back, that it didn't matter, but on the inside of his lids he saw a great door of ebony and ruby, wealth enough to buy them a secure place in the world. He sighed, opened his eyes, and finished tying the knot about his waist.

Jago took the offered rope without comment, knowing the battle Raulin must be fighting with himself in order to go on. He'd seen his brother shake when he'd had to lean out a third-story window. No words could make it easier, so he offered his silent support.

Crystal felt Raulin's fear, felt Nashawryn twitch in answer, and hoped that if anything happened she would not have to fight the dark goddess for Raulin's life.

"Remember," Sokoji told them when they were all securely tied, "the ledge holds me; you are in little danger."

Little danger, Raulin repeated to himself. *Not* no danger. *Little danger. Great.* He shuffled forward as the rope stretching back from the giant grew taut—shuffled, for if he picked up his feet he would be left for an instant pecariously balanced on one leg. Inside his mittens, his hands grew clammy. His heart thumped so hard he felt sure the vibrations against his ribs would throw him off the precipice. He tried holding his breath. It didn't help. His focus narrowed to the rope tied around Sokoji's waist. The knot bobbed as she walked and it distracted him enough so that he could keep moving.

Gradually, he began to relax. The combination of the slow and steady pace and Sokoji's bulk—his mind simply refused to acknowledge that the giant could fall—calmed him. Then Sokoji turned to face the mountain, her hands flat against the rock, her feet sliding sideways.

"Hey!" Raulin stopped and as Sokoji felt it through the rope she looked back over her shoulder at him. "What are you doing?"

"There is a narrow place here," she explained. "We must pass carefully. Do as I do. The path will not become less wide than your feet are long."

Less wide than your feet are long? What kind of a measurement is that? Raulin wondered. And he looked down.

Down.

A long way down.

He swayed. His head felt heavy, almost more than his neck could support. The world began to tilt.

Suddenly his cheek pressed hard against rock. His arms were outstretched, his fingers trying to dig into the granite. His toes attempted to root. He didn't remember turning. He couldn't make the world stop sliding back and forth. He needed to throw up. His pack. His heavy, heavy pack. It was out over the edge. It would pull him down. He couldn't catch his breath. He couldn't remember how to breathe.

"Raulin!"

Jago's voice slapped against him.

"Take deep breaths. Slow down. Make it last. That's it. In. And out. In. And out."

The world began to still.

"In. And out."

"I'm okay," he managed. The rock near his mouth was wet with drool. His muscles felt like porridge and that weakness brought back the terror. He couldn't stand. He wasn't strong enough to hold his own weight. Before the world began to spin again, Raulin ground his cheek into the rough face of the mountain and drove the fear away with pain.

"I'm okay," he repeated after a moment, and this time he was. "At least, I think this is as good as it gets."

"Can you walk?" Sokoji asked softly.

The laugh he dredged up went beyond strained to

just this side of hysteria. "If it'd get me off this mountain, I'd dance."

He heard the smile in Sokoji's voice.

"I don't think that will be necessary. If you could just slide your left foot. . . . Yes. Now, the right. . . ."

One sliding step at a time, they crossed into Aryalan's valley.

Safely away from the edge, Raulin took Crystal into his arms and buried his face in her hair.

She held him tightly and whispered. "I wanted to help . . ."

"Why didn't you?"

"Tayja said you needed to make it across on your power, not mine."

He could still feel the fear knotting the muscles of his back. "Yeah," he said, after a moment, "she could be right."

Doan stayed close to the Mighty One as he stomped up into the gully. Unless they looked straight down, the tiny figures on the ledge would not be able to spot him.

At the north end, where a sheer cliff rose up two hundred feet or more, he scanned the rock closely then ran his fingers along a crack invisible to any eye but a dwarf's. A perfectly rectangular door swung open, folding back into the mountain.

Muttering about the dust, he stepped inside and pulled the door shut behind him. His eyes were red lights in the darkness and when they'd adjusted enough he started up the stairs. The watchtower had been destroyed with the mountain, but the lower gate into the valley should still be clear. Dwarves built to last.

Even destroyed by the Wizards' Doom, and with all its majesty hidden under snow and ice, the remains of Aryalan's tower drew the eye. Bits and pieces of half buried buildings jutted up in the center of a perfect circle, the shore of the lake still clearly delineated by a subtle difference in the shading of the snow. From where they stood, distance blurred detail, but the sense of what had once been, the power, the evil, the beauty, was strong.

"I think we have enough light left to get to the lake," Raulin noted, squinting west. "It'll give us less distance to cover tomorrow and we can hit the tower still fresh."

Sokoji nodded. "That would be best."

"There's not much cover down there," Crystal pointed out, scanning the valley with her wizard-sight. She sighed and shifted her gaze to the immediate area. The shattered mountaintop had a greater air of desolation than the land below. "Still, there's not much cover up here either. I suppose we might as well get as close as we can."

"The air feels heavy," Jago said quietly as they started single file down the slope. "It's almost like we're being watched."

Raulin snorted, blowing a great silver cloud into the cold air. "Thank you very much, Jago." He placed his feet carefully in the giant's bootprints—stepping anywhere else left the brothers floundering hip-deep in snow. "All we need is to have spirits haunting this place."

"As to that," Sokoji's voice floated back, sounding thoughtful but unconcerned, "who knows what happens when a wizard dies? My sisters and I spent some time considering it but reached no answer."

"Some time?"

"Ten years and four months."

"And came up with no answers?"

"Perhaps the Mother's son knows, but he keeps the secrets of his people."

Raulin twisted to look at Jago. "I don't suppose he's around?"

Jago shook his head. It didn't seem necessary to mention that Lord Death hadn't been around for a number of days. Whenever the Mother's son was mentioned, a combination of yearning and fear sang along the link stretching between him and Crystal and as he saw no way to help, he had no desire to add to her burdens.

Behind them, the mountain rumbled.

Slowly, like puppets pulled by a single string, they turned.

A ball of snow, a hand's span wide, smashed against Crystal's legs.

Another followed, then another.

The rumble came not from the mountain, but from the mass of snow beginning to move down it.

Crystal's face paled as the hint of a power she thought she should remember brushed lightly across hers. Not a wizard's power, not quite. Then the memory slipped away in the need of the moment. Her eyes flared and she grabbed Raulin and Jago each by a hand. She could feel their trust in her and it gave her strength.

She met Sokoji's eyes.

The giant nodded. "I can hurry when I must."

The snow beneath their feet began to shift.

"Run," commanded Crystal.

And so they did.

Crystal wrapped the brothers in her power and the three of them almost flew over the snow. Their feet barely touched before lifting again, the packs weighed nothing on their backs, and the wind helped carry them along. In spite of the knowledge that they raced disaster, both men felt a thrill of pleasure in the effortless speed.

Sokoji moved a little ahead, running with great bounding strides.

With a screech, the avalanche finally broke free and surged down the slope, gathering force as it roared toward them.

"Chaos," Raulin swore, risking a glance back over his shoulder.

And Chaos it appeared to be. Boulders ground together along the front edge of the mass of moving snow, a churning wall of destruction rising thirty feet into the air. The screaming rumble grew in volume until it drowned out thought and reason.

They'd covered two thirds of the distance to the wizard's lake, nearly deafened but unharmed, and Crystal began to feel secure. Even without drawing from the barriers, she had sufficient power left to carry the three of them to flat ground where the beast behind would die of its own weight.

Then Jago stumbled and fell.

By the time she yanked him to his feet, the avalanche was upon them, dragging both brothers from her grip.

"NO!"

She whirled, fingers spread, and threw her power at the enemy.

The wave of snow and stone slammed into a wall of green.

And stopped. And fused.

The green faded.

Ears ringing in the silence, Crystal stared at the white cliff rising above her. She felt whole, complete in a way she hadn't since Kraydak's defeat. *But how?* she wondered and almost cried when the question shattered something fragile within her and the goddesses returned.

She turned as Jago gently touched her arm.

"You were whole," he said softly. "I felt it." That Crystal had saved them seemed of less importance than this.

"Was whole," she agreed and swallowed the lump that had formed in her throat. "Was."

The whole, added Tayja's voice, *is greater than the sum of its parts.*

Not now, Tayja. The finding—then the losing—of self left a pain too deep for even those goddesses who had proven her friends to be endured.

"Come on," Raulin slipped an arm about her and Crystal rested gratefully against his side, "just a little farther and you can sit down. You'll feel better with a cup of tea inside you and a fire lighting the night."

"Raulin . . ."

"What?"

"Oh, nothing." Jago decided against explaining. He almost wished he had his brother's calm acceptance of the world. He knew that in Raulin's eyes Crystal had merely done what wizards do and now, like a porter who had strained something carrying too heavy a load, she needed taking care of. With one last awe-filled look at the towering pile of snow, he fell into step behind them and wished, for Crystal's sake, it could be that easy.

Sokoji waited for them at the end of the lake. She studied Crystal's face as the wizard approached. Satisfied with whatever it was she saw, she pointed up at the blasted peak of the Mighty One.

Against the pink granite of the mountain, almost glowing in the last of the afternoon sun, lay a great black dragon. The Doom of the ancient wizards.

Crystal's mouth went dry and then she realized the beast was stone.

She reached out with what little power she had left and touched only rock.

The path of the avalanche began at the dragon.

She recalled the power that had brushed against her just before the mountain shook off its load of snow. When she woke Kraydak's Doom—the dragon created in his arrogance from the body of the Mother—she had felt the same type of power.

"What is it?" Raulin asked, squinting in an attempt to make out details. At this distance he saw only black on pink.

"Aryalan's dragon. Aryalan's Doom."

"Is it alive?"

"No, not for years."

The brothers traced the swath of destruction left by the snowslide and exchanged identical glances.

"Are you certain?"

"Yes." She tore her gaze from the graceful line of limb and scale and met first Raulin's then Jago's worried eyes. "Whatever memory of power my presence may have triggered is gone now. There's nothing there but stone." She sighed and added in a small voice, "I thought someone promised me a cup of tea?"

And the marvel of the dragon was banished in making camp.

And if Crystal lay awake that night and wondered what else would be triggered by her presence, no one knew.

Twelve

The wind had rippled the surface snow into a parody of the lake it covered and the tiny ridges were all that disturbed the unbroken expanse of white. Staring across from shore to island, the lake appeared wider than it had from up on the mountain. Jago rubbed his eyes and tried to bring the remains of the gatehouse into focus, but the entire area persisted in wavering; one moment sharp and clear, the next no more than a soft gray shadow against the white. He snapped his snow goggles down off his forehead but, although he no longer needed to squint, the scene remained unchanged.

"Crystal," he called without turning, and felt rather than saw her step to his side. "Look toward the island and tell me what you see."

Crystal looked out over the lake, frowned, and shook her head. Her eyes began to glow, living emeralds reflecting the morning sunlight. "I see . . ." She paused and shook her head again. "I don't know what I see, exactly."

"You see one of Aryalan's remaining defenses," Sokoji told them, moving to stand at their backs. "Do not try to puzzle it out for too long."

"Because we can't?" Jago asked.

"Because you'll soon begin to think of nothing else, neither food nor sleep nor drink, and will eventually die still staring across the water." The giant waved a hand at the snow covered ice. "Or what passes for water these days.

The full effect may not be working, but I advise you not to risk it."

Jago pointedly turned his back on both lake and tower. "Okay," he said slowly, "if we can't look at the island, how do we cross?"

"Why, by not looking at it."

Raulin grinned at the implied "of course" on the end of Sokoji's answer. "Really, Jago," he teased, bending over the campstove where their breakfast cooked, "use your head."

"Why not use yours? We'll need something solid to test the ice." Jago leaned forward and grimaced at the pale brown mass in the pot that was just beginning to bubble and steam. "And then again, we could just throw that stuff in front of us, let it harden, and we'll have a bridge."

"Ignoring the insult to my cooking," Raulin sighed, "I have to agree with the sentiment. I am definitely tired of oatmeal. Even if Crystal does power out the lumps." He raised the wooden spoon and the sticky clump on the end fell back into the pot with a loud and unappetizing splat.

Clicking her tongue, Crystal dropped a handful of snow into the pot. It turned to water as it hit and began to loosen the gluelike consistency of the porridge. "To begin with, you've got your proportions wrong." She added just a little more snow water and the spoon briskly stirred the liquid in.

"Do mortals usually waste time on trivialities before going into the unknown?" Sokoji asked, her head to one side, her expression both puzzled and faintly amused as she watched the trio gathered around the campstove.

The two mortals and the wizard looked up from the porridge pot, looked at each other, had no need to look out toward the tower, and said simultaneously, "Yes."

Sokoji nodded and sat down on the well-packed patch of snow she'd been using since the night before, her weight having sculpted it into comfortable contours. "That explains your behavior. I had always believed mortals preferred to get danger over with quickly. Perhaps some cinnamon would help." She offered a small bag pulled from one of her many pockets.

"Help to get it over with?" Raulin asked.

"Help the porridge."

"Oh. Right. Do you always carry cinnamon with you?"

Sokoji reviewed the recent contents of her pockets.

"No," she said at last.

Breakfast lasted longer than the oatmeal—even improved by the cinnamon—warranted. No one offered an opinion as to why they were so strangely unwilling to start on this, the last leg of their adventure. Conversations started, stopped, restarted, and sputtered out.

"I'll never forget," Raulin broke into the uncomfortable silence that had fallen after the last abortive attempt to find an acceptable topic, "the look on Crystal's face when she picked herself out of that snowdrift." A laugh hovered around the edges of his voice.

"When?" Crystal shifted around to face him. "After you blithely pitched me off the sleigh?"

"Yeah," he admitted, winking, "then."

And that began a series of reminiscences, as if this were their last evening together and the next day they would all be back in separate and safe lives.

Raulin and Jago traded banter. Raulin and Crystal traded glances almost physical in intensity. Crystal and Jago shared a quiet moment in complete accord.

We've redefined ourselves, Jago realized, when talk shifted away from the personal to the dwindling supply of tea. *Reinforced who we are and what we mean to each other.* He glanced in the direction of the tower, not attempting to keep his eyes on it when it slid out of view.

"I've changed my mind," he muttered into his tea. "I don't want to go."

"You never wanted to go," Raulin pointed out.

No, he hadn't. But he couldn't let Raulin go alone, not back in the beginning, not now—and Jago knew Raulin would go on. Not because he didn't feel the menace radiating from the island—menace that kept Jago's mouth dry and his stomach in knots—but because he wouldn't let the fear it caused stop him. An admirable trait, Jago had to admit, remembering the battle his brother had fought and won on the ledge into the valley, but not one likely to allow either of them to die comfortably of old age.

By the time the last cup of tea was finally finished, the pot dried and stowed away, the sun was a pale yellow disc high in the silver sky.

"I'm better at beginnings," Raulin admitted to Jago as they hoisted on their packs. He looked back at Crystal and then forward at the still shifting tower. "I've always been lousy at endings."

"Then think of this as another beginning," Jago told him, yanking a braid free from under the shoulder strap. "Things change, but they don't end."

"Oh, very profound, junior."

Jago tied on his hat, his violet eyes twinkling under the fur edge. "That's why mom liked me best."

Crystal stared up at the distant dragon, her wizard-sight caressing each strong and graceful curve. Life had left it thousands of years before and yet it still had a beauty that caused the breath to catch in her throat. She stood almost perfectly still, mesmerized, only her right hand moving, blindly weaving her hair around the fingers of the left.

"What are you thinking of, child?" Sokoji asked, coming silently up beside her.

"How it must have looked in the air with the sun turning its scales to black fire and its eyes glowing red."

"Its eyes are closed. How do you know they were red?"

"Weren't they?"

The giant nodded. "Yes. But how did you know?"

"Kraydak's colors were gold and blue and so was

Kraydak's dragon. Aryalan's colors were black and red and this was Aryalan's dragon."

"Not *her* dragon, child. That is the mistake the ancient ones made, claiming ownership of the Mother's body."

"I wonder," she said dreamily, giving no indication she'd heard Sokoji's last words, "how a dragon would look in silver and green."

"A dangerous thought, wizard."

At the giant's tone, Crystal shook herself free of her fascination with the great beast and turned to face Sokoji. "But only a thought," she said clearly. "I am not like those ancient wizards." Under Sokoji's continuing gaze, she drew herself up, her shoulders went back and her chin rose. Her hair spread out around her, a living silver frame, and her eyes flashed like jewels amidst the ice and snow.

Sokoji, whose memory went back almost to the world's creation, smiled. "No," she conceded, "you are not like the other wizards."

"Hey!" Raulin yelled from the edge of the ice. "You two going to stand and talk all day? These packs are heavy!"

"I will never understand mortals," Sokoji muttered as the two women walked forward. "First they spend the greater part of the morning dawdling and now they must instantly be off."

"An unpredictable race," Crystal agreed, conveniently forgetting for the moment her own mortal heritage.

"Unpredictable." Sokoji turned the word over in her mouth. "Yes, I suppose that's one word for them."

The snow covering the lake was dry and hard packed and it squeaked under boot soles.

"How do we know the ice is thick enough to hold us?" Jago asked, when they were about twenty feet from shore.

"Well," Raulin drawled, "if you're not breathing water, it's thick enough."

"Maybe we should be checking it." After weeks of

traveling through the mountains, crossing such a large open area left him feeling exposed and vulnerable. The ice wasn't really the problem, but it would do until something else came along. He could hear Raulin's own nervousness in his flippant answers.

"We are checking it out; we're sending Sokoji out ahead. Anything'll hold her will hold us."

"Don't worry, Jago." Sokoji smiled back over her shoulder at him. "During the second and third winter moons, the ice is as thick as it ever gets. We will not fall through."

Raulin reached out and tugged on a floating strand of Crystal's hair. "You're very quiet," he said. "Copper for your thoughts?"

"I was just thinking that this is really the only time of the year you could get to the tower, when the lake is frozen solid enough to walk across." She waved a hand back at the shore where clumps of stunted trees raised twisted branches barely above the level of the snow. "In the summer you'd need a boat and you certainly couldn't build one from those. Nor could you get one over the pass. In the spring and fall, while the mountains are saturated with water, you couldn't get into the valley at all, the footing would be too treacherous."

She paused and looked up at Raulin. "And if I hadn't gotten to the demon before you, you'd be dead and I'd be . . ." The memory of Nashawryn breaking free tightened her throat around the words. ". . . I'd be . . . well, I wouldn't be, and the map would have never been used. And if Sokoji hadn't met with us, we'd still be heading toward the wrong valley."

"Your point?" Raulin asked.

"Why did you decide to travel in winter? You've got to admit, it isn't when people usually go north."

"In the winter we could use the sleigh and carry a lot more gear. No bugs, few wild animals. It just seemed to make the most sense."

"What about the weather?"

Raulin tucked his chin deeper in his scarf. "The

lesser of a number of evils. You were traveling in the winter . . .''

''But seasons don't mean anything to me.'' She searched for other ways to convince him. ''If I hadn't met that brindle, I would never have used enough power for the demon to hear me and call . . .''

Maybe. Maybe not.

''Crystal . . .''

''. . . and I'm sure Sokoji has a logical reason for being in these mountains as well.''

Maybe. Maybe not.

''Crystal, what are you getting at?''

She sighed and pushed both her hands up through her hair. ''I think someone, or something wants us—you, me, and Jago, possibly Sokoji too—at that tower.''

''What!''

''Well, you've got to admit, it's a few too many co-incidences to be plausible.''

Raulin threw one arm around her shoulders. ''I've got to believe nothing of the kind. You're just a little spooked is all.'' He noticed the giant watching and added, ''Right, Sokoji?''

''In the world of the Mother-creator,'' Sokoji said solemnly, ''coincidences are few and far between. Nothing happens without reason.''

''Are you telling me you believe what Crystal just said?''

''Maybe. Maybe not.''

''Don't you start,'' Crystal growled.

Sokoji looked puzzled.

''I'm sorry.'' Crystal hoped she sounded sincere. She couldn't tell over Eegri's giggles.

Jago wondered if he should mention that he'd been mulling over the circumstances that had brought the four of them to this place at this time and had come to much the same conclusion. He opened his mouth to speak, caught sight of the expression on his brother's face—Raulin clearly anticipated what he was going to say—and decided to keep silent.

With the remains of the gatehouse, and the island it stood on, unreliable as a guide, it was difficult to determine both how far they'd walked and how far they still had to go. Judging distance by the shore they'd left helped very little, for the farther they walked over the lake the more the shore took on the same characteristics as the island.

"Look at the bright side," Raulin remarked as they continued, "this is some of the easiest walking we've done for weeks. It's flat, it's clear, we're not plunging through drifts, we're not . . ."

The ice groaned, a long drawn out sound that set teeth on edge and could be felt up through the soles of their feet.

". . . we're not likely to live to see the other side," Raulin finished, white showing all around his eyes. "What, in the name of Chaos, was that?"

"Just the ice settling," Crystal explained, moistening her lips. Knowing the cause barely lessened the sound's chilling effect. "Something to do with thermal patterns in the lake." The centaurs had spent a great deal of time, many years before, teaching her the ways of the world. Knowledge, they reasoned, brought respect. She wished now that she could remember more of it. "We're perfectly safe."

The ice groaned again.

Raulin and Jago went rigid. Even their clothing seemed to stiffen.

"Look," she realized they believed her reassurances and she understood that belief had little to do with their reaction to the sound, "Sokoji hasn't stopped."

The giant had pulled four or five body lengths ahead and continued to walk unhurriedly toward the island.

The brothers glanced at the giant, at each other, and simultaneously stepped forward. The footing remained solid.

Jago sighed deeply and banished thoughts of plummeting down into icy depths, the cold and the water racing to see which could kill first. *I've got to do some-*

thing about my imagination, he thought as he kept moving, watching Raulin shrug off even the memory of the fear. Raulin lived wholly in the present and Jago envied him the ability. He grinned as he pictured his brother, resplendent with new wealth, amid the corrupt and fearful aristocrats of the Empire who would, like so many others, take Raulin's bluntness for stupidity. The vision so enthralled him, he didn't notice he'd struck a patch of clear ice until it was brought forcibly to his attention.

"Oof!"

The pack and his many layers of clothing acted as a cushion, but the unexpected fall knocked the breath out of him. He glared up at Raulin and Crystal, who, seeing him unhurt, began to snicker. Even Sokoji's mouth twitched although she, at least, made no sound.

"No need to help," Jago hid his own laughter under an exaggerated sigh—it probably had looked pretty funny—"I can get up by myself." He threw himself over onto his stomach, silently cursing the weight of the pack, got his knees under him, and paused a moment, gathering the strength and balance necessary to stand.

The ice, an arm's length from his nose, was a greenish black. No, he realized with wonder, the ice—ice thick enough to support the giant's passage—was perfectly clear. The water below it was a greenish black.

If the glassmakers could learn to do this . . . he thought admiringly.

And then his thoughts froze.

A shadow, darker than the water, solid, and large, passed below the ice.

And the ice became, in comparison, very fragile.

"Hey, Jago, you all right?"

The shadow passed again and Jago knew, beyond any doubt, it was aware of him. Aware of all of them.

A long, trailing something, as thick around as Sokoji's thigh brushed against the lower surface of the ice.

Panic controlling his arms and legs, Jago scrabbled

back onto the nearest patch of snow and sat panting. He could no longer see it and that helped, but he still knew it was there. Knew it waited. Knew it wanted.

"Jago?" Raulin dropped to one knee and took hold of the younger man's shoulders. "What is it?"

"Something . . ." He took a shuddering breath and tried again. "Something under the ice."

"Are you certain?" Sokoji asked.

Jago looked up at the giant and nodded.

"Then perhaps it would be best if we kept walking."

"Good idea," Raulin agreed, standing. "Present a moving target."

"And get *off* the ice," added Crystal, pulling Jago to his feet.

He clung to her hands for a moment, taking comfort in the strength that had all but lifted both him and the extra weight of the pack, feeling the warm pressure of her fingers through his mitts.

"Take a wizard to breach a wizard's tower," he said, a plea for reassurance in his voice.

Crystal met his eyes and, for an instant, openly wore the mantle of her power. Even shattered as it was, held together by the wizard's will alone, it blazed with a painful glory. Then it faded, replaced by the concern of a friend. "I didn't stop an avalanche," she told him with exaggerated pique, "in order to feed you to a fish."

The remaining distance to the island became the longest distance Jago ever walked. With every step, he expected the ice to crack and break and let the hunger that it sheltered out to feed. He didn't doubt Crystal's power. He didn't want to test it.

The others were nervous, he saw it in the way they carried themselves; movements a little jerky, heads cocked to one side and brows drawn down as if to give eyes and ears a better chance to give warning. They all avoided the clear patches of ice.

When he stepped up on land at last, relief hit with

such force that if Raulin hadn't grabbed his arm he would've sagged to the ground.

"I'm okay," he protested, embarrassed at his weakness.

"Sure you are," Raulin said noncommittally, and held on until he felt Jago could stand on his own.

As they walked away from the shore, Jago viciously buried the thought that threatened to immobilize him. To get off the island, they would have to recross the ice.

The island looked very little different from the lake; a smaller circle, about a hand's span higher, and covered by that same hard snow. They could see the ruin of the gatehouse clearly now. Here, a wall, still vibrantly red even after centuries, stood alone and unsupported. There, the flip of a tiled roof poked out of the white. From the center of the island rose a small square building, still half buried under drifts.

"But it's only . . ." Raulin raised his hand horizontally to about mid-chest. "We won't be able to stand up."

"I stood in it," Sokoji reminded him. "It was not built level with the surface of the island. There are stairs around the corner."

"Is that where you sprang the trap?" Crystal asked, flexing long fingers, her hair rippling on the still air. She could feel power waiting in this place and it grew stronger as they neared the center.

"One of them. The ancient wizards trusted no one, least of all their fellows. Their towers, their strongholds were built to keep out," the giant paused and searched for the correct word, "visitors."

"Don't you mean intruders?"

She shook her head. "No, their paranoia was never that justified."

Crystal considered what it would mean to trust no one and to have no one trust you. "They must've been very lonely," she said softly.

Sokoji studied the last living wizard, her face thoughtful. "Yes, they must have been."

Indicating Raulin with one hand and Jago with the other, Crystal smiled. Here was her trust. "Don't worry, Sokoji."

Sokoji nodded and half-smiled, understanding what Crystal was telling her, but still looking thoughtful.

"The traps . . ." Raulin prodded. They were still advancing toward the gatehouse and he wanted to know what they'd face before they arrived.

"All the traps I sprang were tied to the life forces of the Elder Races."

"Which means?" Jago asked, although he had a nasty suspicion he knew.

"Others must exist tied to the life forces of mortals and wizards."

"Which we'll have to find?"

"Yes."

"But Aryalan's been dead for thousands of years," Raulin protested. "How much trouble can something this old give us?"

"It almost killed me," Sokoji told them, her voice even slower and weightier than usual. "If Aryalan were still alive and able to feed power and direction to her guardians, I could not have won."

"Lovely."

"Thank you."

Raulin flushed. "No, I didn't mean . . . oh, never mind."

Jago, whose line of sight took in Sokoji's face, smiled in spite of the situation. He simply hadn't been able to convince his brother that the giant possessed a sense of humor.

In the years since Sokoji had been inside the tower, winter had refilled the stairwell leading down into the gatehouse, leaving only a dimple in the surface of the snow.

Raulin let his pack crash to the ground and straightened up with a groan. "Looks like shoveling," he sighed.

They could see the top lintel of the door, carved with fantastic birds and beasts, but nothing more.

"At least a body length of shoveling if that door's standard size," Jago added, dropping his pack with a little more control but an equal mount of relief. "And if Sokoji went through it, I'm betting we've her body length to clear, not ours."

Crystal stepped into the dimple and spread her hands. The snow flashed green and disappeared. She stood at the top of a broad flight of black marble stairs. At the bottom loomed a door, also black, and large enough for the giant to enter without so much as having to incline her head.

"That may not have been wise," Sokoji said solemnly. "Any power remaining here will now know a wizard has returned."

"Any power remaining knew the moment I entered the valley." Crystal pointed back to where the dragon rested. "That avalanche was no accident."

"What's done is done," Raulin declared philosophically. "And what's done beats shoveling." He slid over the lip of snow and onto the stairs. The small flurry he brought with him melted away as it touched the steps. He shook off a mitten, bent and drew a finger along the slick surface. The luster of the marble made it look wet. It wasn't.

"I destroyed the trap set on the stairs for my kind," Sokoji informed him, "but there may be others set for yours. Shall I come with you, or will you descend alone?"

Raulin looked down the length of black, each step as perfect and sharp edged as the day it had been set. "Alone," he decided. "Less distractions."

"Careful," Jago warned, advancing to the edge but no farther. "Check everything."

"Don't teach grandma to suck eggs, little brother." A memory stirred and he heard his master sergeant screaming orders. *Amazing the things you pick up amid the rape and slaughter,* he thought, inspecting each step before moving onto it. He knew marble could be trapped in the same ways as wood—stairs were stairs, after all—but he suspected he was missing any number of nasty . . .

Stone snapped down on stone.

Raulin froze. Until he saw which way the danger lay, going back could be as deadly as going ahead.

A panel in the base of the door burst open.

Raulin got a vague glimpse of scales and claws and teeth. He had time to shape them into a large and ugly lizard but no time for fear before the thing was on him. He twisted, fell, and slid almost half the remaining distance to the door.

The lizard overshot. Claws scrabbling for purchase on the marble, it whirled to attack.

A piercing noise split the air.

It reared, tail lashing.

Jago whistled again.

It charged.

Jago stood unmoving, smiling slightly.

As it struck, it disappeared.

His heart loud in his ears, Raulin levered himself up onto his knees and yanked his scarf away from his mouth. He felt like he couldn't get enough air. "Thanks, Crystal," he panted. "That's another one I owe you."

"I didn't do anything," Crystal told him. "It was Jago."

"Jago?" Raulin twisted around to face his brother. "What did you do?" he demanded.

Jago shrugged. "It was a gowie lizard," he explained. "They live in very hot climates. Coming out into this kind of cold would stop it dead." They all watched—as if noticing for the first time—while he huffed out a white plume of breath illustrating the temperature. "In fact, the cold would probably kill it."

"Fascinating," Raulin growled. "But what did you do?"

Jago shrugged again. "I disbelieved it."

"An illusion?"

"Seems that way."

Raulin flushed. "I feel like an idiot." He got to his feet. "That was a mortal trap?" he asked Sokoji.

The giant spread her hands. "I saw nothing."

"Illusion!" Raulin spat out the word. "I should've known. Kraydak used illusion all the time. I've seen them before. Chaos, I've fought with them."

"Well, I've created them and I didn't identify it until it disappeared." Crystal's self-mocking tones lifted Raulin out of the guilt he seemed ready to fall into. "Next time you'll know."

"Next time," Sokoji put in, standing on the top step, "it will be real and you'll die. A wizard's tower holds stranger things than gowie lizards."

"That's not very encouraging." Crystal frowned at the giant.

Sokoji thought about it for a moment.

"No," she agreed. "It isn't."

"Do you want me to come down?" Crystal asked, eyeing Raulin with concern.

He shook his head and rubbed an elbow that had slammed into the marble. "I'm okay, just bruised. Anyway," he measured the distance he'd fallen and the distance he still had to go, "I'm almost there."

The next seven steps were clear. He reached the door safely, turned and grinned. "If that was her attempt at keeping mortals out, I can't say as I'm very impressed." He pulled off his hat and wiped beads of sweat off his forehead. "It's warmer down here."

"And warmer still inside," Sokoji said.

Inside.

Raulin turned back to the door, feeling dwarfed. It rose taller than the giant and spread almost twice Sokoji's not inconsiderable width. Its six lacquered panels were carved with marvelously detailed scenes of wild animals nearly impossible to see at more than a few inches away, for the black absorbed all the light that fell upon it. The ruin of a large brass lock dominated the middle right side.

"What a mess." He ran his fingers over the broken metal. "Looks like Sokoji put her fist through this on that last visit.'' Peering back over one shoulder, he raised an eyebrow in the giant's direction. Sokoji inclined her head, admitting the action.

"Okay, there's no sense putting all our eggs in one basket. You three stay there until I check this out.''

Crystal began a protest, but Jago gripped her arm and shook his head.

"He wants us out of the way when he opens the door.''

"But what about him?''

"He knows what he's doing.''

But both of them realized that if something came out the door, knowledge would do little good.

"It swings in,'' he called, placing his hand against the shattered lock. He took a deep breath, pushed, and dove to one side in the same motion.

Silently, the great door swung open.

Soft golden light spilled out over the threshold.

"Anything?'' he asked as Crystal and Jago dropped to their knees and even Sokoji bent to get a better line of sight.

"Nothing.'' Jago said. Crystal and Sokoji nodded agreement.

"Nothing?'' Raulin repeated, shrugged, pushed away from the wall, and stepped inside.

The gatehouse appeared the same size on the inside as on the outside. Based on what Crystal had told him, Raulin knew that wasn't always a given in wizard created buildings. The soft golden light radiated down from all but one corner of the ceiling where the tiles were broken, dull, and gray. A great diagonal gouge marked one wall; the others were smooth and all four were bright red. They reminded him of raw meat. Not a particularily comforting analogy.

The floor was the same black marble as the stairs and in the center was a massive slab of ebony. It took Raulin a moment to understand why the ebony appeared to have been splashed liberally with blood and then he remembered what Sokoji had said. Rubies;

stones ranging in size from tiny flecks to ovals too large to completely fit on his palm.

Their beauty as much as the wealth they represented tugged at him, drew him forward. So many and so red. Burning . . .

He caught himself in midstride, shook his head like a dog coming out of water or a man out of a dream, and put the foot back where he had lifted it from. Slowly and methodically, keeping his eyes off the gems, he searched the room for less obvious traps. At the spot beside the ebony slab where feet would have to be braced to raise it, he grunted and stopped a careful arm's length away.

"Never a rock around when you need one," he sighed, unlacing his boot. He unwound his scarf and wrapped the boot in the center of it. Holding both ends in one hand, he swung the whole thing around like a flexible hammer and slammed it down on the pressure plate.

Sword blades immediately thrust up from the floor at random points throughout the room.

"Raulin!" Through the open door, Jago saw the flash of steel and flung himself down the stairs.

Crystal tried to follow, but Sokoji held her.

"Wait," said the giant, "until you know he needs you."

Jago reached the door and clutched at the frame to stop his headlong rush.

"I'm okay," Raulin reassured him, stepping back. The razor edge had only parted the hairs of his heavy coat and not even cut the hide beneath. "Dumb luck strikes again." He glared. "And who told you you could come down here?"

"Just seeing if you'd fallen asleep, you were taking so long."

"You always were lousy at waiting for things."

Both men wore expressions much gentler than their words.

Raulin rapped the boot he held against the flat of a

blade. "You might as well come in, this is as secure as it gets. Call Sokoji and Crystal."

Sokoji reacted to the call by lifting both abandoned packs. With one dangling from each hand, she turned to Crystal.

"Go," Crystal told her. "We know it's safe for you. I'll wait until you're off the stairs."

The giant nodded and descended.

Crystal waited, readying her power, trying to remain calm. Doubt would only rouse the goddesses and leave her less able to deal with whatever traps Aryalan had left. *I dealt with a living Kraydak,* she reminded herself. *This should be nothing in comparison.*

Sokoji reached the bottom and Crystal started down.

And it was nothing. Nothing at all.

Standing safely in the doorway, Crystal forced herself to relax. Apparently Aryalan had set no traps for her fellow wizards on the stairs. Or the traps that had been set had faded over the years. Or the trap was too subtle to be immediately obvious. The litany tightened her stomach back into knots and she sighed.

"Hey, Crystal," Raulin's voice came muffled around the finger he'd stuck in is mouth, "Could you do something about these?" He waved at the blades with his free hand. "They're a little in the way."

"Are you all right?" she demanded.

"He's fine," Jago said, grinning like an idiot. "Just clumsy."

Raulin's grin grew just as wide. "You're the one who suddenly wanted to dance."

"Dance?" Crystal frowned, then caught sight of the rubies. "Ah, dance."

The blades glowed briefly green and slumped to the floor.

"The use of power may set off other traps," Sokoji pointed out.

Crystal shrugged. "It didn't. And I don't think it matters."

"She's right, Sokoji," Raulin enthused, stripping off his overcoat and dropping the heavy fur to the floor by his hat and mittens and scarf. "It doesn't matter. There's more than enough treasure here. We don't have to go into the tower. *This* is as bad as it gets."

Only Jago saw Crystal's face at that moment. It was so carefully blank he grew suspicious.

"Are we still in danger?" he asked.

"I think not," Sokoji answered. She stretched back her arm and pushed the door shut. "As your brother said, you have no need to go into the tower."

Shrugging out of his own coat, Jago allowed himself to be convinced. Crystal could have any number of reasons for hiding what she thought, any number.

"Sokoji," Raulin sat down to pull his boot on and prodded one of the now flaccid swords, "why didn't you set off this trap? Didn't you try to lift the slab?"

"I saw the plate—I think it is meant to be seen—and leaned over from the other side. A position only one of my kind would be both tall and strong enough to use." She paused, remembering. "I loosed something else."

All eyes turned to the gouged wall and the dark corner of ceiling, then back to the giant.

"I won," she said, and fell silent.

The silence lengthened.

Raulin rose to his knees and pulled his dagger. "Well, come on," he waved the point at Jago, "our future isn't going to pop out of that door unaided."

"Are you sure it's safe?" Jago asked, tossing his braids back behind his shoulders as he knelt beside his brothers.

"The gems will not be trapped."

All three, Raulin, Jago, and Crystal, turned to look at Sokoji who paused in pulling the teapot from a pocket to return their multiple stare.

"To you this is a fortune," she explained. "To Aryalan it was merely a decoration. Wizards have no use for wealth."

Raulin nodded, accepting the statement at face value. He slipped his dagger point beneath a small rectangular jewel and began to pry it loose.

Jago watched Crystal's face for a moment, wishing their link was stronger. He'd heard a double meaning in Sokoji's words and didn't understand what it was. Crystal knew, he'd bet his share of these "decorations" on it. Then it hit him. Wizards *have* no use for wealth. Not had. Have.

"Crystal."

When she turned to face him, he knew the answer.

"You're going into the tower, aren't you?"

"Yes."

Metal rang on ebony as Raulin's blade fell from his hand.

Thirteen

"We're going with you and that's that."

"No, you aren't." Crystal thrust both hands up through her hair and paced the length of the room. At the far end she turned, marshaled her arguments for what seemed like the thousandth time, took a deep breath, and sighed. "What can I say to convince you two to stay here?" she asked plaintively, leaning against the bright red wall and sliding down it to the floor.

Raulin came over and sat beside her, wrapping one arm around her shoulders. "If you go down there, so do we."

She twisted to face him. "I *have* to go down there. The tower is too dangerous to just leave. If even a small fraction of Aryalan's power remains . . . You know the sorts of weapons a wizard wields."

"We know."

"I'm the only one who can destroy the threat and I've got to do it now, before someone else stumbles on it, learns to use it, and tries to start the madness all over again."

"We understand that."

"If you go with me, I'll be too busy taking care of you to look out for myself. You'll be putting me in danger."

Raulin caught Crystal's flailing hand and held it. "And what if you need taking care of? Who's there for you?"

Crystal looked across to where the giant sat by the door. "Sokoji?" she pleaded.

"He is right," Sokoji said placidly. "If you are not like the ancient wizards, prove it now. In their pride, they denied friendship and thought only they were capable. They refused to admit others could stand beside them; saw no strengths but their own."

Crystal winced, but Raulin flashed a triumphant grin at his brother.

"Crystal," Jago dropped to one knee before her. "Could you watch a friend you loved go into danger while you stayed safely behind?"

"No," she murmured, and then louder, "no."

"Then don't ask it of us. Please."

She rubbed her cheek against Raulin's arm where it rested on her shoulder. "You two are crazy. You know that, don't you?"

Recognizing capitulation, Raulin smiled in agreement and Jago laid his hands on both of theirs. "We know," he said softly.

Later that night, Sokoji watched the two mortals and the wizard sleep, a tangle of arms and legs, and gold and silver hair. One of Jago's braids had come undone and his hair and Crystal's had wound in and about each other until they were so completely entwined only power would be able to get them apart. She looked from them to the ebony door, now plucked clean of its rubies. The tower did need to be dealt with and the last living wizard was the only one who could do it; the giants had long since come to that conclusion.

That the last living wizard was also the only one who could fully use the mysteries of Aryalan's tower, the giants were well aware. Nor had they, like Doan, dismissed the centaurs' fears out of hand. If they had not felt there was some basis for those fears, they would not have offered to watch; the wizard was at the time an unknown and unknowns should be investigated.

It hadn't taken much watching for Sokoji to decide that the centaurs had no real knowledge of the child they'd raised and the wizard they'd trained. If Crystal broke, it would be duty that struck the blow, not license. Duty the centaurs had taught her. In Sokoji's opinion, Crystal's greatest fault was her self-doubt, her fear that a very normal and healthy self-interest would lead her down the paths of the ancient wizards.

Raulin muttered in his sleep and tugged at the cover. Jago snorted and hung on. Neither woke.

Sokoji wondered if the brothers suspected how much they had remolded the shattered bits of Crystal between them.

"Are you ready?"

Raulin and Jago clutched at their daggers, Crystal wrapped her power about her, all three nodded.

Planting her feet firmly, Sokoji leaned across the width of the trapdoor, slipped two fingers beneath the ebony bar, and lifted.

Smoothly and quietly, the door rose.

Another black marble staircase, broad and wide enough for the giant to descend, spiraled down into Aryalan's tower. The walls were a familiar red. The air drifting up into the gatehouse smelled strongly of roses. The soft, golden wizard-light continued down the stairs, although they saw no visible source.

"Okay," Raulin transferred his dagger to his left hand and wiped the palm of his right on his pants. Like Jago, he wore his jacket but left the fur overcoat behind with the packs. Besides the dagger, he carried a waterskin and the belt pouch that held the rubies. He didn't know why he brought the rubies. He supposed the answer he'd given Jago, *If I'm going to die, I might as well die rich,* was as good a reason as any. "Okay," he said again. "I go first, then Crystal, then Jago. Keep one step apart, no more, and sing out if anything seems the slightest bit suspicious."

He put his right foot down on the first step and slowly shifted his weight onto it. Nothing. Then the next step . . . then the next. . . . When his head dipped below the level of the trapdoor, he suddenly felt as if his ears had been stuffed with lamb's wool. Slowly, he reached up and touched Crystal's leg. Rubbing his fingers against the rough cloth of her pants made no sound.

"Crystal?" He felt her hand wrap around his. As far as he could tell, that was his only answer. Holding on to her tightly, he backed up until his head was once more in the gatehouse. The ambient noise seemed very loud.

"Did you hear me call?" he asked.

Crystal shook her head and looked worried. "No."

Raulin chewed on one end of his mustache. "I think it's just soundproofing. Crystal, keep hold of my hand, and Jago, take her other one. Don't follow her down until she tugs twice. If we can't talk to each other down there . . ." He shrugged. "Well, only one way to find out."

He backed down the stairs, not taking his eyes off Crystal's face. Her expression told him when she hit the effect. "Can you hear me?" he asked.

She smiled in relief, her hair lifting out a little from her ears. "Perfectly."

"We'd better test it." He kissed her fingers. The kisses made no noise, but the words were clear. "You're the most beautiful woman in the world."

"You haven't met my mother." She flicked a fingertip against the end of his nose. "We'd better let Jago know everything is all right."

"I suppose so." Raulin sighed dramatically—and, he was pleased to note, audibly.

Crystal grinned and drew his hand up to her lips. She kissed his palm and closed the fingers over it. "For later," she pledged.

He laid the hand against his heart and waggled his brows in his best lecherous manner. Then he turned and started carefully down the rest of the stairs.

Jago, upon entering the soundproofing, merely murmured, "Interesting," and continued to place his feet precisely where Raulin and Crystal had stepped. He wished he had the comforting bulk of Sokoji at his back, but the giant had remained in the gatehouse. No one had asked her why, and Jago suspected it was because they hadn't wanted to hear the reason.

Crystal kept both arms tight to her sides so they wouldn't brush against the walls accidentally. Perhaps Kraydak had been unique in mortaring his tower with the trapped souls of the dead. Perhaps not. She didn't want to find out.

Why not? If they're there, they'll call their Lord, and he'll have to come. Avreen's voice slid like silk through her mind.

Crystal gritted mental teeth but made no answer and Avreen's mocking laughter accompanied her down the next few steps.

Raulin squinted but couldn't see into the gloom that hid the bottom of the stairs. Although their immediate area remained brightly lit, the wizard-light staying with them as they descended, he'd have preferred a little less light where they were and a little more where they were going. He weighted the danger of Crystal sending light ahead against the probable consequences of her depleting her power and decided the gloom would lift eventually on its own. But Chaos, he hated not knowing what he was walking into.

Sokoji watched Jago's golden head disappear around the first turn in the spiral staircase. She could've gone with them to the stair's end but didn't see the point as she could go no farther whether she wished to or not. Nor, she admitted to herself, did she want to take a chance that what had waited for her at the bottom waited there still. It was no danger to the others, but she didn't think she could defeat it again.

She smiled as she heard a faint sound outside the gatehouse door.

"Come in, Doan," she called.

The door swung open and the dwarf stood on the threshold, his sword drawn and a crescent shaped slice of black marble lying at his feet. "Damned step tried to fold up on me," he explained when he saw the direction of Sokoji's gaze. He kicked the piece of stone

out of his way and stepped into the room, his brows
rising at the limp blades scattered about on the floor.
''Had a bit of trouble?''

She shrugged. ''Not really.''

Doan shoved the door closed and slammed his sword
back into its sheath. ''When did you know I was following you?'' he demanded.

''I never thought you wouldn't. Taking another's
word for something is not your way.''

He jerked his chin at the hole in the floor. ''They
gone down?''

''Yes.''

''All three of them?''

''Yes.

''And I should stay right where I am?''

''This is her chance to prove herself to herself. Don't
ruin it by upsetting the balance she had achieved.''

''Pah!'' He thrust his hands behind his belt and
snarled, ''So what do we do now?''

Sokoji's expression saddened. ''We wait.''

Doan snorted. He hated waiting. ''And we think,
no doubt,'' he added sarcastically.

''No. We try not to.''

They reached the bottom of the stairs without incident. Crystal couldn't understand why. Surely Aryalan
would've trapped the only entrance to her tower. Raulin paused on the last step and Crystal watched anxiously as he lowered one foot carefully to the floor.
And then the other. He walked three paces away and
then it was her turn. Nothing.

The room they stood in had been done in the same
combination of red and black.

Enough is enough, sighed a voice Crystal thought
was Sholah's and she had to agree with the sentiment.
The vibrant colors only added to the tension.

She heard Jago step off the stairs behind her, then
she heard Raulin gasp.

''What . . .'' she began to ask, then fell silent.

Out of the shadows that hid the corners of the room,

stepped a woman. Strands of gold wove through the thick chestnut of her hair, flecks of gold brightened the soft brown of her eyes, and a sprinkle of gold danced across the cream of her cheeks. She stood almost as tall as the wizard and almost as slender. Her smile, although touched with sadness, brought such beauty to her face that beauty seemed a word completely inadequate to describe it.

"Mother?"

Tayer, the Queen of Ardhan, held out her hands. "Have you no welcome for me, Crystal? I traveled far to speak with you."

"Mother?" Crystal cursed the break in her voice and reached out with power. This had to be of Aryalan's making. But it felt like the memory she held of her mother. "You can't be here."

The sadness on Tayer's face deepened. "The dead can be anywhere," she said softly.

"Dead?" Crystal's mouth went dry. "You can't be dead. I'd know." She turned her probe into a spear and drove it into the heart of whatever it was that stood before her. Nothing blocked the blow. Not a woman with a life of her own. Not a creature created by wizardry.

"Your power can't affect the dead." Tayer shook her head and sighed. "I've never lied to you, child, why should I start now?"

"But I'd know," Crystal repeated, suddenly unsure if she would. "If you were dead, I'd know."

"Perhaps not. We've grown apart lately, you and I. I blame myself for that."

"No, Mother. I . . ." With a shock, Crystal realized this—this something—had more than half convinced her it—she—spoke the truth.

"You were a miracle, Crystal, and I was never sure of how to treat you. I suppose if I'd treated you like my daughter, and that alone, things would have been better between us." Tayer gazed sadly into emerald eyes. "But that's behind us now. I've come for another reason. Your father needs you. I'm afraid for him."

"Father needs . . ." The words wrapped around her and made it difficult to think. Something was wrong. Something was missing.

"Mother . . ." *No!* she told herself. *This is not my mother.* "How did you die?"

A blush stained Tayer's perfect cheek, the expression making her appear absurdly young. "I thought it was only a cold; that it would go away . . ."

"Oh, mother." Crystal took a step forward, turned away, then turned back. Tayer had always argued with the Royal Physicians, insisting she was perfectly healthy long before they thought she should be up. This was exactly the sort of thing Crystal had always been afraid would happen one day. Her heart caught in her throat. "Mother?"

Tayer nodded. "Yes, my darling. I'm sorry."

Crystal reached out a trembling hand. It passed through Tayer's shoulder. Not even a wizard could touch the dead.

"Crystal, you must go to your father. Now."

"I, I can't."

"I never asked you for anything when I was alive, my child."

"But I can't!" Crystal wailed. "I can't."

"Is it because . . . because he isn't your father by blood?"

"No!" Forgetting she couldn't touch, Crystal reached out in shock. "I never . . ."

"He always loved you as if you were his own."

"Mother, I . . ."

"Please," Tayer pleaded, her eyes filling with tears. "Your brothers are too young and hurt too badly themselves to help. Your father is so alone now. If you should die in this place, I'm afraid he wouldn't survive the loss of us both. Go to him, please, prove to him you still love him. He took my death so hard."

Death. Lord Death. Where the dead were, so was he.

And he wasn't.

Still speaking, the image of Tayer faded away.

Built on a memory, Crystal realized as the mists cleared from her mind. *And as real as my memories are.* And hard on that thought came another. *I would know if mother had died. I would. We haven't grown apart. And father knows I love him.* She gained a new respect for Aryalan's powers then, for, even defeated, the trap left guilt behind to slow the intruder.

"No . . ."

Jago, his hands raised in supplication, backed toward the stairs. His eyes were fogged and the expression on his face was that of a man torn between duty and desire.

Gently, Crystal reached along the link they shared, found the place where Aryalan's power had lodged, and twisted Jago free. She caught just a glimpse of a brown-haired woman, weeping, and she touched betrayal.

Jago cried out, a strangled sound of loss and pain, and then his eyes began to focus. His hands fell to his sides and clenched into fists, the knuckles white against his tan.

"Not really there," he said huskily. "I should've known." He scrubbed the back of his wrist across his eyes. "A trap?"

"Yes."

"Emotional blackmail?" At Crystal's nod, his mouth curved into something not quite a smile. "Nasty lady, Aryalan, glad I didn't know her when she was alive. Everybody's got something they . . ." He paled. "Oh, Chaos, Raulin."

Raulin, who had served as a soldier with Kraydak's Horde.

Blood trickled down his chin from where he had bitten through his lip. His cheeks were wet with tears. Gray eyes stared at nothing visible, and, although his shoulder blades were hard against a wall, Raulin's feet kept moving, trying to back away.

"Raulin?" Crystal touched his arm. The muscles felt like rock. Without a ready pathway into Raulin's mind, she had to go slowly and carefully, balancing her need to get him free against the damage she could do if she hurried.

Gradually, she became aware of an unending parade of the dead. Not the dead as Lord Death presented them, ready to be received back into the arms of the Mother, but bodies, mortally wounded, risen up from their graves. Every one of them—men, women, and children—named Raulin their slayer, demanded justice, and advanced on him to claim it. And Raulin was almost at the point where their justice would be a small price to pay.

Crystal knew the focus had to be here, somewhere. Desperately, she searched among the bodies, trying not to acknowledge them as real in any way lest Raulin's guilt absorb her as well. She could feel Raulin's will weaken with every second.

There!

A surge of power, green enveloped the dull red glow, and the victims of the Horde were gone.

Under Crystal's hand, Raulin's muscles went suddenly slack. He swayed, Jago grabbed him, and they both sagged to the floor. With Jago's arms tight around him and his head against his brother's chest, Raulin sobbed once, then lay shaking.

While Jago held him, Crystal stroked his back, her power smoothing away the sharp edges of his pain. She didn't care if her power attracted something. In fact, she hoped it would. The last time she'd wanted to hit back this badly, she'd leveled a mountain.

Finally, Raulin pushed himself up into a sitting position. He nodded at Jago, who looked relieved, and met Crystal's eyes.

"I never killed any children," he said.

Crystal leaned forward and kissed him, putting all her trust and all her understanding into the action. When their lips parted, she murmured, "I know," against his mouth. And he had to believe her where he might not have believed words alone.

The three of them stood together, Crystal positioned within the circle of Raulin's arms and both of them feeling better for the contact. Eyes were carefully averted from the shadows in the corners.

"Well?" Jago asked. "Do we go on?"

"Why not? It can't get any worse," Raulin declared, but his usual jauntiness sounded forced.

Crystal didn't mention that it very well could. There didn't seem much point.

The door leading into the tower was locked.

Raulin eyed it speculatively, his color beginning to return. "Two traps tied to the lock that I can see. Figure on at least two more I can't. Jago?"

"Two anyway," Jago agreed." "Well, I've got the steadier hand, so . . ." He slipped a small leather case out of his jacket pocket.

"You pick locks? Both of you?"

The brothers exchanged speaking glances.

"Growing up in the Empire," Jago began.

"Gives you an excuse to develop a wide variety of skills," Crystal finished, shaking her head. "But I'd rather neither of you risk this when there's a better way." She reached up and pulled free a hair which changed to a slender silver rod in her hand.

"You're going to do it?"

"No. Tayja is."

"The goddess?" Raulin's voice rose almost an octive. "Crystal, have you gone crazy?"

"I trust her, Raulin. She took control once before and gave it back."

"I'd rather take my chances with the traps."

"I'd rather you didn't!"

They glared at each other.

Jago cleared his throat. "If you're sure . . ."

Crystal tossed her head. "I'm sure."

Raulin transferred his glare to Jago.

A surge of joy, that could have only come from the goddess, accompanied Tayja as she moved up from the depths of Crystal's mind.

Crystal watched as once again her hands took on a life of their own, manipulating the silver probe with amazing dexterity. This time, however, she wasted no energy fighting the possession. Raulin and Jago peered over her shoulders and counted off the traps.

"Four!" Raulin advanced on the door, hands raised.

"Wait." Crystal's mouth formed the word, but it wasn't Crystal's voice. She shoved the probe into the lock and twisted it violently to the left. A sharp crack sounded deep inside the mechanism. "Five!" declared the same voice, smugly. "That is all of them and that one had to be last or it would set off all the others."

Still under Tayja's control, Crystal's hands turned gracefully in the air. *You take a great chance allowing me this much freedom, child.* The long, pale fingers flexed. *I am a goddess, after all, and as proud and arrogant as my sisters.*

But I know you, Crystal reminded her. *And I know you are more honorable than some.*

In her mind's eye, Crystal saw Tayja smile. *Yes,* she admitted. *More honorable than some.*

As you come to know me, you better know a part of yourself. But the words were so faint, Crystal couldn't be sure if they came from memory or if Tayja had actually said them as she retreated.

Then Crystal's hands were her own again. She stared down at them and frowned, remembering the goddess' joy as she rose to help. She'd felt it herself, back when Dorses had seen her power as a tool rather than an abomination to be feared. This was important; important to her perception of herself and her perception of the goddesses. She reached for the word that would pull it all together.

"She got them all." Raulin pulled the door open a finger's width. Nothing; no steel plates, no poisoned darts, no cascade of acid, and nothing tried to get through the crack. "I'm impressed."

Chaos! Crystal swore. Raulin's voice drove the word she reached for from her mind.

"I think your goddess must've hung around with a number of less than holy characters." Raulin readied to open the door wider. "She never learned how to pick locks like that in a temple."

I taught how to pick locks in a temple.

Crystal laughed and passed on Tayja's message, ignoring Sholah's indignant, *You did nothing of the sort.*

The door, when fully opened, revealed nothing more threatening than a long red and black expanse of corridor fanning to a half circle into which were set three more black lacquered doors.

"This wizard liked her doors small," Jago observed. "Sokoji might have made it through this one, but she'd never have got through those."

"Surely it's just the distance," Raulin protested. "They can't be as narrow as they seem."

"Well, there's only one way to find out." Crystal lifted a foot to step over the threshold, but Raulin jerked her back.

"Not until we check the corridor for traps." Only when he knew for certain that the first section was safe did he allow her to advance, followed closely by Jago.

Behind them, unseen, dull red runes crawled for an instant along the edges of the doorframe, then faded, leaving no sign of their existence.

They found no traps in the corridor.

"Maybe this is the easy part," Raulin suggested as they reached the wider area and paused to study the three doors. Not only were they unlocked and untrapped, but they had no locks to trap.

"Maybe." Jago sounded dubious as he measured his shoulders against their width. "We'll have to go sideways to get through."

"And which one do we go through?" Crystal wondered. "They're identical."

Claws dragged against the marble floor. The prevailing smell of roses changed abruptly to rot.

As one, they turned.

The creature advancing toward them supported its weight on its knuckles as much as on its feet. Scimitar-shaped talons scraped as it swung each arm forward.

"Where did it come from?" Jago gasped.

"Does it matter?"

Their daggers looked pitifully small next to the creature's natural armament.

Its eyes showed black from lid to lid, it had no nose that they could see, and its mouth, a lipless gash across the width of its face, bristled with a double row of triangular teeth. No neck separated the head from the powerful torso.

Crystal threw up her hands. An arching green bolt struck the creature full in the barrel chest.

It hissed, staggered back a step, then continued forward, moving surprisingly quickly on its squat legs. It was on them before they had time to consider flight.

"Get in close!" Raulin yelled, dropping to avoid a wild swing.

Jago hit the floor and rolled. Talons gouged the marble near him.

Raulin grabbed an arm on its next attack—the gray skin felt like wet cork—and used the momentum to slam himself and his dagger point into the creature's body. He yanked the weapon free, raised it to strike again, and realized his first blow had left no wound.

"Chaos!"

The smell of rot grew overpowering and Raulin found himself staring between four rows of teeth.

Silver hair wrapped around his head and snatched him back just as the massive jaw crashed shut not a finger's width from the end of his nose. A blaze of green, bright enough to leave spots dancing before his eyes, slashed downward.

The creature screamed. A line opened along its jaw, oily black liquid beading the length.

Crystal appeared to be wielding a dagger formed of power.

"Got another one of those?" Raulin yelled, scrambling backward, slicing into a massive arm and again doing no damage. "Plain steel ain't worth spit!"

An elbow drove into Jago's stomach and slammed him up against a wall. He slid to the floor gasping for breath.

Throwing herself between Jago and the creature's next blow, Crystal caught a talon on the shaft of green she held. The talon smoked and snapped off. She reached behind her with her free hand and dragged Jago to his feet.

"Distract it!" she shouted. "Let me get close enough to use this." A sword of power, she realized belatedly, would've been more practical. She tossed bands of green around the creature, slowing it by the smallest of margins.

Raulin and Jago agreed on strategy with a glance and raced to opposite walls of the corridor.

Crystal swung at the creature twice more.

"You're cutting it," Raulin told her, panting. "But I don't think you're hurting it much." The effort of keeping himself alive was beginning to tell. He'd taken only glancing blows so far and suspected a solid hit would break bones at the very least.

The creature ignored both its gaping wounds and the fluid dripping from them.

Rocking with the force of a blow that clipped his shoulder, Jago kicked with all his strength at the rear of a bony knee.

Taking advantage of the resulting lurch, Crystal opened a diagonal gash across its chest.

Free me, Zarsheiy demanded. *Free me and it will burn!* The fire goddess beat at the barriers containing her.

Suddenly, the creature concentrated its attack on Crystal. Both huge, taloned hands reached for her, curved around the shield she threw up, and began to compress it.

The power dagger faded as Crystal reinforced the shield. It lasted maybe three heartbeats longer.

She heard Jago scream her name as she went down.

"We're dead," she thought, and prepared to pull power from the barriers.

Yes! Zarsheiy shrieked.

"Mustn't, mustn't, mustn't!" caroled a high pitched voice.

The sound of a strangely muffled explosion echoed off the walls of the corridor. Something wet dropped onto her cheek.

As she could feel her power repairing shattered ribs, she didn't try to move. Lying motionless hurt sufficiently.

An iridescent face poked into her field of vision. "Are you mashed?" it asked brightly. "Pulped? Crushed? Scrunched?"

"Yes," Crystal answered.

"Oh." It looked concerned and withdrew.

"Crystal?" Raulin's face was smudged with black and his mustache was caked with blood. "Can I do anything?"

She shook her head, carefully. "Just let me lie here for a moment and tell me what happened."

"The creature blew up."

One eyebrow rose slowly. "Just like that?"

Raulin grinned. "Pretty much."

"Is Jago all right?"

"I'm not sure the solution wasn't worse than the problem," Jago answered, off to one side, "but yeah, I'm fine."

"Jago was closest to the center of the blast," Raulin explained, smiling strangely "and the whole thing was kind of . . . messy."

"Oh, I see." She didn't, but Jago *sounded* all right. "If you'll help, I think I can sit up now."

He slid one arm behind her shoulders and lifted gently until her back rested against his chest.

The corridor—walls, ceiling, and floor—was awash with black ichor and fist-sized bits of steaming flesh. She noted with disgust that Jago—especially Jago—Raulin and herself were covered with the stuff. Surprisingly—fortunately—it smelled no worse than it had when alive. The demon she'd freed from Aryalan's cave sat cross-legged in midair, about the only place it could sit and stay clean. Its resemblance to the larger creature was illuminating.

"One of yours?" she asked, prodding at a misshapen lump with the toe of one boot.

"Was," the demon agreed. "Warned you not to come here. Told you it was dangerous." It looked down at her, as close to a serious expression on its face as its features were capable of. "No more debt between us," it said. "All debts are paid."

Crystal nodded. "All debts are paid," she repeated.

The demon nodded as well, a motion that set it bobbing in the air. It spun about once, and vanished.

Jago pulled a sodden sleeve out from his arm and summed up the situation with an emphatic, "Blech!"

"Could be worse," Raulin reminded him. "You could be dead."

"I think I'd prefer it," Jago muttered, flipping a braid back and wincing when the movement jarred his shoulder. Using the wall for support, he stood and stripped off jacket, shirt, and undershirt. Where his torso wasn't black with ichor, purple bruises were already beginning to show.

Crystal pushed power across their link and left it to sort out what needed healing. Then she turned to Raulin and drew her finger along the shallow gash that ran the length of his thigh. Behind the finger's path, only a fine white scar remained. "Anything else," she asked.

"Well, I've got a lump the size of an apple on the back of my head, but I can live with that." He brushed her hair back off her face. Not a single drop of ichor clung to the silver strands. "Save your power for when you need it."

"It's not as bad as that," Crystal protested. She reached into her pocket and pulled out a handful of crumbled horse-cake, wishing she'd landed on her other side when she'd fallen. "Sokoji planned for this; I'll eat and I'll be fine."

"Fine," Raulin repeated. "When you're not putting yourself at risk, you can heal whatever you want but now you've got to be close to drawing on the barriers."

Crystal stared at him in astonishment. "How did you know?"

He pinched her chin. "I'm smarter than I look."

He'd have to be, Zarsheiy snarled.

"In the meantime," he continued, unaware of Zarsheiy's remark, "let's get out of this mess." He took a step and had to windmill both arms to keep his balance.

"Careful," Jago pointed out mildly, "It's slippery."

Raulin glared at his brother, then turned his attention to the doors. As Crystal had mentioned earlier, they were identical; which one then to open first? Ready to slam it shut at the first sign of danger, he broached the door on the left.

Nothing.

He picked up Jago's discarded jacket and slapped it over the threshold, both breaking the line of the door and spraying the room beyond with black.

Nothing.

He peered into the room and blinked at the red and black checkerboard on walls and floor and ceiling. Both side walls and the one opposite held archways but from where he stood he couldn't tell if the openings led to rooms or corridors. Turning his head, he could see the backs of the other two doors. He examined the floor carefully.

Nothing.

Moving next to the central door and then to the right he repeated the process with the same results.

"Okay," he said at last. "It seems safe. Shall we go on?"

"Which door?" Jago asked.

Raulin shrugged. "Why not all of them? I don't like the idea of one of us being in there while the other two are still out here; those doors are too narrow if someone gets into trouble. If we go through at the same time, at least we'll be together. Are you going to get dressed?"

Jago clawed congealing ichor out of his beard.

"No," he growled, "I'm not." Even his undershirt had been soaked through and he didn't want it touching his skin.

"Good thing your legs didn't get hit," Raulin muttered shaking his head, "or you'd be wandering around bare-assed."

Jago ignored him and turned to Crystal. "Your decision," he said graciously.

Crystal hid a smile. "We'll go through together like Raulin suggested." She waved Jago to the right and Raulin to the left while she took the center.

"All right." She drew a deep breath. "On three, open the door and step through. Freeze on the other side until we're sure of what to do next. Ready?"

Jago gave her a thumbs up and Raulin blew her a kiss.

"One, two, three!"

In unison, they pulled the doors open, turned sideways, and stepped through.

Crystal found herself alone in a room with an open archway cutting through the checkerboard wall opposite her.

She spun around.

No door.

"RAULIN! JAGO!"

No answer.

Fourteen

"CRYSTAL! JAGO!"

The answering silence seemed to mock him and Raulin lost his temper.

"Chaos' balls and the Mother's tits!" he screamed and threw himself against the wall that should've held a door but didn't. He kicked it, he pounded on it, and he slammed his shoulder into it all along its length. When he finally calmed down, he had a sore foot, aching hands, and a bruised shoulder but no better idea of what had become of his companions.

"This can't be happening," he muttered, and slumped against the offending wall. Drumming his fingers on his thighs, he reviewed everything he'd done to check for traps. His memory held no clue to what had happened.

He'd seen a room with three archways and three doors.

He stood in a room with an archway in the left wall and no door.

The red and black checkerboard pattern was the same, and so was the size as near as he could tell. The remaining archway had neither moved nor changed.

He hoped Crystal and Jago were together, but he very much doubted it.

"Okay," he said to the silence, "I have two options. I can stay where I am and maybe Crystal or Jago will find me. Or I can go looking for them myself." He picked at the torn hide where the demon's talon had ripped through his heavy pants, then, squaring his shoulders, pushed himself off the wall. "Right. I go looking." Every second that he delayed increased the chance he would arrive too late to help either lover or brother or both survive.

Of the sixteen red and black tiles in the floor, he'd already effectively tested four by his mad race up and down the wall. Hugging the walls, therefore, seemed the least hazardous path to take as it gave him only one more tile to risk. This proved out as he reached the arch safely and sighed in relief at seeing the plain gray stone beyond the opening. The red and black motif was apparently at an end.

Giving the single stone of the threshold a quick inspection, he stepped completely over it. The fine crack surrounding it might have been the result of ancient mortar crumbling away to dust, but he didn't think so.

The hall he now stood in had a high vaulted ceiling and about half the width and twice the length of the room he'd just left. A clear white light banished shadows from even the farthest corners. An archway, identical to the one behind him, cut through the far wall. At equal intervals along each side of a central aisle, were statues of strange and impossible creatures.

"Well, maybe not so impossible," Raulin muttered, staring up at the first, "considering what else is wandering around down here." He scraped a bit of caked ichor off his sleeve. The statue appeared to be a demented combination of snake and bear. He peered closer. Each scale had been intricately carved. He lifted a hand to touch the stone; and stopped, suddenly remembering nursery tales of carvings coming to life.

Hands shoved deep into his pockets, he headed toward the exit, carefully keeping his eyes straight ahead.

Just on the edge of his vision, he thought he saw a giant cat with too many heads twitch slightly. He walked faster.

". . . thirteen, fourteen," he counted as he reached the arch, teeth clenched from the effort of not breaking into a run, "and each one uglier than the last. Interesting taste this Aryalan had."

Although the hall behind him sent icy chills up and

down his spine and he wanted nothing more than to be out and gone, he bent and examined this second threshold. The same fine crack ran around it. Satisfied, he straightened and lifted a leg to step over.

The first tile on the other side protruded slightly higher than the others.

Raulin jerked his stride short and brought his foot solidly down on the stone of the threshold. It settled and he felt, rather than heard, the mechanism it controlled click into place.

The first tile now lay level with the rest of the floor and Raulin advanced into one end of a long corridor leading off to his right. Opposite him was a large, wooden, brass-bound door. *Just the sort of door you'd expect to find in a wizard's tower,* he thought, *not like those little lacquer things.* Looking to his right he counted twelve more doors, as far as he could tell, all exact copies.

The door he faced led farther away from Jago and Crystal, so Raulin ignored it. He turned and walked to the first in the right-hand wall. His only plan was to circle back until he passed the checkerboard chamber. If the trap that got them into this followed any sort of logical pattern when it split them apart, his chamber would've been the farthest left. Using their initial orientation, he had to go right.

The lock on the door was huge and ornate and had, he saw, a keyhole large enough to look through.

So he looked.

Something looked back. Its eye was large and yellow and bore no resemblance to the eyes of either of the two Raulin searched for—or for that matter, to anything Raulin had ever heard of.

"Jago can't be in there, he hasn't had time to get this far." But a small, illogical part of him kept insisting he go back and check as he walked away; kept supplying him with visions of his brother lying wounded and helpless in the creature's den.

Nothing looked back through a second, similar keyhole but the line of sight was too limited for Raulin to see much of the room beyond.

"It's going in the right direction," he muttered, sliding out a lock-pick. "Good enough."

A few moments of careful examination identified the trap and a few moments more was all he needed to spring it. When the dart flew out of the frame, his hand was nowhere near its path. Satisfied, he pulled open the door.

"Empty," he grunted. "Good." Through an archway directly opposite, he could see another small room. It appeared empty as well but he decided he'd better check. The door that led back to his brother might be just out of sight.

He stepped into the room and paused. Both side walls had peculiar scratches running diagonally from the near corner to the ceiling. Under normal circumstances, Raulin preferred to stay near the walls, but those scratches didn't look like normal circumstances so he started across the middle of the room.

About three-quarters to the other side, the entire floor tipped suddenly down like an unbalanced teeter-totter, dropping Raulin with it.

Raulin threw himself at the archway.

The threshold hit him in mid-chest. He clawed at the stone, feet scrabbling against the wall below, and managed to stop his fall.

Then he remembered to breathe.

Bracing his elbows, he levered himself up and flopped the top half of his body over into the second room.

The floor moved.

He jerked away, almost overbalanced, and spent the next few seconds stabilizing again.

The side walls of this room bore scratches as well, running diagonally from the far corner to the ceiling.

"Chaos. Chaos! CHAOS!" Raulin swore, blinking sweat from his eyes. His dangling lower body had never felt so exposed and vulnerable. He could feel his balls drawing up into safer territory. He didn't blame them.

He risked a glance back over his shoulder.

All he could see was a gray stone wall, slightly angled away from him.

"Wonderful," he muttered, steeled himself, and looked down.

The bottom appeared to be no more than two body lengths away.

He snapped his head back and tried to calm the pounding of his heart. It wasn't very far. Next to no distance at all if he lowered himself on his arms before he dropped. He swallowed and wet his lips. His chest hurt where he'd slammed it into the stone. His choices seemed to have narrowed to staying where he was or taking a chance down below.

Slowly he began to inch back, taking his weight on his forearms and then on his hands alone.

Kicking out a little from the wall, he let go.

One leg twisted under him when he landed. He fell heavily, then lay for a moment while he writhed in time to the waves of pain pulsating out from the injured joint. When the demon had slashed his leg during the battle, the blow had wrenched his knee as well, a minor ache in the wake of the other and until this moment he'd forgotten about it. He had a feeling he wouldn't forget about it again for awhile.

Finally, the pain began to ebb. He straightened his arms, pushing his body into a sitting position, and dragged himself around until the floor/wall supported his back. Yanking his waterskin forward, he managed to remove the stopper. Although the water had the slightly brackish taste of melted snow, the action of getting the drink helped to calm him.

"What I wouldn't give," he sighed, taking another mouthful, "for even a mediocre brandy." He looked up. " 'Course it could be worse. If I'd followed the wall like I usually do, I'd have been near nothing I could grab, would've fallen the whole distance, probably broken my leg, at the very least, and lain here until I rotted. Which raises the question,'' keeping much of his weight on the wall at his back, he stood, ''how in Chaos do I get out?''

The area he found himself in was about twelve feet long, about twelve feet wide, and about twice that height. He bent, ignoring as well as he could the protest from his bruised ribs, and prodded at the bottom of the floor/wall. Although there wasn't much space, he found he could grip it with his fingertips. To his surprise, the massive block of stone rose easily when he tugged at it. When it reached his shoulder height, he ducked beneath the rising edge and shoved it hard enough to level it out.

The wizard-light stayed with him, he was happy to discover. He'd half anticipated exploring this lower level in the dark. Looking up, he could see the pivot mechanism and the ledge that supported the one end of the floor; supported it until some Chaos-born fool walked too far.

The new room had the same dimensions as the one above and had a single door in the long wall to Raulin's right.

''Right angles to the way I should be going. Still,'' Raulin sucked on his mustache, ''I haven't much of a choice.''

He limped to the door exercising more than his usual caution. The lock was untrapped and, even allowing for the painful distraction from his knee, it gave him no trouble. He stepped into the middle of a long corridor, a t-junction at each end with nothing to choose between them except his need to find Jago and Crystal. He turned to the right and began walking. At the corner he hesitated, his way no longer clear.

He shifted his weight off his bad leg and sighed, his chin sinking down on his chest. Then he blinked. In the wall in front of him was the faint but unmistakable outline of a door. He raised his head. It vanished. He lowered his head. It reappeared. With his chin tucked in, he ran his dagger around the edge, found the catch, and freed it. A rectangular section of the wall swung silently outward.

"Now this has got to be an illusion." He closed his eyes, disbelieved as hard as he could, and opened them again. "Still there." Stepping forward, pushing a gem encrusted goblet away with his foot, Raulin stared at more wealth than he'd ever suspected existed. Gold and silver coins, jewels, both loose and in ornate settings, ropes of pearls, beautiful and gleaming things he couldn't identify; all of it heaped and piled and thrown about the room.

"We could live like kings on this." He bumped into a chest and the lid snapped shut on the bolts of silk and cloth of gold. Bemused, he sat down, his eyes wide with trying to take in the glittering display.

He scooped up a handful of coin and poured it from one palm to the other . . .

. . . from one palm to the other . . .

The clinking of the metal sounded almost like music . . .

. . . almost like music . . .

He'd never noticed before that gold had a texture. That pearls felt like satin. That diamonds could never be mistaken for anything but what they were. That weapons could be beautiful.

He stroked a dagger, its hilt set with emeralds, and thought how well the stones would match Crystal's eyes.

Crystal.

The dagger fell from lax fingers.

Crystal. And Jago.

He had to find them. Suddenly the glitter was only that, and unimportant. He stood and the pain in his knee drove the last thoughts of the treasure from his mind.

"Why in Chaos couldn't they gild a walking stick?" he grumbled, limping out the door.

"RAULIN! CRYSTAL!"

Jago called until he was hoarse and then slumped against the wall in despair. The tiles were warm against his bare back, perversely comforting as those tiles should've been the door he'd entered through. He glanced at the archway to his right, now the only way of exiting the room, and wondered if he should use it. Raulin, he knew, would not sit quietly waiting for rescue. Raulin had never been very good at waiting for anything.

The logical thing to do was to stay right where he was, assume Crystal would find both Raulin and himself, and then the three of them would go on together.

But there was nothing to say that Crystal would even be able to look for them. That Raulin wasn't lying hurt or confined or both. Nothing to say that he, Jago, wasn't the only one able to move about and find the other two.

Logic argued against it, but logic had no proof and logic was no comfort and Jago found himself standing at the archway almost before he'd consciously decided to leave.

The cool, gray stone of the adjoining room soothed his raw nerves and he bent to examine the threshold in a less frantic frame of mind. Nothing, so he straightened and looked up. Not quite touching it, he ran his finger along the crack that split the lintel and continued halfway down the supports on both sides. He couldn't identify it as a trap, but that, he knew, didn't mean a Chaos-inspired thing.

Preferring embarrassment to dismemberment, he squatted and waddled through the opening, careful to keep his head lower than the bottom edge of the crack.

The hall he entered stretched long and narrow to an identical archway at the opposite end. Tapestries, brilliantly colored and glittering with gold, hung at equal intervals along each wall.

They had to have been created by power, Jago realized, standing before the first and gazing at it in wonder. No mortal hand could have done so perfect a job for the terror that twisted the man's features was as extreme as the beauty it twisted.

He moved to the next and although it was a different man, it was the same expression.

And then he realized that these men, so perfect of face and form, all stared in terror across the hall, and he turned.

And recognized the tapestry he now faced.

Red-gold hair, sapphire eyes, and a mocking smile; Jago had grown up in Kraydak's Empire and once he'd seen its lord. The blue eyes of the tapestry seemed to glow and Jago felt his palms grow damp. Fighting over half a lifetime of fear and oppression that threatened to drop him to his knees, he raised his head and met the wizard's eyes. And saw they were nothing but bright blue thread.

He wiped his hands and swept his gaze along the rest of the wall. The tiny woman with the ebony hair and eyes, with the lips as red as rubies and the smile as cold, had to be Aryalan. He didn't need to put names to the rest.

He turned again to the wall he'd first examined and saw the terror repeated seven times as the seven gods stared out at their wizard-children who had killed them.

Curious, Jago looked more closely at Kraydak's sire. His shoulder-length hair and full beard had been picked out in gold thread and pieces of amethyst had been worked into the color of his eyes. Falling from one limp hand was a scale and from the other a sword. Kraydak had murdered justice.

"And he continued to destroy you, all the rest of his days," Jago said softly to the god. "But for what peace it gives, he too was destroyed in the end."

He looked at no more tapestries as he walked to the archway that would take him out of the hall.

It took him some time to find the trap—his mind kept drifting back to gods and wizards—and he'd almost decided no trap existed when he spotted the false lintel. But the trigger eluded him still. Finally he gave up, put the point of his dagger between the stone and the overlapping masonry, and threw his weight against the hilt. The blade bowed but held and the lintel sprang free, slamming down to shatter against the floor.

Jago waited until the dust had settled and the echoes of the noise had died and then he stepped over the rubble and looked left down a corridor that held twelve huge, wooden, brass-bound doors.

"Twelve," he mused, pushing a chunk of stone back toward the archway. "And fourteen tapestries. And, if I'm not mistaken, sixteen tiles in each wall and in the floor of the checkerboard room." He smiled grimly and began searching for the next number in sequence. At one of the not-quite-identical doors he stopped; ten rivets held the lock to the wood. The door opened a route to the left as Jago suspected it would. He had to go left to find Crystal and Raulin.

Pulling out his lock-picks, he dropped to one knee and set to work. When the eighth tumbler fell, the door swung open.

The room was empty, and, as far as he could tell, untrapped. In the center, a flight of stairs led down to a lower level. There were no other exits.

Jago paused in the doorway and frowned. He'd either solved the riddle, and the rest of his way was clear, or he'd solved the riddle and was walking into a major setup.

"How in Chaos do I out-think a wizard dead for centuries?" he wondered, decided not to try and headed for the stairs.

He reached the bottom in a small anteroom, with padded leather benches against the side walls and a dark red carpet on the floor. A smell he recognized drifted through the open door that faced the stairs; dust and leather and . . .

"Books?" Jago ran forward into the largest room he'd seen inside the tower and rocked to a stunned halt. The room was filled with books—books on shelves, books on tables, books stacked haphazardly on the floor.

"These can't be real," he murmured as his feet, under no conscious control, carried him farther into the canyons between the cases. His disbelief had no effect on either the books or the room in general.

He bumped up against a table, picked a book at random off a pile, and opened it. The lettering remained as clear and sharp as on the day the Scholar had put pen to paper. Jago drew his fingers lightly over the page and began to read. A while later he put it down and picked up another and, later still, he began to wander—scanning titles, dipping occasionally into the pages, marveling at the knowledge stored away.

In a corner, he found a rack of scrolls and carefully unrolled the uppermost. The crackling parchment gave the first indication that time did, indeed, operate on the objects within the room but then, the scroll had been written before the Age of Wizards. He read over half of it before he realized he shouldn't be able to read it at all. None of the words looked familiar, but he knew what they meant.

Thinking back, Jago remembered other books in other languages but never any book he hadn't understood. Aryalan had obviously taken steps to ensure all parts of her library were accessible.

". . . and the Lady of Grove," he read aloud, his voice touched with wonder, "came from the heart of her tree. Greatly daring were the bards who sang of her beauty for she walked in beauty beyond words. Tall she stood, and slender, with silver hair, and ivory skin, and eyes the green of sunlight through summer leaves." Tossing a braid back over his shoulder, he smiled. "Sounds like the spitting image of Crystal." Then he paused, one arm outstretched to grasp a black leather tome. What had he just said? Parchment rustled under his other hand and he looked down.

The scroll.

Silver hair, and ivory skin, and eyes the green of sunlight through leaves.

Crystal.

And Raulin.

He wet lips suddenly dry.

"Mother-creator, I'd forgotten about Crystal and Raulin."

Close to panic, Jago backed away from the scroll and began to search frantically for another door. There had to be another way out. He found it at last, tucked back behind a shelf of geographies, half buried behind stacks of maps. It had no lock, only a brass hook, and he was afraid, until he opened it, that it was just a closet. He checked the way for traps, moving faster than he knew was safe, and stepped through, pulling the door shut behind him.

The air in the narrow stone tunnel seemed cleaner somehow and he stood for a moment just breathing it in.

"So," he said to the silence, "were the books a trap of Aryalan's making or my own?"

The silence made no answer.

"Did she cause me to forget? Or did I do it to myself?"

He pulled the stopper from his waterskin and took a long drink. He didn't really think he wanted to know.

The tunnel ran, by his best guess, parallel to the hall of tapestries, although a level lower. He started down it, back toward his companions, leaving his questions by the door. He hadn't gone far when the walls began to close in and the ceiling lowered. For the first time since he'd entered the tower, he remembered that it was not only underground, but underwater.

He touched the stone. Was it damp?

And then the wizard-light went out.

It was more than Jago, nerves already frayed, could endure.

"Not alone," he begged. "Not in the dark."

He could feel the weight of rock all around him.

Closing his eyes helped only a little, just enough for him to force his feet to move. With his shoulders pushing against the walls and one hand running along the ceiling to protect his head, he inched forward. It was never so bad when Raulin was with him and he used that as a goad. If he couldn't make it through this, Raulin might never be with him again.

He had no way to tell if time was passing until the blackness against his lids turned gray. And then orange. He opened his eyes and could see the end of the tunnel.

With his whole mind on the open area ahead, he stumbled forward and out.

He thought of traps one step too late, felt the stone give under his foot, saw the steel plate begin to drop. He had no idea what the steel was to close him in with—fire, flood, or wild beast—nor did he care. He dove forward, rolled, and the plate crashed down behind him.

When his ears stopped ringing, he tried to stand and found he hadn't rolled quite far enough. One braid had been caught between the metal and the floor.

Laughter seemed the only appropriate response . . . until he felt a touch against his boot sole and looked up into the tiny black eyes of a male brindle.

Raulin stood and stared at the narrow stone bridge, his back pressed so hard against the wall he was sure his shoulder blades would leave imprints. Mentally, he retraced his route and decided he'd head back to the last cross corridor and try the other direction; just as soon as he could get his feet to move. He'd caught only a glimpse of the depths the bridge spanned, but that had been enough to send him staggering back to safety and freeze him there.

"Just as soon as the memory fades a bit," he told himself, the wall under his palms growing damp, "I'm out of here."

And then he heard Jago scream on the other side.

He was across the bridge before he knew it and running as fast as his bad knee would allow toward the sound.

"Chaos!" Skidding around a corner he only just managed to avoid slamming into the hind end of a brindle. A brindle that appeared to have his brother pinned. Well, he'd dealt with *that* once before.

He pulled his dagger and leaped at the animal's back, aiming for a pale patch of fur at the top of its spine.

A pale patch of fur . . .

Jago watched mesmerized as the brindle swayed above him, both his legs held easily beneath massive paws. He remembered claws and teeth tearing his flesh from the bone. He remembered pain. He waited for it to begin again.

The brindle bent its head to feed. Jago forced himself to look away.

"Jago! Chaos blast it, Jago, look at me!" Raulin grabbed Jago's chin and yanked his head around. "It isn't real! It's illusion!"

To Jago, caught up in the memory of old torment, Raulin's voice seemed to come from very far away. But Raulin's voice shouldn't have been there at all, so he listened and dragged himself free of the words. When he finally managed to focus, Raulin crouched where the brindle had been.

Raulin saw reason return to his brother's eyes, and started to breathe again. "If you believed in that thing so strongly," he growled, "why didn't you run?"

Jago jerked his head to the limit of the trapped hair.

Raulin's gaze ran along the golden braid and back and Jago tensed for the roar that was sure to come. Raulin didn't disappoint him.

"I TOLD YOU TO GET YOUR HAIR CUT!"

With a half-smile, Jago pulled his dagger and handed it over. "Be my guest."

"Serve you right if I shaved half your head," Raulin muttered, bending to the task. "I told you this would get you into trouble one day, but you wouldn't listen. You can sit up now."

Jago sat and tried not to wince as the other braid was cut to match. "What are you doing?" he asked as Raulin coiled the length of hair and crammed it into his belt pouch.

"What does it look like," Raulin snapped. "I can't

see how you managed with two. This thing weighs a ton.''

"I am feeling a little light-headed." The ragged ends just touched his shoulders.

"That's because there's nothing between your ears." And in a much softer tone he asked, "You okay?"

"Yeah. You?"

"Yeah."

They held each other then, and everything was all right.

"Tested . . ." Raulin nodded. "It makes sense."

"It's the only thing that does. If Aryalan wanted to keep people out of her tower, she wouldn't have bothered with false floors and falling walls and the rest of this nonsense, she'd have thrown up a power barrier or made the tower invisible."

"So what are we being tested for?"

"I don't know."

Raulin sighed. "Great. Lost in a dead wizard's tower, being tested for reasons that probably died with her, and we know what happens if we fail."

Jago stood and offered Raulin his hand. "Frankly, I'm more worried about what happens if we pass. Come on, let's find Crystal."

"RAULIN! JAGO!"

Crystal let the echoes of her voice fade and reached out with power. Nothing. She could feel the link with Jago, but she couldn't use it to track him. She couldn't touch Raulin at all.

"I told them this was going to happen. I told them!"

Feeling better after that short burst of pettiness, she started across the checkerboard room to the archway. Raulin would not stay put, that went without question. Jago might, but she rather doubted it as he had no way of knowing if either of his companions still lived. She had to find them before they found something they couldn't handle. Or something found them.

Raulin could be dead, Avreen pointed out. *Why*

don't you call the Mother's son and find out? He did say he'd come if you called.

Raulin isn't dead. Crystal's voice was edged.

You could know for sure. What is it about Lord Death that frightens you lately?

Crystal slammed a barrier down so hard she felt her other shields tremble. She couldn't keep Avreen locked away for long, but she'd enjoy the peace while it lasted. Afraid of Lord Death, indeed. He was her oldest friend. Why didn't she call him?

The center four tiles of the sixteen in the floor dropped out from under her.

Her power caught her just before she hit the spikes. She drifted up and out of the pit, furious at herself for being distracted.

"What a stupid way for a wizard to die," she muttered. "I keep this up and someone's going to have to rescue me."

When she reached the arch she paused and pushed a wave of power through before her.

Glyphs flared up both sides and the opening pulsed red then black then red again. A binding, similar to the one that had imprisoned the demon. With nothing to hold, the binding faded and the way was clear.

She stepped into a long hall, the archway in the middle of one side. Fourteen windows stretched black and featureless almost floor to ceiling across from her. The ends of the hall held identical doors.

As she approached the nearest window, the glass glowed green. When it cleared, she looked out into a snow covered garden where three children were building a fort. One of the children turned to yell instructions and Crystal recognized her half-brother, the Heir of Ardhan. The two smaller children had to be the twins. She laughed as a disagreement turned into a wrestling match, the twins, as usual, ganging up on the older boy but never quite managing to pin him down.

Maybe, she thought, leaning against the window frame, *when I'm finished here, I'll go . . .*

Zarsheiy tried to force her barriers and Crystal suddenly realized what powered the window.

She threw herself back and the scene faded.

"Clever," she acknowledged. She hadn't felt it draining her.

Idiot, snorted Zarsheiy.

Staying a careful distance from the rest of the windows, Crystal made her way to the door in the left end of the hall. Finding Raulin first seemed the only choice; Jago, at least, she knew was alive.

On the other side of the door were twelve steps, leading down.

Crystal slammed the door.

"Games!" she snarled. "Twelve, fourteen, sixteen, this isn't a tower, it's a puzzle board."

Boredom had been the greatest enemy of the ancient wizards. The world had fallen at their feet and left them nothing to do.

"This *isn't* a tower," Crystal repeated. "And yet the tower must be close or Aryalan wouldn't have been able to watch her games played. Watch and influence the outcome." She pushed her hair back off her face and thought.

After a moment, she smiled.

With lines of power, she drew a door in the air, opened it, and stepped through . . .

. . . into the center of a circular room, its seven walls made up of seven mirrors.

She turned slowly, hoping to catch sight of Raulin or Jago but saw only Crystal. She touched one mirror with power and let it reflect onto all the others. Nothing. If Aryalan had watched from this place perhaps it was turned only to her, or there was a trick to activating it that Crystal hadn't yet discovered.

Or Aryalan might have anticipated Crystal's move and the room was itself a part of the game.

Idiot.

Trust your instincts.

Reason must be the key.

She should follow her heart.

Maybe, maybe not.

"Be quiet!" Crystal snapped. "All of you." she buried her face in her hands, trying to think, and when that didn't help, began to spin slowly on the ball of one foot.

"The ancient wizards were not only bored," she said, seeing herself surrounded by herself, "but vain."

The reflections wavered, and changed.

Eegri laughed out at her, tossing brown curls.

Tayja smiled and spread a mahogany hand against the glass.

Zarsheiy's eyes burned with fire contained but far from under control.

Sholah opened wide her arms, offering refuge.

Nashawryn, stars caught in midnight hair, only stared, her silver eyes impossible to read.

One mirror showed a graceful line of shoulder and back, as Geta, still grieving for her brother, continued to hide her face.

And Avreen. The goddess of love pushed auburn hair away from amber eyes.

"Have I no reflection left at all?" Crystal whispered.

Avreen shook her head, and sighed. *All the reflections are you . . .*

. . . you . . .
. . . you . . .
. . . you . . .
. . . you . . .
. . . you . . .

Red light played over the lowest level of the tower as the most powerful of its guardians stirred. While not exactly aware, it was capable of independent thought and actions within the boundaries Aryalan had set for it centuries before. Until she created her dragon, the ancient wizard had considered it her greatest achievement and it had given her many hours of amusement.

The Wizards' Doom had not affected it, nor had the centuries it had lain dormant.

It had watched the intruders and now it knew them; knew their strengths and knew their weaknesses; followed the lines that joined them and knew how to tie them in place.

It judged them worthy of its attention.

It gathered together the power still at its disposal and prepared to use the knowledge it had gleaned; prepared to place all three pieces in the final configuration.

Had Aryalan been there to watch, she would have been very amused indeed.

—WIZARD—

The mirrors faded and Crystal found herself suspended in blackness. Red lines, sullenly pulsating, held her securely and where they touched they brought torment. Hurriedly, she threw shields up against the pain and found it left her no power to get free.

—YOU HAVE A MOVE STILL REMAINING IN THE GAME—

Fury banished fear.

She bit off each word and spat it out. "I'm not playing."

Lines of red flashed out from those that bound her, wrapped about and illuminated two bodies; Raulin to her left, Jago to her right. They had no protection from the pain and screamed wordlessly and continuously, thrashing and fighting as the light spun out between them and completed the triangle.

The voice sounded clearly over the brothers' cries.

—TO FREE YOURSELF, WIZARD, BREAK THE BALANCE—

Raulin shrieked her name and she spun toward him. The motion caused the lines about Jago to flicker and brighten. He threw back his head and his screams grew shrill. When she turned to Jago, Raulin writhed in new agony.

—ONE MUST BE SACRIFICED, WIZARD, IT IS THE ONLY WAY—

To free herself.

"No." Her chin went up. "I am not like the ancient wizards," she said. "I don't play games."

She dropped all barriers and threw wide her power. This time, she didn't fight. The word she'd searched for, the word that pulled it all together, was acceptance.

All the reflections are you. . . .

The pain hit first, from the lines of red, then Zarsheiy burned and the pain was lost in fire. She felt Sholah and Tayja give themselves joyously to the new matrix and she felt Eegri dance through the flame. She acknowledged Avreen, acknowledged the face the goddess wore and added to the reforging the sorrow of love admitted too late. Darkness surged forth with the eldest goddess. But there came no answer from the light.

Only the threat of Kraydak had convinced Geta to help in Crystal's creation. Kraydak, like Getan his father, had died. Geta mourned her twin and would not be moved.

Then Jago screamed and chance alone made the words the last that Getan had cried.

"Mother, it hurts!"

And the goddess looked to the image of her brother writhing in pain.

No!

Freedom rose to stand against the darkness.

Crystal looked to Raulin, now hanging limp in his bonds and remembered the strength in his arms and the pleasure they had shared, the warmth that had banished winter's nights. She looked to Jago, who still twisted and fought, and gently touched the place where his life touched hers, savoring the knowledge that, for a time, she had not been alone. Gathering up the memories, she placed them where she hoped they would survive what was to come, for friendship was too rare a thing to lose. All this in less than a heartbeat . . .

. . . then Crystal let go of self.

The red lines disappeared, for the wizard they had held was no more.

"Mortal! Mortal, wake, or you will go to my Mother by my hand!"

"Bet you wish you could shake him."

Lord Death whirled and glared at the dwarf. "Do not mock me, Elder, lest I misuse the power I wield. You can be killed and I am Death."

Doan spread his hands, his face unwontedly serious. "I do not mock you, Mother's son. I spoke without thinking. Forgive me." He dropped his eyes to the two men crumpled on the ground. "The mortals live?"

"They live. But I cannot get them to wake."

"Perhaps I can help." Sokoji pushed passed the dwarf, her arms full of fur. She wrapped both bodies in the overcoats, then bent over Raulin. After a moment, she shook her head. "If he wakes at all," she said sadly, "it will not be for some time." She moved to Jago and her expression grew more helpful. "This one has something in him that fights what was done and is almost healed." Lifting Jago's head onto her lap, she held out her hand to Doan. "Give me your flask."

"There's not much left," Doan warned her as he passed it over.

"It won't take much." Sokoji waved the open flask under Jago's nose.

Jago coughed and opened his eyes. "What . . . what happened?"

Doan snorted. "We hoped you'd tell us."

With the giant's arm a firm support across his back, Jago sat up and looked around. The tower, the island, and the lake were gone. In their place, a perfectly circular bowl of bare rock curved up around him, Sokoji, the dwarf, Lord Death, and the still body of his brother.

"Raulin!" He twisted out of Sokoji's grasp. "Raulin?"

"He lives," Sokoji told him, "but he needs help I cannot give."

She paused, and in the silence, Doan prodded: "Perhaps Crystal . . ."

Jago shook his head, spattering the rock with tears. "Crystal is . . . she . . ."

"She what, mortal?"

Jago met Lord Death's eyes. "I don't know," he whispered. He laid his hand against Raulin's cheek, comforted by the feather touch of breath, and tried to describe what he'd seen in the instant between pain and oblivion.

"Her face was perfectly still and her arms were open. It sounds crazy, you couldn't see through her or anything, but she looked clear," his mouth twisted, "like crystal. She'd been wearing clothes she'd borrowed from us—from Raulin and me—they were gone. Silver light began to pour out from her hair, then from her eyes, then from her skin, then there was only light so brilliant it burned. That's all."

He couldn't describe what he'd felt when Crystal had dissolved into light, the searing glory that had burned along the life-link and threatened for an instant to consume him too. He didn't have the words for it. He doubted the words existed.

He wanted to turn away from the expression of Lord Death's face. He didn't.

"She called me," Lord Death told him. "I heard her."

"I'm sorry." And Jago cried for more than just Crystal and his brother.

Sokoji stood and scanned the sky. "From out of darkness came the Mother, but in what fire was she forged?" She glanced down at Doan who stared at her in puzzlement. "It is a question my sisters and I often think on."

"Yeah, so?"

The giant smiled. "And now it has been answered. There will be new worlds born from this day."

"Let me get this straight," Doan shoved his hands behind his belt, "you think that Crystal just became a new . . ." His mouth opened and closed unable to get around the concept.

"A new creator?" Sokoji nodded. "Yes."

"No." Lord Death's hands curled into fists and he staggered forward, fell to his knees and howled. "NO! Crystal, come back! I love you!"

The words hung in the air for a long moment and then they faded.

A silver spark danced along the path of a wandering breeze. And then another. And then another. And then the breeze danced in silver hair and Crystal opened her arms to Lord Death.

"I can touch you now." Her words were a promise.

Lord Death laid a trembling hand in hers and let her pull him to his feet.

"I heard you call," he told her. "I heard you say you loved me."

Back before the remaking, when love had been separate, and love had worn his face. . . . "Yes," she said, drawing him close, "I called."

"I came."

Her lips parted.

Then his arms were around her and the glory enfolded them both. The silver light grew brighter, and brighter still, and then, abruptly, it was gone.

Except for one small spark that settled gently on the very tip of Raulin's nose and flared, wrapping his body for an instant in light.

When it faded, Raulin blinked and yawned. "S'it over?"

"Yeah." Jago managed to get the word out past the lump in his throat.

"Then why are you crying? Didn't things work out?"

Jago glanced from Sokoji to Doan. The giant only smiled, the dwarf rocked back on his heels and shrugged, so Jago came to his own decision.

"It's okay," he said, and wiped his eyes. "Everything worked out."

End

Raulin tossed the purse on the table and grinned at the way the clerk's jaw dropped.

"Go on, man," he prodded, "open it; this *is* the day the Council admits new members."

The clerk glanced nervously over his shoulder at the six councillors and with trembling fingers untied the purse strings. Twice a year, in the spring and in the fall, the Council opened its doors, allowing new members to buy their way in. This was the first time anyone had tried for the seats cost more than most citizens of the crumbling Empire saw in a lifetime and the price had to be paid in gold. Twice a year the four men and two women who ruled the city ranged themselves at one end of the council chamber and waited while curious citizenry ranged themselves at the other. And also waited.

When Kraydak had fallen, many of the weak and corrupt he had put in power hung on.

". . . 28, 29, 30." The clerk looked back again, and waved one hand over the stack of freshly minted coins. "It's, it's all there, milords." He obviously had no idea of what to do next.

One of the councillors stepped forward, glared first at the coins, and then at Raulin.

"Where did you get this?" she demanded.

Raulin winked at her. "It used to be my brother's." In fact, it used to be Jago's braid, but he had no intention of telling her that.

"It must be tested."

"Go ahead." Nor did he intend to tell her of how,

on the long trip back, Doan had melted down the soft, pure strands of gold Raulin had found in his pouch and doubled their volume by reforging them into a metal less pure but more acceptable.

The clerk was sent to find a goldsmith and the councillor withdrew back to her fellows where they muttered and fretted and planned. A rustling noise came from the crowd as something very like hope drifted through their ranks.

Although Jago had gone that morning to the Scholar's Hall, Raulin could feel his brother at his back, and knowledge he'd learned was as formidable a weapon as wealth or steel. He touched the jewel he wore on a silver chain about his neck—one of the two emeralds inexplicably mixed in with the rubies; Jago wore the other—and thought of the patch of light in the center of his palm. The kiss Crystal had given him, for later. If Jago had been changed by their journey— and there was no denying the younger man had picked up a number of interesting abilities, not the least of which was self-healing—Raulin had only had something he'd always believed reinforced.

Anything is possible.

He smiled at the row of councillors. One by one, they tried to stare him down. One by one, they dropped their gazes.

That's right, he said silently, *squirm. 'Cause there's going to be some changes made.*

Other places might look gray and depressing in early spring but the Sacred Grove, Tayer felt, bore a promise for the renewal that lay ahead. Delicate new growth already touched the ground with green and, even with their branches bare, the ancient silver birches ringed the Grove in beauty.

"Majesty."

Tayer started and stared at the squat, broad-shouldered man who had so suddenly appeared. Her brow furrowed. "Do I know you?"'

Doan bowed. "We met once, many, many years ago."

"Here?"

"No, in the wood. But you had just come from the Grove." His eyes moved for an instant to the space in the circle where a tree no longer stood.

Tayer smiled sadly. "I don't remember much of those days." She remembered light and love and not much more.

"Uh, yes." Doan's gaze dropped to his feet, for he remembered those days very well; back when he'd guarded the Grove and the hope it had contained. "Best that you don't."

"Have you come then to renew our old acquaintance?" Tayer asked, brows raised.

"No." He took a deep breath. Sokoji had offered to bring the news to Tayer but Doan, having been in on the beginning, felt he should see it through to the end. "I've come about your daughter."

"Tell me." The Queen of Ardhan squared her shoulders and waited for the blow. "Has she been killed?"

"No!" In his rush to wipe the pain from Tayer's face, Doan snapped out the word so hard she winced. "No," he repeated, more gently, "she isn't dead." He saw again the glory that Crystal had become wrapped in the arms of Lord Death and added, "Exactly."

"Exactly?" Tayer repeated, looking both relieved and confused.

Doan snorted. "It's a long story."

"Well . . ." Tayer crossed the Grove and sat down on a protruding root. Both her council and her children would have recognized her tone of voice. "Why don't you start at the beginning."

So he did.

When he finished, Tayer sat quietly for a long time. "Is she happy?" she asked at last.

"Yes. I believe so."

Tayer felt the tug of a baby's lips upon her breast.

Smelled the soft scent of sunlight on silver hair as a child snuggled on her lap in the garden. Saw a girl stand to face an ancient evil, green eyes blazing defiance. Heard the voice of a young woman who shared her heart.

Her lower lip trembled. "I shall miss her."

Doan nodded and reached out to wipe a tear away. "And I," he said softly. "And I."